Sue Dent's
Forever Richard

Do enjoy!
Sue Dent
1-10-9

The Writers' Café Press
Lafayette, INDIANA

This is a work of fiction. All the characters and events portrayed in this novel are either fictitious or are used fictitiously. And by the way, these vampires and werewolves are fantasy . . . fiction . . . not real.

FOREVER RICHARD
First Edition: January 2009
by Sue Dent

Copyright © 2009 by Sue Dent

All rights reserved, including the right to reproduce this book, or portions thereof, in any form.

Cover photography by Hauns L. Froehlingsdorf
Cover model: Stephen McLellan www.shoutlife.com
United Kingdom Consultant: Peter Stephen Martin

A Lost Genre Guild Book
Published by The Writers' Café Press
Lafayette, IN 47905

ISBN: 978-1-934284-03-2
Library of Congress Control Number: 2008936520
Cataloguing Information available upon request.

Printed in the United States of America

Acknowledgements

A heartfelt thanks to all who've waited so patiently for Forever Richard. I hope you enjoy reading it as much as I enjoyed writing it.

A special thanks to my publisher, The Writers' Café Press. Without you, readers would still be waiting for this novel.

And to Frank Creed of The Finishers.biz, manuscript critiquer extraordinaire—well, what's there to say? Just wow!

Finally, to the overwhelming number of my readers who favor CBA/ ECPA fiction—who'd have thought a horror book, written for the broader general market, would appeal to you! The big Christian publishers certainly didn't think it would but I guess you showed them. I'm glad I could give you something to read and enjoy.

To my daughter Amanda—read Never Ceese. All your friends have.

And to my top salesman Reece, I wish I could pay you what you're worth.

Prologue

Port Hampton, Wales—1785

Richard sprinted and slipped down the steep slope behind the mission. "Slow down," he shouted at Brendan's back, "tell me what's going on!"

"No time!" Brendan called over his shoulder as he charged ahead, widening the gap between them. Richard, though older than his brother by two years, struggled to keep pace. Brendan's long legs and athletic ability provided the edge.

Brendan smiled and nodded as he strolled through the picnicking parisioners. His eyes roamed until they settled upon his brother. He discretely picked up the pace until he stood at Richard's side and grasped his shoulder hard. His brother looked up from the plate of food with raised eyebrows. Brendan angled his head past the mission grounds and forced another smile until Richard stood up and excused himself. The brothers strolled off around the building. Brendan looked back over his shoulder then grabbed his brother's arm, this time with more urgency, and hissed, "Run!"

Richard, at eighteen, was expected to help his father at parish functions, not go running pell-mell down a hill to . . .

what? But he had no time to consider this. He had to find out what Brendan found so urgent.

High bluffs marked the landscape of Port Hampton, a small port on Swansea Bay. Level grounds surrounded the mission and to the rear the land sloped dramatically. Brendan ran down it with relative ease, but Richard's slick-soled shoes didn't offer much traction, and his lack of experience didn't help either. The unmowed grass grabbed at his ankles. He'd tug to break free, then slide with his very next step. He risked looking up to check the distance between him and Brendan and both feet slipped out from under him.

He went down hard.

Momentum and gravity propelled him forward and he slid then rolled down the slope. Richard stopped when he hit level ground near the bottom of the hill. He lay flat out, unmoving for a moment. All at once, he pushed up with his hands and stood back on his feet. Brendan stood just a few yards away, his back to him. Gasping for air and in pain from aching muscles he didn't know he had, Richard headed over and swung Brendan around by an arm. "You *will* tell me what this is all about."

Catching his breath, Brendan said, "I need your help, and I . . . I can't trust anyone else!"

Richard held tight to Brendan's arm and stared into troubled green eyes framed by thick, dark brows. "You expect me to believe this has something to do with trust? Tell me the truth, or I'll not help you at all."

"I can't . . . I promised."

"Promised what?"

Instead of answering, Brendan pulled away and headed for a stand of trees. He knelt at the base of one and began to dig through damp leaves. Richard followed and hands on knees, he studied what his brother pulled out from the debris.

A hangman's noose? What the devil—?

Brendan stood. "Dalia's fallen in the river. We need to save her." He gathered the long rope up as he spoke. "Isabelle found me after it happened; asked if I'd help. Said Dalia's clinging to the branches of a submerged tree. And you know that water's freezing cold! We have to hurry—"

Richard grabbed Brendan by his shoulder when he'd turned. "No. We need to get help. To tell someone—"

Brendan shook his head. "I promised Isabelle I wouldn't tell. She was supposed to be watching Dalia. She's afraid she'll get in trouble."

"You should've known better than to promise something like that. That's . . . well, it's just insane!" And, very like his impetuous younger brother, to lumber ahead without thinking things through. *What else would I expect?*

Brendan's face turned brick-like just before he slung the rope over a shoulder. "Even if I hadn't promised, there's no time to get help. Isabelle is with Dalia now, watching her from the shore. When she sees me on the Mill Creek Bridge, she's going to tell Dalia to let go."

Wild-eyed Richard prodded, "And?" There had to be more.

Beaming a prideful smile of which their father would most definitely have disapproved, Brendan replied, "The current will carry her downstream, and I'll be there to catch her."

"Oh that's it. I am going back for help. That is the most ridiculous idea I've heard of."

"Do what you will," Brendan replied. "But Dalia's already been in the water too long. She's so little. Any longer, and she could freeze to death."

Richard looked back toward the slope. It would take more time to climb it than it did to roll down. There had to be a better way to save Dalia but any further discussion was futile. When he turned back, Brendan was already jogging toward the bridge. He followed.

As Richard ran to the bridge, he searched for a sign of the five-year-old Dalia. There amongst the fallen tree limbs bobbed a little head. Her face streamed with tears—or river water droplets—he couldn't tell. He could see her mouth open and close with desperate cries that carried away on the breeze. Isabelle, her ten-year-old sister, stood on the bank, staring toward the bridge, wringing her hands.

Richard heard once that the Mill Creek Bridge was built high above the river to remain passable when other bridges were submerged. Spring rains and melting snow often pushed the river over its banks. At its hump, the bridge deck sat thirty feet above the bitterly cold rapids. *But what is Brendan think-*

ing? And why had the girls left the picnic to begin with?

When he reached the bridge, he found Brendan rushing to rework the hangman's noose into a loop. He watched him slip the loop over his head and down around his chest.

"Here." Brendan handed the bulk of the rope to him.

Richard's jaw dropped. "No. You can't be thinking—you're heavier than I am. You don't seriously expect me to lower you down into the river?"

Brendan scrambled over and sat on the very edge of the bridge. Then, a second later, turned around and slipped off the side to dangle by his hands.

Richard set the coil of rope down, got on his hands and knees and looked over the side. "This is ridiculous. You aren't going to help anyone. You'll end up drowning as well!"

"Not if you hold onto the rope."

Richard took a frantic look around. "Brother, there's nothing for me to brace myself against. The bridge . . . it has no rails—"

"My life is in your hands," Brendan said. "Dalia's life, too."

And Brendan let go.

As his brother fell, the rope beside Richard uncoiled.

Reverend Merideth Porter had just moved the family to Port Hampton. In May of 1785, he'd been called to Llandyfan, Wales, and although he'd never questioned this, circumstances had forced a move to Port Hampton. A month ago, on the very eve of her birthday, his beloved Julia had been taken by a stranger into the woods, then handed off to another who had his way with her. The first stranger returned, transformed into a wolf before Julia's eyes, and scratched her on her side. He said it was for proof of the encounter. He left another message to give to her husband—that they should leave Llandyfan and never come back. If they didn't leave, he would come after their children next.

Merideth knew instantly that the message was meant for him; he'd heard the warning before. Several young men from the mission in Llandyfan said similar things. They, too, had seen the message-bearer transform into a wolf. Only they hadn't survived; those warnings came as they breathed their last breaths.

He wasn't sure how to take the words of the young men, but he knew how to take what Julia told him. Port Hampton was in need of a minister. They'd contacted him once before. He'd turned down their offer because it meant he'd have to move his family. Things were different now and the Porter family left as soon as they had their possessions packed.

The move proved more difficult than Merideth had imagined. He had to plan for Julia's condition. The scratches on her side had not completely healed and they caused her much pain. Then they discovered she was with child. She and Merideth decided not to tell anyone. He cared little what others thought but he wanted to protect his wife. He was more concerned that Julia understood he would love the child no matter what—it was a part of her, therefore a part of him. He'd meant it. Julia was his life.

Today Julia smiled, even laughed as she sat surrounded by new friends. The scratches had healed, and the melancholy that first plagued her appeared to have lifted. Standing close by, he heard a young matron ask his wife if she had a name for their child.

He held his breath. They'd had no discussion so far on the matter, and her reluctance to decide, or even to talk about it, had worried him. Julia had names for all their other children long before they were born.

She looked down at her folded hands, and her lips formed a quiet smile. "Meri has always favored the name 'Cecil' for a boy and 'Cecilia' for a girl. I think I shall humor him this time."

A sly look in his direction told him he'd been discovered eavesdropping. "And what fine names they are," he said, coming over to kneel in front of her.

"My dear Meri," she chastised with a broader smile as he took one of her hands in his, "it's not proper to eavesdrop."

Julia looked as beautiful and animated as the day he'd met her. He grinned and patted her hand. "I'm so glad I did. To learn of the names you've chosen . . . Cecil or Cecilia . . . I couldn't be happier." His smile widened. "After you let me name Richard, I was certain that would be the end of it."

She addressed the amused looks from ladies seated around her. "I told him he could choose the name of our first child, *if it was a boy.*"

"Well, at least he chose a respectable name," an older lady laughed. "I don't think I'd be so brave as to let my Henry choose."

"It's actually Meri's name. Merideth Richard Porter. And Richard is so much like his father, it was the perfect choice. He's going to be a minister as well. He's already been called by Our Lord."

"One day," Merideth added, squeezing her hand before standing. "I shall leave you with your friends now. I see Lyle Witherspoon, and I need to speak with him about the addition to the main building."

The light laughter he heard as he walked away was a balm. *If only I could reverse time to undo what happened to her. Or perhaps stop time now, so she could be this happy forever.*

Daydreaming was interrupted when Isabelle rushed in with a drenched and coughing Dalia. With an anguished cry, Dalia's mother rose from her chair and hurried toward them, closely followed by her husband.

"She fell into the river," Isabelle cried out, handing Dalia over. "Brendan saved her, but I fear his brother has drowned!"

Her words drove like daggers into Merideth's soul. He quickly scanned for their lads. *Raewyn and Sophie are with Julia. Christian is with Rolland. But where is—?*

"Richard," Julia gasped behind him.

He turned on his heel to see her wilt into the chair. The women on either side grasped her shoulders to steady her. He stepped toward her, but stopped when someone grabbed him from behind. He turned to see Lyle, his face somber and tense with concern, and the other men standing behind him.

"We'll go with you—"

"No." His reply came too quick, Merideth realized, not to be followed by an explanation. "I mean, there's no point. I'll take Isabelle with me; she'll know where they are." But how could he explain the feeling he had, the one that told him to come alone?

Lyle nodded. "Then we'll make sure Julia is taken care of. Go find your sons."

Merideth ran back to where Isabelle stood beside her mother, who held a blue-lipped Dalia. She rocked her back and forth to calm her shivers while other ladies clustered around, helping her wrap the child in their shawls.

"Can you take me to them, Isabelle?" he said. "Can you take me to where you last saw Richard and Brendan?"

She nodded, and he followed her.

At the bottom of the steep slope, Isabelle stopped and looked around.

"What is it?" He tried not to sound impatient. But the girl's lost stare worried him.

"I . . . don't remember the way. I know I came down the hill . . ." She gave a frustrated sigh. "But then I . . . I'm just not sure."

Merideth considered her young age as he continued to prod. The wrong tone could have her shut down altogether. "Just take your time," he encouraged. "Maybe it will come to you."

Moments later, she said, "I'm sorry, I don't remember!"

He was quick to console. He wiped her tears and sent her along with the assurance that she'd done the best she could. He then set out on his own.

At least he knew the boys had to be somewhere on the river. He followed its course. Then, for what reason he couldn't tell, he had the overwhelming urge to stop and turn around. When he did, he saw an area of beaten back grass. For a moment he considered what made him stop and look, decided it was divine intervention, and followed the path he'd just been shown.

His heart lurched in his chest when he heard feet thrash the grass as Brendan headed toward him.

"Your brother—"

"Back that way," Brendan shouted and pointed. "Just over that mound. On the other side. I think he's—"

Merideth didn't let him finish. "Your mother . . . go back to the mission. Tell her I found Richard, and he's all right."

"But Father—"

He shook his head at Brendan's protest. "Just tell her. He *will* be fine."

Meredith scrambled up over the mound and Brendan reluctantly took off in the other direction.

Soft, cool grass all around, but his hands seemed on fire. And why couldn't he get out from under the heavy weight pressing down on him? The same pressure, pressed in rhythmic succession, as he fought to take a breath that wouldn't come.

Panic swelled and with one final push, water gushed up from his lungs and out his mouth. On his side now, he sputtered, coughed and gasped for air.

Faint threads of reality formed, then broke. "Dalia? . . . Brendan—"

"—are both fine, thanks be to Our Lord. But Isabelle said you fell into the river. If Brendan hadn't found you . . ."

He squinted to make out his father's form. "Brendan . . . *found* me?"

"Yes. He told me where you were. You don't remember?"

Richard tried to quiet his mind, tried to recall. Nothing came to contradict his father's words.

He wasn't sure how much time had passed, but now Brendan's face appeared over him. His hair hung in damp, heavy ringlets.

"I thought this might help with the burns from the rope." Brendan knelt down beside Meredith with strips of cloth and a tin of salve. "You did a very brave thing, Richard."

His eyes, Richard couldn't help thinking. *And he's never this helpful without being told. He's hiding something.*

"He doesn't remember anything, Brendan."

Richard watched Brendan's face carefully, curious to see his reaction.

His brother said, "I'm sure he'll remember soon enough."

"Your mother, she'd fainted. Did you manage to tell her Richard is all right?"

Richard gasped. *Mother must be overwrought—*

A dismal Brendan shook his head. "She didn't believe me. She wants to come see for herself."

Meredith rose from his kneeling position and brushed grass from his knees. "She can't come. It would be too difficult. I must go tell her myself."

Richard watched his father leave. "Wait," he said, unable to bear the thought of his mother being upset over him. She was so fragile after the wolf attack. He pressed his hands against the ground to push himself up. "I'll come—"

He cried out in agony. A glance at his hands showed a mass of raw, blistered flesh on the palms. *But how did they get like this?*

Brendan took charge once their father ran out of sight. "Don't be such a baby. This will help."

The salve had a dramatic cooling effect. The strips of cloth, loosely wrapped, helped as well. Finally, he could think past the pain.

"What happened? You have to know something."

"You fell in the river while helping to save Dalia. What's there to tell?"

There had to more to it than that. "One doesn't just fall in the river." Perhaps Brendan pushed him. He certainly got mad enough sometimes.

Taking his other hand, Brendan began to apply salve there. "You wouldn't have fallen in the river if you'd just lowered me the way you were supposed to. Instead, you let the rope slip through your hands."

"Rope? What rope?"

Brendan finished the second palm and sat back on his heels. "You really don't remember anything, do you? You were going to lower me from the Mill Creek Bridge."

Richard propped himself up on elbows. "Why would I lower you from the bridge? You weigh more than I do. And besides, there's nothing for me to brace against . . ." he paused, "*which,* I now seem to recall telling you right before I was pulled in."

The memory was not a refreshing one, only more troubling. "And why was there a knot in the end of the rope?"

Brendan gathered up the supplies and stood. "I don't know what you're talking about."

Richard stood as well, slowly. Once steadied, he said, "I think you do. I think you'd decided I might not be able to hold on."

Brendan faced him, scowling. "Are you suggesting I intentionally tied a knot in the end of the rope so you'd be pulled into the river? What an absurd notion! How would this benefit me?"

"I . . . don't know, Brother. That's why I'm asking."

"Maybe I thought a knot would help you hold on *better*. Did you ever consider that?"

They'd been down this road many times before, if on other subjects: Brendan's defense was never believable.

"You might as well admit it," Richard said. "Weave your story however you want, but it was a bad idea, and you're going to have a difficult time explaining to Father what really happened."

Brendan caved. "I didn't know the rope wouldn't be long enough. I didn't know you'd be pulled in."

Richard remembered everything now. "None of that would've mattered if you'd just gone back for help."

"I suppose you're going to tell Father, since you enjoy seeing him angry at me."

Richard sighed. "I nearly drowned, Brother. And all because you had to do things *your* way. When will you learn?"

Brendan's shoulders dropped. "Perhaps I'll never learn."

His despondent tone triggered a memory—back to when Brendan had found the rope. It made him reevaluate his brother's mood. Since they'd moved to Port Hampton he'd become withdrawn, and would go to the woods often, staying for hours.

"What was the hangman's noose for?" He kept his voice gentle.

"I wasn't trying to kill myself, if that's what you think. And it's only called a hangman's noose if you intend to hang someone with it. I wasn't planning on hanging anyone."

"Then what?"

Brendan moved closer, looked to his left, then to his right. "I know something," he whispered. "Something you wouldn't believe. I was setting a trap with the rope."

"What were you hoping to trap?" Richard asked, not sure he wanted to know.

"Not *what*. *Who*. The one who hurt Mother. The one who scratched her."

"What do you mean, *who*? Mother was attacked by a wolf. You know this as well as I do. You also know Father asked us not to speak of it again."

"But there's more than what Father told us. Much more. It—he followed us here—to Port Hampton. And there's something else too—"

Richard wouldn't listen to this. He wouldn't! "You're mad! Mother was attacked by a wolf. We moved from Llandyfan to Port Hampton because of the attack. Anything else is a lie. You're wrong, and that's all there is to it."

"It isn't a lie. Joachim told me—"

"Who is Joachim?"

"A . . . friend. Why?"

"Because, Brother, the truth is only as good as the one telling it. If I don't know of whom you speak, then why should I put stock in his words? How do you know this . . . this *Joachim* isn't lying? Father said we shouldn't speak of Mother's attack, and so we shouldn't."

Brendan's body tensed and his hands fisted. Whatever he'd been told or imagined clouded any good sense he might have had.

"I'll tell you what," Richard said, "if you promise to keep quiet about what this Joachim has told you, I'll promise not to tell Father the truth about what happened today. You'll very possibly look like a hero."

"You wouldn't lie," Brendan said, skeptical. "The good son would never lie."

"Don't call me that. And I didn't say I'd lie. I said I wouldn't tell him the truth. I'll just let him believe I don't remember. But only if you promise. Only if you swear."

"But, the rest of what I know . . . it's a great secret!"

Richard's concern grew. Brendan was always so gullible, so easily drawn in. He'd believe anything, just because he wanted to. This time, however, the alternative was to have Father angry with him, once again, if the truth came out. He decided it was worth pressing. "I promise you, I will not hesitate to tell

Father the truth if you don't keep quiet about whatever *great secret* you supposedly discovered."

Brendan didn't answer. His eyes darted from the ground to the sky to a nearby tree. His fists opened and closed. Richard had never known his brother to consider anything for so long.

"All right," Brendan said finally. "I promise."

"And you'll never speak of the matter again?"

"Yes," he hissed.

"Good. Then we should be getting back to the mission."

He stepped out from behind the tree and stared after the two as they left. Sadly, matters were once again out of his hands. Even after he'd led the father down the right path, and kept the son alive until he got there. All in vain. Brendan would not tell his secret, which would have warned the minister. This forced him to consider another line of action.

Yet Zade was too powerful to fight one-on-one. So perhaps he'd just wait for the child to be born. Yes, Joachim decided. That would give him roughly eight months to plan, eight months to foil whatever plan Zade had for the child.

"Yes," Joachim whispered to the still air.

The pack would wonder where he was. He didn't need them suspicious of his treachery. With that thought, he transformed back into his wolf form and raced into the woods.

1

The blazing mid-morning sun laid a haze over the southwestern landscape. José squinted at the distant horizon. "*Mirada que está viniendo,*" he said. "It's him."

The day laborers loitered on corners hoping for work in the fields—backbreaking work that paid little. Not the type of work they wanted but because most of them lived in the country illegally, they hadn't a lot of choice. The laborers worked long hours for little pay, which was attractive to employers—so attractive they'd risk breaking the law to hire them.

The men had to watch for Border Patrol agents, so they scrutinized every *gringo* with a careful eye.

José's buddies squinted in the direction he'd indicated. Raul pushed himself off the wall where they sat. "I thought you saw him leave town—for good."

"Yeah," Antonio seconded. "*Qué tal?* You can't see good or something? Maybe you don't know what you're talking about."

For several weeks they'd watched this stranger. No one knew when he'd arrived or how long he planned on staying. They did know they wanted him gone. Both a *gringo* and an outsider—the combination usually meant trouble.

José watched the giant of a man approach. His long black duster billowed; his boots stirred up a dust storm around him. José boldly took a step forward. Raul watched and his lips curled into a smirk. *Who did José think he was kidding anyway?*

"What you gonna do, *hombrecito*? The little man gonna take the big man on? He'll squash you like that little bug."

José, desperate to earn respect among his peers, ignored the comment and squared his shoulders.

The small immigrant town of Rio Lobos could have easily been a mirage. Surrounded by dry, flat desert, like the desert he'd spent the past two days walking through, he considered this possibility. Not until he stepped onto solid pavement did he believe otherwise.

Heavy boots marked each step as he moved along. His long duster no longer billowed but flapped freely. He'd tucked his left sleeve into a front coat pocket to prevent it from blowing about but with no left arm inside, the sleeve hung slack.

In town, he stepped onto a sidewalk. Worn and beaten by the elements, sections of it were in dire need of repair—the curbs crumbling chunks of concrete. The entire town needed a facelift. Colorful pennants, strung about and flapping in the hot, arid breeze did little to disguise this.

The most modern building was the bank. It sat on the adjacent corner and boasted a display below the bank name that alternated time and temperature: 9:47 AM and a scorching 97 degrees. Sweat beaded and rolled down into his thick beard. He scratched at it but stopped short of complaining. After all, the beard had offered his face some protection against the stark rays of the blazing desert sun. Yet, a curse for the one responsible for his present condition was never far from his lips.

Blasted werewolf! If it hadn't been for the creature, he wouldn't have to worry about hair that grew twice as fast as normal. The bite wasn't the only thing to worry about when battling a werewolf.

His stomach growled. Two days had passed since he'd eaten anything. The five young migrant workers on the corner watched him arrive and stared belligerently as he drew near. One of the five took an aggressive step forward. The stranger slowed when he saw the young worker but walked on by. No one followed.

La Tienda sat next to the laundromat. The tantalizing aroma of authentic Mexican cuisine lured him across the street.

Those standing around the entrance scattered. Startled patrons inside moved as far away as possible as he stood between them and the door. Mothers gathered their small children. The young lady who worked the counter wore a nametag, *Maria*. She stifled a scream and backed up against the wall. Someone hissed the word *gringo* and he understood.

"Aye, *gringo*," he said, his Scottish accent strong. "I get that. I'm different. But I don't want any trouble."

Trapped in bodies that wanted to run, a dozen pairs of eyes watched him go about his business. Careful not to make any sudden moves and frighten the patrons further, he walked slowly to the counter and gathered up foil-wrapped burritos from beneath a heat lamp. One by one, he placed them in a deep pocket of his coat.

"See," he told them. "I just want to eat . . . and now I'm going to pay." He reached into his pocket for cash but had to guess at what he owed. Maria wasn't talking. He laid down a ten, grabbed a styrofoam cup and filled it with coffee, then headed to a group of tables and chairs near the back of the store and sat. A mass exodus followed as anxious patrons darted out. Maria disappeared into the back.

A ceiling fan warbled overhead and kept the hot air circulating. He set his coffee down and took the burritos from his pocket. He devoured the first one in no time. After a few more bites of another, he could finally think about more than his next meal—like the events of the previous evening.

Tobias had eluded him for years, but he hadn't given up looking. The werewolf had information and he was desperate to hear it. After nearly a century of traipsing across continents—Europe, Asia and now North America—he'd finally found him.

Tobias knelt and drank from a stream, his shirt beside him. The moon's glow heightened the appearance of well-defined muscle. Tobias could easily overtake him. He had to move with care.

He took a cautious step closer, pushed the fabric of his duster back, giving him easy access to the pistol-grip sawed-off shotgun holstered on his thigh.

Tobias tensed; he sniffed the air—his cupped hands froze in mid-drink. His head turned a sliver to stare at the abstract reflection in the stream. The stranger drew his weapon and in one fluid motion Tobias stood and turned. Eyes black and narrowed, his nose wrinkled at the odor of silver.

"Aye, did ye think I'd come unprepared?" When Tobias didn't answer he asked, "Do ye speak English, lad?"

Tobias tilted his head, his thick brows furrowed in confusion. Maybe his accent confused, so he worked to tame it before speaking again. This time Tobias nodded.

"Then tell me why ye have run from me all these years." He kept the shotgun level. "All I ever wanted was to ask some questions." *Why had Tobias let me sneak up on him tonight? Maybe it's a trap?* He pressed the gun barrel against the chest of the werewolf. "Ye don't have friends around waiting to pick me off, do ye? If so, then ye should know—I'll kill ye first."

The breath of the werewolf turned to vapor in the cooler night air. "Tobias alone." Stilted werewolf English, but still English. "Tobias wait for you. Tobias need—help. Help Tobias."

Stunned eyes stared back. "Help Tobias? Away with ye! Why should I help when ye have been running from me for so long?"

Tobias glanced over his shoulder and found the moon where it hung, crescent in shape. "Tobias forget."

"Tobias forget?" He followed Tobias's gaze then nodded. "Ahh, Tobias forget—forgotten how to become the wolf. Ye have gone too long without transforming." *They never saw the danger until it was too late.* "Yet ye remember ye need the moon, don't ye . . . to draw the blood up, to get things going."

Tobias turned back to face him. "You help Tobias remember more."

As a subtle reminder, he shoved the gun barrel against Tobias' chest. "Tell me what I want to know. Besides, what makes ye think I can help?" He could help, of course. But he didn't give this information away freely. He didn't need every werewolf who'd *forgotten* tracking him down.

"You help Gideon."

His expression fell. "Great. Gideon shared." Even after he promised that he wouldn't.

"Help Tobias like you help Gideon."

His eyes narrowed. "Aye, but first, ye pay my price. Tell me. You know the werewolf Joachim. Ye ran with his pack. What became of him? Where is he now?"

"Joachim? Joachim is no more."

The words hit him hard. All these years of waiting, hoping—it couldn't be true. "Ye lie!" he growled. He had to be. He moved in closer to Tobias and forced the end of the gun under his chin. "Ye'll tell me the truth or I'll blow your head clean off!"

"Tobias show you."

"All right." He brought the gun back down to chest level and allowed Tobias to put an open palm to his forehead.

The first image: two wolves thrashing it out, teeth bared and bloodied, eyes blazing with intent. It ended when one of the wolves went down and *she* rushed forward. He gasped and Tobias removed his hand.

"*She* killed Joachim," Tobias spat out. "*She* the reason he is no more."

"Ye will not speak of her like that. Ye won't!"

"Joachim is no more because of *her*! He fight Zade for her."

"Where is she now? Ye have to know."

Tobias reached into a pocket, took out a trinket on a thin chain and held it up.

A lump formed in his throat; moisture played in the corner of each eye. "Where'd ye get that, lad? Where in the world did ye get that?"

"Tobias take it from Joachim."

He batted back the moisture to regain some composure. "Doesn't prove anything. Ye still haven't told me where she is or *if* she is."

"Hold tight. If she is, you know. If she isn't, you know too."

He considered this. "Aye, but I'll need my hand for that and I canna say I trust ye enough to holster my weapon. But—" he said, "if *ye* hold the locket—maybe that will work."

Tobias placed his left palm back to the stranger's forehead and held the trinket tight in his other hand.

Images flashed. A castle, a feeling. "Aye, I see her. She's alive." He furrowed his brow. ". . . sort of." Tobias took his hand away. "Now put that necklace in my breast pocket."

"You help Tobias?" the werewolf replied.

"Aye, of course." After all, that was the deal. He couldn't use the information himself. He wasn't cursed. But, having the information and the ability to share it—on occasion there had been a definite advantage to that.

He'd have to holster the shotgun to free up his hand to initiate the action. "This is going to be bit tricky," he admitted, not certain he wanted to risk putting his weapon away and give up the advantage. But Tobias seemed ready to cooperate. He put his apprehension aside and slid the gun back into its holster.

With his hand on Tobias' forehead, the flow of information could begin. Several attempts to get things going ended in failure. *What was wrong?*

"Ye block me. I canna help if ye block me."

With no more coercion than that, Tobias let his mental guard down.

"Aye, that's better." He'd helped several other werewolves remember the way. Some took the information quickly. Some didn't. Often he could help speed things up by focusing. He closed his eyes but they shot back open when he felt sharp claws dig into his wrist. Tobias had already begun the transformation.

"Aahh!" He fought the instinct to pull away. Tobias could take his only arm if he wasn't careful. The pressure increased. "For the love of God," he exclaimed.

Tobias stiffened and his hand jerked before he fell backwards onto the ground. The stranger ratcheted his shotgun from his holster. "Aye. That'd be a word ye canna tolerate."

On the ground, Tobias continued the rapid transformation—the human form faded further until the new looked at home on all fours. Soon, it sprinted off into the woods.

"Good riddance," he yelled out after him, "you ungrateful beast."

The migrant workers still loitered. The same young man who'd shown aggression the first time moved directly in his path.

When he angled to go around, the guy matched him step for step. Dark intimidating eyes met his. "I don't want any trouble," he said. "I just want to get by." He searched the young man's face for any sign of compromise.

"You gotta pay to get by, *gringo*."

That word again. "I can't give ye what I don't have."

A quick look over his shoulder to the others and the young man tensed his forearms. "Well, you better come up with something or you'll have to deal with us, right, *muchachos*?"

Arms crossed, they nodded.

"All right," he said. "I do have one thing." He reached into a pocket and drew out his hand, closed. Slowly, he opened it to reveal—nothing. In another instant, his palm covered the young man's forehead and the ringleader sank to the ground, unconscious.

The others backed away. "*¡Él lo mató!*" he heard one say before they all broke and ran.

"Nay," he yelled after them. "He's not hurt. It's not what ye think."

It was pointless to explain further. They'd disappeared around the corner. He sighed deep and pulled the young man along by an arm. He left him to rest under the shade of an awning.

On the outskirts of town sat the Alamo Plaza Apartments, remnants of a not-so-successful motel chain that dared defy the odds. No traveler would stop here now, only locals. You could pay by the week or ten dollars an hour, maximum two. His third prepaid week at the motel. He headed straight back to his unit.

When the stranger saw another tenant leafing through mail, he quickened his pace. He was expecting something. Perhaps it had arrived. The mail had come, but no package waited. A notice stuck to his door, the "Attempted Delivery" box marked. Tomorrow the post office would try again. He pushed past disappointment and went inside. Calling the post office did little good. The mail truck with his package was still out making deliveries and wouldn't return until after the post office closed.

He removed his duster and let it fall across a chair near the door. He placed his shotgun on a table next to the unmade bed and lay down. Two days of walking through the desert had taken its toll. He needed to rest.

Sleep came easily enough. He recalled waking up once to find the room dark. The sun had set. The next time he awoke, it was morning, 9:45 according to the digital clock on the small bedside table. He sat up and rubbed the back of his neck. He felt rested but antsy. How would he kill time until his package came? A long shower helped, as did shaving his thick beard. But he still had at least an hour.

He settled onto the end of his bed, television remote in hand, and began channel surfing. *Jeopardy.* He stopped to watch. The category: Famous Wars.

The unyielding presence of this single Highland regiment caused the Russians to abandon their intention of taking Balaclava.

The contestants jumped all around the correct response. "What is the Charge of the Light Brigade?" one said. "Who fought the Crimean War?" another chimed in. The third contestant merely shrugged.

His deep-set eyes misted over in remembrance. "Aye, the thin red line—what was the thin red line."

The thunder of hooves, the smell of death, he remembered it all. *To die like they did. That would be an honor.* Yet dying wasn't an option for him. Neither was aging in a timely manner. It had something to do with the battle he had with that werewolf. He did age, though much more slowly—about a year for every fifty he'd lived, but death never came. He'd been run clean through during the battle at Balaclava, an injury that left more than a few men dead where they fell. Not something he understood—in fact, quite frustrating. He switched the television off to avoid further memories.

A solid thump against his door and then a knock. "Aye. I'm here," he said jumping to his feet. A short sprint to the door and—no one there. He looked down to see a package at his feet.

He checked the box and brought it inside. The postage showed it had come all the way from New Delhi, India. He carefully opened it. The seller had done such a fine job of packing that it took him more than a minute to reveal the knife inside.

Its pitted blade and wooden handle reinforced with bone plates attested its authenticity. He ran his fingers over the traces of Aramaic and Hebrew inscription. "Aye," came his breathless whisper. This had to be it, the knife of the *Aqedah*, the very one used by Abraham on Mount Moriah. The one he'd been searching for. He'd combed sacred parchments for any mention of the knife past Abraham, looked around at *Djebel Thebeyr,* where a granite block, purportedly split in two by the touch of this knife, drew tourists. Still the knife had eluded him . . . until now.

"Finally." He stared at what he held in reverent awe. "Finally I can end this madness."

2

Bring them home. Stirred from her sleep by the voice, Cassie raised her head and rubbed her eyes. "Wh-what? Bring who home?"

She scanned the hospital waiting room, curious to see who had spoken. The voice came from right next to her but there was no one there. A couple of chairs down and across from her sat a middle-aged woman flipping through a magazine.

She felt awkward asking but had to know. "Excuse me. Did you by chance say something to me a second ago?"

The woman looked over the top of her glasses. "Why? Did you hear something?"

What an odd response. Why would she ask if she hadn't? "Never mind."

The woman went back to her magazine.

She hadn't dreamt it. The voice was too real. And she'd heard the voice before, on two separate occasions. The first occurred two days ago in the apartment she shared with her unaccommodating roommate, Rodney. Their friend Ceese, at that time a werewolf, sat across from her at the small kitchen table and stared with those intimidating green-gold eyes. During the conversation, Ceese spoke of Cassie's dead grandmother. "Penny talks to me," she'd said. "Sometimes her thoughts fill my head."

In the process of explaining to Ceese that this wasn't possible, Cassie had heard Grandma Penelope's voice herself—the same one she'd heard a moment ago. She'd discredited that experience because Ceese had the ability to "get inside someone's head," as Rodney put it. Cassie could never rule out Ceese's involvement when the werewolf was near.

The second time she'd heard Grandma Penelope's voice, Ceese was nowhere around. Neither was she around now.

Cassie thought again of the words she'd just heard and decided to speak them aloud. It might help her think. "Bring them home."

She shook her head, frustrated. No. She still didn't get it and to make matters worse, the woman with the magazine stared. She must've heard her. But Cassie knew she hadn't spoken loud enough to draw attention. Nevertheless, the woman asked, "Did *you* say something?"

Cassie bristled at the condescending tone. She squeezed together red sleepless eyes. Her tolerance level low, she snapped, "No, did you *hear* something?"

Offended, the woman gathered her things and left. Cassie sighed. She hadn't meant to upset the lady but six hours of sleeping in a chair with her head propped against a wall, hearing voices no less—she wasn't quite at her best. She tried to put the incident out of her mind but couldn't. *I'll just go find out what's taking Richard and Ceese so long.*

She leaned to get her backpack and pulled it on over her shoulders. She walked out into the main hall and headed toward ICU. Though Richard and Ceese had made remarkable recoveries from their gunshot wounds, the hospital still wanted to run tests. By now they should be finished—why hadn't they come for her? She'd told them where she'd be. It was time to go check.

Just before she stopped at the nurse's station to get information, Cassie saw a water fountain and headed over. Holding her auburn hair back with one hand she leaned to drink. Out of the corner of her eye, someone approached. Slowly, she straightened to see . . . *Richard.* His pale blond hair hung to his shoulders. His smile seemed softer and less than arrogant. The hard edge of the vampire had disappeared. As she stared, she neglected to take her thumb from the button and the water still arced out.

Richard remedied this. "You wouldn't want to flood the place." His accent held as much interest for her as he did—sophisticatedly English but with subtle variances that left her curious. Cassie now understood Grandmother Penelope's infatuation with his voice. It intrigued her as well.

"Oh—of course not," she said. "I was just—well, I guess I was just caught by surprise. You look so—I mean you *seem* so different."

"A good different, I hope."

"Oh, yes. It's definitely a good different." Could she have sounded any more adolescent?

Richard looked down at his clothing. "The clothes fit all right, don't they? The nurses brought several items in for me to choose from."

For the past three days, she'd only seen him wear black—black pants, black shirt, and black coat. The white button-down shirt and khakis were definitely a change.

"Apparently the hospital gets donations every now and then," he added. "I'm just not sure something else might have fit better."

He seemed desperate for confirmation. "You look fine, Richard. Trust me."

"I guess I shouldn't worry so much. It's just that Mamá—" He stopped short. "Your grandmother used to help me with this sort of thing, since I couldn't see my reflection. She had an impeccable eye for fashion, much like you."

He couldn't be serious. She wore the same jeans she'd had on the day before. The fitted tee matched, but other than that . . . She studied him with an intrigued eye. This wasn't about her. "You miss her, don't you? You miss Grandmother."

Cassie's grandmother Penelope had died shortly before Richard and Ceese left England to find her.

"I suppose in some small way, I do. The vampire wouldn't allow me to care much about anyone."

He paused and Cassie waited to see if he'd say more. Grandmother was such a mystery to her. She'd found Cassie online, told her she thought they might be related. Cassie's adoptive parents had no information on her biological ones so

Cassie was ready to listen. The information she provided was hard to prove or disprove so Cassie chose to believe.

Penelope had given up her only child years ago because she wasn't financially able to support her. After years of regret, she began a search. She found that her daughter had married and settled in a small suburb very near where Cassie lived in New York. This daughter had given up her own daughter for adoption, though the reasons weren't clear. Penelope tried to find out more but the records were sealed.

As Cassie stood and thought about what her grandmother had told her, Richard slid his hands into his pockets. He had nothing further to add.

She looked down at her watch. "Weren't you two together?" she asked. "Did they have to run more tests on Ceese?"

Richard nodded towards the other end of the hall. "There she is now."

Hand in hand, she and Rodney walked. Ceese also wore different clothing. It was clear Rodney had made some input. Together, they pulled the grunge look off quite nicely.

"Take a picture," Rodney said as Cassie stared. He held his head at an angle so that his long hair, black at the roots, neon blond at the ends, slightly covered one eye.

Rodney took advantage, as usual. He had to know how Ceese looked up to him and depended on him. Cassie worried this might become an issue and now she had proof. "You must be proud."

Rodney strutted and grinned. "Hey, she picked out her own clothes."

"And you didn't influence her at all."

Rodney shrugged. "She asked me what I thought."

Ceese pulled away from Rodney and took the few steps over to where Richard stood.

"I want to go home," she said. "I want to leave this place." Ceese too had an accent. Not like Richard's. Hers was much more Gaelic.

"Home?" Richard said, confused.

"Yes, home—back to England."

Bring them home, Cassie heard again. She could've sworn the voice came from behind her. At once, she swung around— no one there. When she turned back the others stared. From their looks, she knew they hadn't heard what she had. She struggled to come up with an explanation that didn't make her sound crazy. "I—I just—I thought I heard someone call me, that's all."

Richard turned back to Ceese. "England isn't your home any more than it is mine."

"I don't care," Ceese said, more like a five-year-old trying to get her way than a rational eighteen-year-old. "I want to go. Today. As soon as possible."

"Maybe we can discuss it after we get back to the apartment."

Cassie agreed. "Yes. That really does sound like the best idea."

Ceese ignored Cassie's comment. "We've done what we came to do. Our curses have been lifted so why can't we just leave and go back home?"

"It's not that simple—"

"Why don't you just tell her you'll look into it?" Rodney said, very diplomatic for once.

"What's that?" Richard asked.

"You can look into it, can't you?"

Richard shrugged. "I suppose."

Ceese brightened. "Then you will check?"

Richard's smile showed his relief to have come to some resolution. "Yes, certainly. I'll check."

⁓⁓⁓

Kyle exited the elevator into a maze of hallways. The nurse had given him directions but in his panic, he'd quickly forgotten them. Convinced he was running in circles, he sprinted around the next blind corner.

"Hey, watch where you're going!"

Kyle turned on his heel. "Rodney, dude, am I glad I found you!"

3

Kyle appeared paler than usual beneath the thin offering of tightly curled red hair cut short to make it manageable. Multiple facial piercings, including eyebrow and nose rings, littered his worried face.

He wasn't the sharpest tool in the shed despite what his grade point average and IQ test results indicated. Rodney had known Kyle too long to put stock in the test scores. "And why are you glad you found me? More importantly, why are you here?"

"It's Josh. He's downstairs, in the emergency room."

Rodney's forehead wrinkled. "The two of you were supposed to wait at the cemetery for the police to arrive. You were supposed to take them to Henderson's body and explain how I shot him in self-defense. You were supposed to tell them where I was so they'd know where to find me with their questions!" Rodney's voice peaked. "So you see why I am confused? . . . and now you say that Josh is in the emergency room?"

"Yes."

"Well, where are the cops? What'd they say? Did they send you to find me?"

"If you'll shut up, I'll tell you," Kyle said. "I'm not here because the police are looking for you. I went back to the main road to lead the police in. Josh decided to stay with the body because he was afraid the cops would know he was high—"

At that, Rodney looked around anxiously, no one but Cassie, Richard, and Ceese within earshot. With a rush of whispered words, he attempted to censor Kyle. "Are you crazy? Do you want everybody to hear you? We all know what Josh's incentive was for helping Henderson. But I'm pretty sure nobody else needs to know."

"Can I finish?" Kyle asked.

"Yeah. Sure. Just keep it down."

"So anyway, Josh had planned to stay out of sight until the police left. I didn't expect to see him when I returned with the police. I figured he'd just stay out of sight until the coast was clear."

"He didn't do that?"

Kyle shook his head. "When the police and I arrived, Josh was on the ground where Henderson's body was supposed to be. Hend—"

"What? What do you mean *where* Henderson's body was supposed to be? What is going on—?"

"If you would listen for a moment instead of . . . oh never mind. Henderson was gone. And Josh . . ." Kyle turned paler, ". . . he—he was on the ground with a set of bite marks on his neck. The paramedics said he'd lost a lot of blood but they didn't know how."

Professor Henderson, the newly elected head of the Bioengineering department at Templeton University, had taken Cassie under his wing. He'd persuaded her to believe they had a common interest: helping vampires and werewolves find a cure for their curse.

Cassie's hands formed fists. "Oh, I wish I had the sense to figure out how conniving Henderson was—how he used me to get to you, Richard and Ceese too. But to hear he's somehow acquired the curse of the vampire? Are you sure his body was gone? Maybe you just missed it. After all, it was dark."

Kyle looked at her and rolled his eyes. "Did you just swallow a big gulp of *dumb*? There were marks on Josh's neck and the paramedics said he needed blood. He was on the ground, very close to where Henderson's body had been."

Cassie didn't argue further.

"So the police," Rodney affirmed, "never saw Henderson's body? They don't know anything about him being shot."

"No."

Rodney rubbed his hands together. "Great. That's good news."

"Yeah, I guess. At least we don't have to worry about explaining that."

"No. I meant I'm off the hook. I don't have to deal with any of this anymore. I can leave and pretend none of this happened."

"But what about Josh?" Kyle petitioned. "You—you can't just leave him."

"Oh yes he can," Cassie said. "You know it's how he operates. He doesn't care about anyone but himself."

"And that bothers you?" Rodney asked. "I figured you'd be glad to see me go."

"Trust me," Cassie said, "I'm glad."

"You can't leave," Ceese pouted. "We have to help Josh. He saved my life."

Rodney's arrogance bottomed out. "He'll be fine here, Ceese. He doesn't need me."

"They're going to run tests," Kyle said. "What happens if they find out the truth about what he's become? What if he tells them about Henderson and how you shot him?"

Rodney hadn't considered that. "Okay, fine. But we'll need to have a plan."

"Well, like I said," Kyle continued, "Josh is in the emergency room. The doctors are still trying to figure out what to do with him. I heard them talking about tests—"

"Which will not be good for Josh if he is in fact cursed as a vampire," Richard pointed out. "We have to get Josh away from the hospital. But how?"

Rodney said, "We could distract the emergency staff by—"

"A distraction is fine but not if you are in charge of it," Cassie interrupted. "The last distraction you came up with involved dirty bedpans, angry hospital personnel, and nearly being caught in the hospital parking lot."

"Okay, let's see a show of hands; who thinks the distraction is a good idea?" said Rodney.

Alliances being what they were, Kyle and Ceese voted in Rodney's favor.

Cassie fumed, "I can understand Ceese voting for Rodney but not you, Kyle. Only seconds ago, Rodney threatened to walk out on Josh."

Kyle shrugged but didn't lower his hand.

Rodney pressed his back against the tiled hospital wall. Ceese leaned forward to peer around him. "Look, there's someone leaving the room."

Outside Josh's room two doctors conversed, their faces serious, their voices low—too low for Rodney to hear. "Sure would be nice to know what they're saying."

"They're taking Josh for more tests," Ceese said.

"Yeah, probably."

"No, certainly. The one doctor doesn't like what he's found. They want to call the authorities. Josh had drugs on him."

Rodney raised his eyebrows.

Ceese added, ". . . probably?"

Rodney's face paled. Cursed as a werewolf, Ceese could often tell what others were thinking and she was far too accurate for anyone to consider she was guessing. But that ability should've gone with the curse unless—Rodney's eyes widened. "Which is it? Certainly or probably?"

Ceese looked down at her feet. "Certainly?"

"Oh, God," Rodney fell back against the wall. "You—you're still cursed. You could turn into the wolf right here." He ran a shaking hand through his hair and muttered again, "Oh, God."

Frustrated tears filled Ceese's eyes. "I'm not cursed otherwise how could I tolerate hearing you say God's name and how would I be able to say such a sacred name myself?"

"Right," he said, relieved. "But if you're not cursed how can you know for certain what those doctors are saying?"

"I'm not sure I can explain it. I've always been able to sense what others are thinking. I thought everyone could."

"Ummmm . . . No!"

The sarcastic bite to his words pushed a tear down Ceese's cheek. "Maybe I am still cursed. Maybe it isn't over at all."

Rodney melted. He used a thumb to wipe the tear away. "If you're cursed, then why is it you're crying? That is, if cursing stunts human emotions?"

Ceese wiped her eyes with a sleeve. "What if it doesn't work that way? What if the curse really didn't go? What if it-it's just waiting to take hold again?"

"I don't know. Maybe Cassie has an idea. Let's ask—"

"No," Ceese said at once. "I don't think we should tell anyone. I think we should keep this to ourselves."

Rodney shrugged. "Sure. Whatever you think."

"You promise then," Ceese insisted. "You won't tell anyone."

"Who'd believe me?"

Rodney leaned forward then to see that the two doctors had moved along. Another walked into Josh's room. "If what you say is true about what those doctors were saying, we're going to have to make a move soon." Working as only his mind could work, Rodney struggled to come up with an idea that might help them. Finally, a distraction dawned.

"Ceese," he said. "Go back to the end of this hall. Get an elevator and hold it. I'll be there in a minute."

Ceese nodded and left.

The archaic fire protection system for the hospital should have been replaced long ago—a topic that surfaced at each and every administrative meeting. Profits and funds won out and the fire system was always relegated to a back burner. Being up to code would suffice . . . and it was perfect for Rodney's plan.

A loud alarm sounded and the sprinkler above Cassie came to life. She cursed Rodney even as Richard pulled her along. "It's not so bad here," he said as they stopped in front of a supply closet. The sprinkler head above them didn't work.

"So what do we do now?" Kyle asked.

Richard took a quick look around at those racing in the midst of the chaos. "I've got an idea," he said before he slipped into the supply closet. He stepped out wearing a lab coat.

Cassie stared uncertainly. "Do you really think that's a good idea? What if someone asks you a question?"

Richard shrugged. "Then I'll answer it. Technically, I *am* a doctor." He'd earned the degree for one important reason: access to blood without having to curse anyone. He took Cassie by the hand again and the three headed across the hall and closer to Josh's location. Traveling a serpentine path, they avoided most of the active sprinkler heads.

Kyle led; Richard and Cassie followed close behind—so close they nearly ran into Kyle when he abruptly stopped.

"What is it?" Cassie hissed.

"There's someone in there with Josh." He pointed to the blinded window. The slats slightly angled and he made out two sets of legs.

Richard pushed past Kyle and entered the room. "You're needed down the hall," he said with no lack of confidence.

Neither intern moved from where they leaned. "We were told to wait here," one replied. Composed, Richard reached into a pocket of his lab coat, found a pad and pencil and perched his hand to write. "I'm sorry, I didn't get your names?"

Clipped to each intern's pocket was a name placard which they covered at once while heading for the door.

Josh lay on a gurney in the middle of the room. Cassie frowned and looked around. No water sprayed from the sprinkler heads.

"What is it?" Richard asked.

"Listen," she said. "The sprinklers have been shut down. We have to hurry."

Kyle found Josh's jeans in a closet, and Cassie helped wrestle Josh into them. They couldn't find his shirt. The hospital gown he had on would have to do.

"What about his jacket?" Kyle asked after he and Richard stood Josh up between them, his Marley-like dreads hanging nearly to his chest.

"What about it?" Cassie tried to keep her voice low. "We don't have time to look." She hadn't seen the bomber jacket anywhere.

"There." Kyle nodded toward a chair on the other side of the room. They worked in panic mode, whispering and staying clear of open blinds and doors. Tense voices just beyond the door brought a complete silence.

"Make sure everyone who needed to be moved got moved," one man said. "This room is empty."

Despite the close call, Kyle turned to Cassie. "The jacket?"

"I'll get it," she hissed. "Just get Josh out of here."

Cassie caught up easily. The floors remained slick from the sprinklers' water—Richard and Kyle had to step carefully.

"This way," Cassie said. She pointed at the sign: ELEVATORS. Richard and Kyle followed. *What luck!* Cassie thought. No one lingered in the hall so they wouldn't have to make explanations. Cassie walked over and pressed the elevator call button several times. She became more concerned each time it didn't light up—it had worked previously.

"Great! They must've cut the power."

Kyle jostled Josh around a little. His larger friend was heavy, even with Richard on the other side to help support him. "Maybe they'll turn it back on when they realize it was a false alarm."

Cassie looked over her shoulder at the closed door behind her and Kyle reacted at once. "No way. I ain't dragging him up no stairs."

"It would be difficult at that," Richard added.

Cassie shook her head. "What choice do we have?"

At that moment, the stairwell door flew open and a dry Rodney walked out with a dry Ceese.

Rodney saw Cassie first and actually laughed. "You look like a drowned rat."

Cassie crossed her arms in front of her so punching Rodney out wouldn't be so tempting. "We need to get Josh out of here and the elevators have been shut down due to your *distraction.*"

"So?" Rodney said nonchalantly.

"So?" Cassie echoed. "That means the only option left is the stairs and Kyle is already complaining. Richard can't do it alone and neither Ceese nor I would be all that much help. Josh is too heavy—but *you* could take Kyle's place."

That got Rodney's attention. He went right over and started pushing the call button, repeatedly. "Gee, I wish I'd thought of that," Cassie said. Then the elevator doors hissed open. "How did you—"

Her words were lost in a flurry of activity as Kyle rushed forward after Rodney, pulling Josh and Richard along. Ceese went in after them and Cassie squeezed in behind.

"Ahem." The doctor already on board protested, "It's against hospital policy for unauthorized personnel to use the elevators during an emergency." They paid no attention.

When the doors closed, Rodney said, "There's no emergency. I set off the fire alarm. We needed a distraction so we could get our friend out of here." He indicated Josh with a quick nod of his head. "See, he's a vampire and he's going to need blood real soon."

The elevator doors slid open at the fifth floor. Those inside rushed out—except for the doctor. Cassie said, "That was a brilliant performance. Perhaps you should've told the doctor a little more."

"What do you mean? I told him everything."

"My point exactly!"

"I also told him the truth, so you should be happy."

They took the first corner with watchful eyes; they didn't want to draw any more attention than necessary. "It doesn't matter if you tell the truth if you don't know when not to."

"I don't know what you're so upset about. It doesn't matter what I told him. If he believes what I said about my setting off the fire alarm, which is plausible, he'd also have to believe the part about Josh being a vampire, which is implausible. What are the odds?"

"Pretty good, I'd say," Kyle remarked after looking back over his shoulder. "Here comes the good doctor now and it seems he's met up with a few security guards."

Five, to be exact, and one of the five pointed directly at them.

That was their cue to run, but fatigue closed in on Kyle. Josh was simply too heavy. The trio of Richard, Josh, and Kyle weren't moving as fast as they needed. Rodney ran back to take Kyle's place, brought Josh's right arm over his shoulder and signaled to Richard when he was ready. "Let's go!"

The small group cut down one hall and turned left down another, hopeful to lose those following. It worked.

"Look." Ceese pointed ahead. "The exit."

An ambulance had transported them to the hospital the night before, but Cassie had taken a taxi back to the apartment to fetch her car. She was suddenly glad she had done so. The group ran towards the glass door with renewed energy.

Then Rodney stopped short.

"Sunlight," he said. "Well, isn't Josh allergic?"

"It will take a while for the curse to take hold," Richard said. "He should be fine for now."

"But what if you're wrong?"

"He was a vampire once, Rodney." Cassie placed Josh's bomber jacket over his head for protection, just in case. "He knows what he's talking about."

"And if it turns out he's wrong, Josh is dust."

"Richard's right," Ceese assured him. "The curse hasn't taken hold yet."

"Okay then."

What? Cassie thought. They should've just had Ceese tell him in the first place. Cassie took note and decided to ask Rodney about it later.

Distracted, Kyle looked back down the long hall they'd just run up. "Great, they found us."

Security had just rounded the corner. The chase was on again.

Cassie pulled her keys from a pocket and sprinted ahead to pop the trunk. Josh could ride there. She jumped in the car and started it, then felt the thump when Josh landed in the trunk. A few seconds after that, the others piled in. Richard took the front passenger seat and Kyle, Ceese and Rodney clambered into the back.

Cassie was backing up the car when Rodney yelled, "Go now!" and slammed the car door behind him.

"Is the drama really necessary?" she asked.

"You didn't see their guns?"

Car in drive, Cassie pressed the accelerator. "They're supposed to have guns. Why does that alarm you? We're not armed so why would they shoot us?"

"They don't know we're not armed."

Cassie took the first corner too fast, nearly hitting a side wall.

Richard gripped his door handle hard. "Perhaps you should just ignore Rodney."

"I'm still trying to figure out how to do that." Cassie checked her rearview mirror. No one seemed to be following so she drove a little more carefully.

"Why are you slowing down?" Rodney shouted.

Richard reeled around in his seat, his lips tight. "Perhaps it would be better if you didn't say anything else."

"Oh, I'm sorry," Rodney said, sarcastically placid. "It's just that if she doesn't speed back up, she'll never be able to bust through that wooden barrier blocking the exit."

Richard stared ahead. They had come out onto the bottom level. He looked to Cassie. "I suppose you'll have to speed up to get through that. I don't think they're going to raise it."

A numb expression and subtle nod preceded Cassie's decision to floor it.

A wood-splintering crack heralded their freedom. Cassie swung the car around hard to avoid hitting parked vehicles in her path. She continued to drive a little over the speed limit but didn't slow down completely until she'd made the turn out onto a side road.

"You're still going too slow," Rodney told her. "We're not out of the woods yet."

Cassie found Rodney in the rearview mirror. "I'm going the speed limit. That way I don't look like someone who needs to be chased." She enjoyed making her point.

His face contorted in a mask of disbelief. "You don't hear the sirens?"

"What sirens?"

"Those sirens," Kyle replied with a nervous twitter to his voice.

"Now what am I supposed to do?" Cassie groaned. "I can't outrun the police!" She sped up nonetheless.

"You don't have to outrun them," Rodney said. "Ditch them. Pull into an alley."

"Yeah," Kyle said. "Ditch them. That always works in the movies."

Perspiring despite the fact her air conditioning ran at full blast, Cassie fired back. "In case you haven't noticed, this isn't a movie!"

The wail of sirens grew. Rodney leaned forward in his seat, pointing as he shouted, "Turn now!"

Cassie did. She handled the maneuver well, everything considered, but couldn't stop the car in time. In slow motion the car slid into a dumpster piled high with garbage. Bag after bag fell onto the hood. Behind the car, a fire truck screamed past. Two ambulances followed. Cassie's heated glare pinned Rodney in the mirror.

"I know, I know," he groused. "When we get back to the apartment, you want me to pack my things and leave."

Satisfied he understood, she looked away and eased the car into reverse. Trash rolled onto the ground as she carefully backed out. They trailed garbage for at least a block.

4

Cassie often told Rodney to pack his things and leave. She told him so regularly that Rodney decided it had to be a biological thing—that is, until it occurred with more frequency. Oh well, so much for theories.

Biological or not, Rodney rarely feared the ultimatum. Given enough time, Cassie would always chill. She needed his half of the rent as much as he needed hers.

Cassie jammed the key into the lock, turned it, and then yanked the key out. She left the door open for the others, switched on a table lamp, headed toward her bedroom and slammed the door behind her.

Richard and Rodney, carrying Josh between them, stopped outside the apartment. The doorway wasn't wide enough for them to step through together. "You're going to have to turn sideways," Rodney snapped.

"Understandably," Richard said through clenched teeth. "But perhaps you could tell me who you think should go first, you or me?"

"You, I guess."

Once inside, Richard and Rodney both looked around. "Where do we put him?" Rodney asked.

A dark corner sufficed and with duct-taped tinfoil in place over every window, any area not touched by the light from the lamp was indeed dark. A few empty tinfoil boxes scattered about—Cassie's preparations for Richard's arrival.

Cassie and Rodney shared a small apartment not far from Templeton University's main campus. The fourth floor apartment had one bedroom. Rodney slept in the living room on a futon. He sank onto that futon now and sighed as though he were exhausted.

"Finally." He exhaled. "At least that nightmare's over."

"Yes." Ceese settled next to Rodney. "And at least we're away from the hospital."

The futon sat three comfortably. Kyle settled at the far end when Richard claimed the chair closest to the lamp. "I'm afraid the nightmare's only beginning for Josh," he said.

Rodney frowned. "Could you be any more pessimistic?"

"I prefer to be realistic. He's going to undergo a complete metamorphosis soon. It will be neither easy nor pleasant."

Kyle, affected by Richard's grave tone, leaned forward onto his knees and asked. "Wh—what do you mean?"

"As the vampire takes control, things will change for him. Of course, the biggest change will be that he's going to need blood to survive and he'll do anything to get it."

Kyle glanced toward the dark corner where Josh lay. He didn't look like much of a threat. "How long until this starts to happen?"

Richard shrugged. "It's different in each case."

Kyle blanched like he might wet his pants right there and so Rodney stepped in. "Okay, enough drama. You have to know more than you're telling, Richard."

"I'm afraid I don't."

"Well, how much trouble can he be? We have blood in the refrigerator, remember? You didn't finish it all."

Cassie had gleaned quite a few pint bags from a few sources who owed her favors. She'd filled the space inside the refrigerator. Richard had worked on the blood supply over the past few days but a few bags remained.

"He'll crave fresh blood," Richard said. "And he won't readily accept any substitute. That's the hardest thing for a new vampire to deal with. The desire for fresh human blood is so overwhelming it's difficult to get them to consider any alternative. It's hard to reason with evil."

"How'd you do it?" Rodney asked. "Don't you have any suggestions? I mean, you fought the *overwhelming* desire."

"And it was a constant battle each and every day. Those first few days, however, were the absolute hardest. You're sort of in limbo. You're neither here nor there. Once you've adjusted some, you understand more. You're subtly aware of the ramifications of cursing another. But those first few days—your best hope is that no fresh human blood is available. That's the only thing that kept me—" He paused and drew a contemplative breath, "—the only thing that kept me from making the biggest mistake of my life."

Mentally perched on the edge of their seats, both Kyle and Rodney jumped when Cassie came out of the bedroom.

"Here's a towel." She walked over to Richard's chair. "A warm shower works wonders." She pointed to her room. "I'll leave the vanity light on and the door cracked so you can find your way. Other than that, I'll be resting in my room should you need me for anything."

It was just after three in the afternoon. Too early for bedtime but the rest Cassie had hardly counted as sleep. She glared at Rodney before walking off. "Why aren't you packing?" She didn't wait for an answer and stormed off to her room.

"Dude, she's mad," Kyle said.

"Shut up," Rodney snapped. A duffle bag sat on the floor next to the futon. He reached down and pulled it in front of him and started throwing personal items into it: a couple of shirts from under the small glass coffee table in front of the futon and a pair of shoes. Ceese took hold of his arm when he reached to get the clock radio that Kyle offered.

"She's not going to make you leave," she told him.

"Really?"

Ceese nodded. "She's just angry."

Richard's sudden interest in their conversation manifested in his staring, and made both turn. "What?" Rodney asked. "It's pretty clear that she's just angry and wouldn't actually ask me to leave. She just has to calm down."

Had they not looked guilty of something, Richard might not have commented. "If it's so clear then why did you have to wait for Ceese to tell you?"

"You know what?" Rodney stood. "I'm thirsty. I'm going to get something to drink. Ceese," he said, turning, "would you like something?"

Kyle quickly asked for a beer and Rodney directed him to the balcony. "Why is it out there?" Kyle got up.

"Cassie had to make room for all the bags of blood in the fridge."

Sunlight streamed in when Kyle stepped outside. Josh moaned from his corner and Rodney ran to close the door. "You can't leave this open. We've got a vampire in here."

"Sorry," Kyle said after popping the top and returning to the futon. "What is it about the whole daylight thing anyway? Why can't vampires handle it?"

"I have a theory," Richard said, "but that's all it is. I *have* had rather a long time to think about it, you know."

"Okay." Rodney handed Ceese her drink and sat down with his. "So tell us."

"Being vulnerable to the light forces one to hunt under the cover of darkness, when it's also easier to hide. It's difficult to sneak up on someone in broad daylight when you're sporting fangs. Those who did brave the light either died from starvation, sun exposure, or those who hunted *them.* Over time, vampires adapted very much the way animals do. The longer they stayed in darkness the more susceptible they became to the light . . . until they couldn't tolerate it at all."

"Well, since that was technically Kyle's question, I have one. You're always talking about the vampire like it's a separate entity in itself. Isn't Josh the vampire?"

"Not until Josh sets his fate by cursing another. Until then, he's merely influenced by the vampire. After that, the vampire has his soul."

5

Just as Cassie had said, she'd left the bathroom door ajar and the light over the vanity on. With carpet muting his steps, Richard started across the sleeping Cassie's room. A shower did sound nice considering he was still a little damp from the sprinklers at the hospital.

He continued across the room but froze when Cassie stirred. It was not his intention to disturb her. She had to be exhausted, and that realization brought him a twinge of guilt. For the past few days, she'd kept the odd hours that he and Ceese favored as vampire and werewolf. She'd gone out of her way to accommodate them when her two guests couldn't have cared less. Richard cared now and relaxed when she settled and stilled.

Even in the muted light, she very much reminded him of Penelope before he started calling her Mamá. After her curse lifted, Penelope started aging again. For the longest time, it didn't matter. But eventually, their growing age difference called for a new protocol to hide his secret. Penelope never minded and often told him how much she loved the way he said *Mamá*, and explained that with his accent it hardly sounded maternal at all. Like Cassie, Penelope was also very accommodating.

He stiffened at the memory, the sting of not being able to mourn her death delivered an unexpected blow. She'd sacrificed so much for him and all he could muster at the time of her passing was extreme bitterness and hatred at her leaving. The vampire wouldn't allow him to feel anything else. At least he'd kept his promise to take Ceese to visit Cassie in New York.

"She's my granddaughter," Penelope had said before revealing she didn't really know *how* they were related, just that they were. Richard continued to stare at Cassie. He remembered the photo Penelope had showed him and Richard wondered why had he ever questioned. He should've put more trust in her ability to research things. Especially after he'd given her the computer as a gift. Penelope had proven herself quite resourceful when she wanted to be.

He stared a while but then grew uncomfortable. What if Cassie woke up? How would he explain that he couldn't stop looking at her? Moving along to his shower seemed best.

"Richard?" Cassie called out as he turned.

"Mamá!" he gasped, then stuttered to recover, "I mean, my—my I hope I didn't wake you."

"You didn't wake me. I can't sleep."

He sighed in relief. She hadn't noticed he'd called her *Mamá*. "Do you want to talk?" He couldn't believe how much he wanted her to say yes. He missed the long talks he and Penelope used to have.

"Yes," she said. "I guess I would."

Trying not to look too eager, Richard moved a small chair over and settled into it. "So what exactly is keeping you from resting? So much has happened."

Sitting up on the edge of the bed, Cassie rubbed a kink out of her shoulder. "You're right about that. I think it might take me months to sort it all out. I just wish I could understand how Henderson became a vampire. He had to be the one who cursed Josh."

"It's certain that nothing else makes sense."

Cassie shook her head. "Why would anyone want the curse? It makes no sense. I know immortality is a compelling aspect but even at that . . ."

"Soulless immortality isn't all it's cracked up to be. Once your fate is set and you've cursed another, you're a walking corpse. When one's dead to life, existing forever loses a lot of its punch."

Cassie's sympathetic eyes stirred him. "I don't believe Ceese nor I thanked you properly for what you did," Richard said.

"I didn't do anything but give you and Ceese more time to do things yourself. I think Grandmother knew that was all you needed. I think she also knew her time was running out, which is why she sent me here." Cassie shook her head. "I just wish things could've been different. But after going through those files I found at Henderson's place, I'm worried more than ever about what he's up to."

"Files?"

"Yes." She leaned to get her backpack from the floor and switched on the low wattage table lamp. "After the ambulance took you and Ceese to the hospital, I went back to Henderson's because Kyle said he had files on all of us. He also had files on you and Ceese. I was worried who might find them." She took out an envelope and handed it over to Richard. "There's a letter inside. I think you should read it."

According to the address, it had come from a Dr. Savine in Russia who was apparently responding to a letter sent to him. Dr. Savine wrote that he was excited at the prospect of continuing his research in the States. Richard looked up from his reading. "There's more, isn't there?"

She handed him a newspaper clipping. The heading read, *Stem Cells to Male Gametes*.

Richard looked it over with a careful eye. "He's successfully coaxed mice stem cells into male sperm—"

"—and has successfully fertilized an egg with that sperm," Cassie finished

"And this bothers you."

"This Dr. Savine is coming to the States to continue his research. Henderson's specialty is stem cell research. The letter was sent out *after* I started working with Henderson, *after* he learned of you and Ceese through Rodney's bad decisions. He's up to something and now he's a vampire."

6

His eyes snapped open. Blackness. He stared at a wall and then over to a small window. It was dark beyond. Night. He had crawled into a warehouse just as the sun's rays hit a spot on his bare arm. The skin reddened with searing pain where the sun touched. It didn't take long to figure out he needed to take cover and hide from the light.

He craned his neck to study his surroundings. Crates stacked high. He brought his arm around to look at his watch. He'd been sleeping for close to twelve hours. Day had given way to night.

He pushed up from the floor and started walking around the large room for a way out. He needed fresh blood and he needed it now. He maneuvered around effortlessly, completely oblivious to the dark. He could see detail and color. He could see as a vampire.

Weekly revival services at the Inner City Mission Church started promptly at eight o'clock. Sister Betty Marshall liked to be on time. In fact, she liked to be early. Stuffed inside her floral print going-to-church dress, Sister Betty bustled along the sidewalk. Worn leather sandals, stretched beyond their original shape, accommodated wide brown feet and slapped the concrete as she went.

Sister Betty clutched her Bible close. She had to make it to the revival center *before* Luella Thompson. Theirs was a friendly competition but a competition nonetheless. When she didn't make it before Luella, Luella never let her forget it.

The walk light turned amber and then red just as she reached the busy intersection. Sister Betty slowed down, resigned to her fate. She wouldn't make it on time. Luella would get bragging rights for this evening. "Unless—" She strained her eyes to see. *Was that a homeless man in the alley?* "Yes, Lord!" She headed over. Sister Luella might beat her to services but what were the odds that she'd bring along a potential convert?

When Henderson first noticed the lone Sister Betty, his fangs pushed down and out. He'd intended to wait until she got closer, and then pull her into the alley. He wasn't prepared for *her* to approach *him*.

Her Bible captured his attention first. He drew back, hissing. The cross around her neck added to his torture. His ears burned from the sacred words she now quoted. Searing pain shot through eye sockets each time he looked at the cross on her necklace. He threw his hands over his ears, closed his eyes against the pain, and ran.

Sister Betty started to pray and he ran faster. Sloshing along through drainage from downspouts, he struggled to recover. He needed to feed. A subtle breeze that rustled plastic garbage bags brought hope. He turned a corner to see a large cardboard box. A mangy mutt came around, its tail wagging its body. He might've been disappointed had he not known that the bigger prize was still inside.

~·~

Richard didn't rush his shower nor did he rush to get dressed. There'd been enough rushing over the past few days. Casually, he pulled on his pressed black pants then slowly slipped on his starched black shirt. *Drab*, he thought as he stared at himself in the mirror. *Too drab*. The clothes given to him at the hospital were still damp. Drab would have to work for now.

Starting at the bottom and working his way up, he buttoned his shirt. He caught his image in the mirror and stopped. It had been so long since he'd had a reflection. He rubbed at the stubble on his chin and smiled. He'd actually be able to see what he was shaving today.

He pulled the canned cream from the travel bag and lathered up. Then with his favorite straight razor, he made the first swipe. It made such a difference to be able to see the results. Clean-shaven on one side, he rinsed his blade for another pass. Straight-edge perched, another image replaced his in the mirror. It appeared so suddenly, it startled him. His hand slipped and the blade cut.

Terror stricken, the gaunt, pale face stared. Richard swung around to look behind him, but no one was there. He swung back around to face the mirror. *What in the world was going on?* Then the man in the mirror cried out, "Vampire."

Richard's face lost all expression and he saw what the old man saw.

"No!"

Cassie rushed in and gasped at what she saw—blood on Richard's face and blood on the razor in his hand. *Why did he just stand there gaping into the mirror?* Cassie pried the razor from his grasp, wiped at his cheek with a tissue, and prayed the injury wouldn't need stitches. The cut was deep but the bit of tissue she tore off seemed to be holding, for now.

"Vampire," Richard whispered harshly—his first word since she'd come in.

"Vampire?"

"Why don't you run?"

Cassie looked to where Richard was staring. "You see someone?"

"He's going to curse someone."

"Who—who's going to curse someone?"

"Henderson."

Penelope, Cassie's grandmother had speculated in her diary that a vampire who sired, or rather cursed, another, would often know when the one they sired was about to curse someone else. Perhaps that's what happened here. But that would mean Henderson had in fact used Richard's blood to become a vampire.

"Can you stop him, Richard? Do you have any control over what he's doing?"

"There's a dog," he said to himself. "I should make him take the dog instead."

"Yes," Cassie encouraged. "You should make him do that if you can." She didn't know if he needed her to tell him this but she didn't see how it could hurt.

After a moment, Richard's shoulders sagged. His head fell forward.

"Are you all right? Did you stop him?"

"Yes," he told her. "I did."

The small bathroom offered nothing to distract them and after his answer, it suddenly felt much smaller. In fact, awkwardly smaller. Cassie noticed Richard hadn't finished buttoning his shirt. She'd seen him once before without a shirt, the day she'd found his cross in Grandmother's diary. She'd wanted to ask him about it, but became tongue-tied when she saw him shirtless. At the time, she'd assumed it was the lure of the vampire, but she had no excuse now. She left before she could embarrass herself further.

With the door between them, she was able to think a little clearer. Even at that, she couldn't ignore how Richard made her feel—like a high school girl with a bad crush. Like she'd felt when she first met Daryl. But she'd sworn off guys after Daryl. What was she supposed to do now?

゛゛゛

Josh attacked the second Kyle got up for the television remote. The room was small. Kyle had nowhere to go. "Help!" he managed before going down hard from Josh's tackle. It all happened before anyone could move.

Rodney knew he needed to do something but froze at Josh's fangs. Cassie's bedroom door opened—he yelled at Richard, "Don't just stand there! Do something!"

Josh reared back to strike, Richard raced, locked an arm around Josh's neck and pulled backward. Kyle saw his opportunity and took it. He scrambled away.

Josh grabbed Richard by the arm still around his neck and pushed to his feet. He pulled Richard around and threw him against the far wall.

Cassie had run to the kitchen. After she'd shoved a bag of blood in the microwave and stabbed at some buttons she turned to Rodney. "You know, you *could* help."

Rodney had fixated on Josh. He started at Cassie's voice. He nodded. "Yeah. Sure." He jumped over to the futon, stood on one end and unhooked the potted plant above. Using its macramé rope, he swung the dehydrated fern over his head, released it, and sent the potted plant flying. It nailed Josh in the back and exploded out of its pot.

"Yes," Rodney hissed.

It made no difference. Josh continued his pursuit of Kyle as if he hadn't been hit—he darted this way and that around the coffee table. He could have simply leapt over the table, but a mad grin showed his drive for the hunt.

"How was that supposed to help?" Kyle yelled.

The microwave dinged. "Here," Cassie tossed the warmed bag of blood over to Richard.

Ceese, who'd stayed out of the way, called to him, "Your face. You're bleeding, Brother."

Sure enough, the tissue on the cut had come off. When he put his hand up to check, he found his cheek moist and sticky. Richard's eyes brightened.

7

Richard smeared his bloodied hand onto the pint bag Cassie had tossed him. The vampire froze in his hunt and slowly turned his leering face to Richard.

In the most tantalizing voice he could muster, Richard asked, "You want this?" He stepped slowly toward the vampire, dangling the bag by a corner.

"Careful," said Cassie.

Josh had just thrown Richard across the room with little effort. No one had the desire to see that again—or worse.

Richard smeared more blood onto the bag.

Josh, still in his hospital gown and ragged jeans, snatched the bag. He pierced it with fangs and leapt to a dark corner sucking greedily.

Rodney stepped off the futon. "Are we safe? Is that it? Can our resident expert give us a hint?"

"He'll need more blood."

"Duh. I think I could've figured that out."

"I mean—he'll need more blood soon."

"What?" Kyle whimpered, not ready for a replay of what just happened.

"He'll be looking to replace what Henderson took."

"Don't worry," Cassie said as she headed back to the refrigerator. "I'm on it."

Kyle rubbed at his neck. "I've got a question," he addressed Richard. "Why, out of everyone in this apartment, did he target me?"

"Like any predator, a vampire, particularly a new one, goes for the easiest meal. It needs blood and it needs it fast. It's the most dangerous time to be near them because there's absolutely nothing to hold them back. The vampire is in complete control. There's no other time in the cursed existence when it'll have such control."

"So, that's why I couldn't see 'Josh' in there anywhere," Rodney said.

"Yes. As soon as the amount of blood taken is replaced, he'll appear more like the Josh you knew."

"I still don't get it," Kyle said. "Why did he come after *me*?"

"What's there to get, Kyle?" Rodney now wore the predatory grin. All knew he was very good at and took great pride in antagonizing Kyle. "Richard just told you a new vampire goes after the easiest meal. The vampire obviously sees you as the biggest wimp."

"Perhaps 'vulnerable' would be a better choice of words," Richard suggested.

"Okay," Rodney said. "The vampire sees you as the biggest *vulnerable* wimp."

"Yeah, whatever," Kyle smirked. "But that hardly makes sense when you consider there were two girls to choose from."

"And yet he came for you and almost chose you over a plastic bag of blood."

Kyle snapped his best witticism, "Shut up."

"Perhaps," Cassie carried in the second bag of warmed blood, "you should spend less time antagonizing others and more time explaining your actions. At what point did it make sense to hurl a potted plant across the room? You hate that fern. You never stopped griping about it."

"I had to do something," Rodney protested. "Josh was going to curse Kyle."

"So you launched a potted plant at him?"

"Things were crazy, okay?"

Cassie looked toward the mess the fern had made. "You just make sure you clean it all up."

"Aye, aye, Captain." Rodney saluted. He took the broom from the front closet, muttering, "Least those little leaves won't shed on me all night long."

At 9:45 PM, Josh finished his second bag of blood and fell back into a deep slumber. He would need to feed again—they just didn't know when.

"I don't want to wake up with a vampire on my neck," Kyle said.

"If we get to him quick enough," Richard surmised, "we could likely avoid another fight."

"We could just take turns watching him," Ceese suggested.

"Not a bad idea," Richard said and they settled on one-hour shifts.

Josh slumbered quietly for the first three watches. Then it came Rodney's turn.

"Rodney?" Cassie whispered.

No movement.

"Rodney." Then after another few seconds she whispered loudly, "Rodney, it's time to get up!"

He stirred and grunted but his eyes remained closed. "Okay, Rodney, I'm going to get a glass of water and pour it over your head."

"I'm up. I'm up," he said. Eyes now open, Rodney stumbled over and settled against the same wall she'd been leaning against a moment ago.

"Are you sure you can do this?" Cassie asked.

"I got it," he said. "Just go to sleep."

"You're not going to mess this up, are you?"

"I'll do my best," came his agitated reply.

Cassie left him to his task.

Rodney did do well for the first ten minutes but the soft sound of people breathing had a pronounced effect. His eyelids grew heavy. It became a task not to let them close—and even harder to hold his head up. *I'll just lay down here on the floor.*

Kyle had yet to recover fully from his first encounter with Josh and slipped in and out of a very restless sleep. His eyes popped open, however, when he sensed someone standing very close to him. Imagination or not, it felt real. "Oh, God," he screamed and Josh fell back.

"What's going on?" Cassie sprang immediately out of bed and into the kitchen. Rodney had fallen asleep and Josh had woken up. Kyle once again became the object of his attention.

Fortunately, Josh was a little easier to deal with this time. He readily took the bag of blood offered. Once settled in his corner to feed, Cassie turned to Rodney.

"I'm sorry," Rodney said. "I guess I fell asleep."

"You guess?" Kyle blared angrily. "I've had it. I'm out of here."

"Can't say I blame him," Cassie said to the slamming front door.

Richard glanced over at Josh in his corner. "It's too bad we can't get him to my castle. It would be so much easier for him to temper his desire there. He could roam the woods freely without coming into contact with anything other than animals."

Ceese's reaction was immediate and enthusiastic. "Yes, Brother! Let's do that! Let's take Josh to England. Let's go home. Plus, you could help him restrain the vampire."

She'd said it again. She'd called England home. Taking Josh to England made a lot of sense. But was it feasible? Richard turned to the person whose opinion he'd learned to trust. "What do you think, Cassie?"

"It would certainly be easier on Josh, although I don't think it's fair to ask you to watch out for him. After all, he's not your burden."

"You wouldn't come along?"

Cassie sputtered. "Richard, I can't just pick up and run off to England. I have classes, responsibilities. Do you have any idea how much money it would cost? I can barely afford this apartment. Traipsing off to England—in my dreams, maybe."

"I'd pay."

"Yes," Ceese said and drew a suspicious glance from Cassie. Ceese had shown no partiality towards her, either before her curse was lifted or after. So why was she so friendly now? "Richard would do that."

Cassie looked back to Richard. "I won't go unless I can pay my own way."

"All right, you can owe me then. You'll pay me back later."

"What about school? I have classes."

"Cancel them. Pick up where you left off when you return."

"What about me?" Rodney said. "After all, Josh is *my* friend and I'm poor too."

"Sure," Richard said immediately. "I'll pay your way too."

Ceese smiled at this but Cassie frowned. "You can't pay him back and you know it, Rodney. You already owe me two months of back rent."

"Look, forget paying me back. Consider it a gift. Ceese and I certainly owe the both of you more than we could ever repay. Please don't turn our gift down."

So much had changed for Cassie over the past few days. A professor had blackmailed and used her. She'd missed several classes and several labs. "All right," she said finally. "I'll go—we'll go. But Rodney, we *will* make this up to Richard somehow."

"Yes," Rodney said with a nod and a grin. "Got ya."

"All right," Cassie said thoughtfully, "who's going to take Kyle's shift?"

"I will," Richard replied. "I'll need the time to work out the details of our trip—and figure out a way to keep Josh from feeding on a plane-load of passengers during an eight-hour flight."

8

Cassie sat straight up. The clock on her bedside table read 6:15. Richard should've come after her already for her turn on Josh-watch. She found her warm-up pants and slipped into them. She couldn't imagine what had gone wrong. Had Josh gone wild and cursed everyone but her while she slept?

But Richard sat relaxed at the table, debonair as ever, coffee cup in hand, reading the paper. "Good morning," he said when she entered the kitchen. "I hope you don't mind. I found the paper by the door."

"No. It'll save me from having to move it later." Neither she nor Rodney paid much attention to the paper. They usually let them collect in a small pile in front of the door before doing anything. "Why didn't you wake me up?" She joined him at the kitchen table.

"I wasn't tired and I was able to get some things done." He stood. "Let me get you some coffee." He didn't give her a chance to say no. "I hope it tastes all right. I've no real idea."

"It's good," Cassie said after a sip. "I couldn't have done better myself." She took another sip and asked, "So, you've been busy?"

"Well, I've been on your computer," he said as he motioned over his shoulder, "and I've managed to get first class plane tickets for all of us."

"When do we leave?"

"Tonight."

"Wow. You *have* been busy."

"Is that too soon? I can change the reservations."

"No. It—it's fine." Had he not considered she'd have to pack and get ready? "The sooner the better, I guess." She placed the cup of coffee down on the table.

Richard covered one of her hands with his. "You have no idea how glad I am you decided to make this trip with Ceese and me . . . and Josh."

She smiled but gently eased her hand away, pretending she needed it to hold her cup. She might not be able to keep her eyes from revealing what his touch meant to her. "I can't wait."

Rodney rose from the futon; obviously, he'd been listening to their conversation. He carefully stepped over the sleeping Ceese and headed across the room. "Can't you two keep your hands off each other? I think I'm gonna be sick."

Spiteful darts shot from Cassie's eyes. "Are you sure about taking *him* along?"

Rodney turned one of the kitchen chairs around and straddled it. "Too late. Richard already bought the tickets."

"Perhaps you could work a little harder to get along with everyone," Richard said.

"But it's so much easier to just be myself."

"It works better if you don't humor him," Cassie said to Richard.

"Very well. Cassie, do you have any ideas on how we can travel safely with our vampire friend?"

Rodney's eyes bulged. "You mean you don't know? Shouldn't you have already worked that out?"

Cassie ignored Rodney's theatrics. "We need some way to keep him from waking up."

"Yes." Richard kept his eyes trained on Cassie.

"Hello," Rodney said, waving a hand between the two of them. "I have an idea."

"Do you hear something?" Cassie asked Richard.

"I'm sure I don't."

Rodney put his hand down. "Fine. Then I won't tell you that Kyle's dad is a certified anesthesiologist who has access to some very *strong* and powerful sedatives—which can also be fun at parties if you know what you're doing."

Both Cassie and Richard turned to face Rodney. "Tell me you didn't make that up," Cassie said.

"Should I waste my breath?"

～～～

Kyle knew what dexmedetomidine was. He also knew about the other sedatives Richard had requested—not because he paid any attention to his father's discussions, but his current course load included a class in pharmaceuticals. Kyle stood with Richard in the hall just outside Cassie's door. "You know, administering these isn't all that simple. Certain medications shouldn't be taken simultaneously. Certain doses aren't healthy for some individuals." He held the bag with the sedatives close to his chest . . . as if he might not hand it over if Richard didn't respond with the correct reply.

"I understand," Richard told him. "I'm a doctor, remember? Josh will be fine. What might kill someone else won't faze Josh. Our only hope is that the sedation will work at all."

Kyle handed over the bag. Richard opened the door and walked back into the apartment.

Rodney went out to talk to Kyle. "You sure you don't want to go to England with us? Richard's paying."

"He couldn't pay me enough." Kyle left without adding anything else.

～～～

Perhaps Josh wouldn't die from a sedative overdose but the vampire could easily adjust to its effects. Richard kept this in mind. Each syringe would have a different mixture.

Ceese walked around Richard as he worked. She stepped out onto the balcony. Rodney turned toward her when the foil-covered glass door slid open, then back to his warm beer as Ceese slid the door shut. The balcony faced east and the late afternoon sun shone on the other side of the building. Ceese walked to the railing and stared out.

"I guess you're all packed."

Ceese nodded.

"You've gotta be pretty psyched about going home."

Ceese shrugged. "I am."

"Well, you don't act like someone who's psyched."

Ceese looked down at the weathered railing and picked a few paint flecks off. "I don't like airplanes."

"But you flew over here on one."

"Richard talked me into it. He took me flying around the castle gardens—on his back, when he was a vampire—to get me used to the idea."

"I don't like flying all that much either. That's why I came out here. I thought maybe a beer or two might help calm me down." He cocked his head in her direction. "But you already know that, don't you?"

Ceese looked away.

"You can't keep doing that, Ceese. You can't keep getting in my head like that. A guy's gotta have some privacy."

The glass door opened again. This time it was Cassie. "Sorry, I didn't know you two were out here. I just came to get a pair of shoes I'd left—" Ceese pushed by her before she could finish. Rodney simply looked irritated. Cassie finished her sentence absently, ". . . to dry. Did I interrupt something?"

"Do you really care?"

Rodney tried to push past as well but Cassie grabbed him by the arm. "I'm not the bad guy, Rodney. If you keep treating me like I am, then Ceese will never give me the time of day."

"Why does it matter if she thinks you're the bad guy and why do you try to make everything my fault? Maybe Ceese decided on her own not to give you the time of day. You know, that *is* a possibility."

"She listens to you, Rodney. She pays attention to everything you do."

Rodney broke away. "Well, at least somebody does."

At the kitchen table, Richard placed the filled syringes back into the tri-fold pouch they'd come in. Josh stirred in his dark corner and Richard stood. It was time to feed their vampire.

9

Heavily sedated, Josh's head lolled at an awkward angle; his dreads fell like a curtain about his face as they pushed him along in the wheelchair.

"He's a passenger?" a heavy-set middle-aged ticket agent droned after they moved up to the counter.

Richard followed her subjective gaze to where Josh sat. "Yes. He has a paralyzing fear of flying. He's been sedated for the trip."

She stared at Richard. "I just need to know who'll be in charge of him, that's all." Her flat, dry tone made it hard to determine just what information would be helpful.

"Of course." Richard took out his wallet to retrieve the physician's card. The ticket agent barely acknowledged it. She stamped this, scribbled initials on that and ripped and punched other pieces of paper with practised hands.

"You'll need to remain at his side at all times—in the airport and on the plane."

Richard nodded. "I understand."

Luggage checked, passports and boarding passes in hand, the ticket agent lost all interest in them. They had only been placeholders in a long line of faceless passengers. They gathered up their carry-on bags and moved along.

They'd arrived at the airport an hour earlier than necessary anxious to get to the gate and closer to their destination. The sooner they got there—the sooner it would be over.

Lined up at the security checkpoint Cassie asked Rodney, "Don't you think you should start taking off all that jewelry? Or, are you going to wait for security to tell you to do it?"

"I'm not taking any of it off unless they make me."

Cassie tensed. "Why wait until you've gone through the metal detector? You're only going to slow us down."

"Not unless they make me," he repeated.

"Remove your shoes and empty his pockets, sir," said a security agent with a detection wand. He didn't give Rodney's jewelry more than a second glance.

Once on the other side, Rodney turned to Cassie and smirked. "See, no problem."

Ceese, who was next in line, slowly started to back away, muttering under her breath, "It's evil."

When they'd made the trip over from England, Richard had heard Ceese refer to many things as evil. If she didn't understand something or it frightened her—it was evil. And because she had chosen to stay in her wolf form for so long to avoid the temptation of cursing another, nearly everything frightened her. He'd prepared her as best he could before the trip to the States but he'd forgotten all about her fears since their curses were lifted. The things that frightened her were still there and she'd had no time to get used to them.

Richard stood and watched. He wanted to go to her, but had already passed through security and technically, he couldn't leave Josh's side. The ticket agent had made that very clear.

Cassie watched Ceese as well. Rodney, the only other person who seemed to be able to get through to her, wasn't even paying attention. He busied himself with his shoes. Finally, he looked up. Ceese had her back pressed against the wall.

Rodney rushed back through the metal detector and over to Ceese. He stopped in front of her and held out his hand. "Here," he said. "You helped me once. Let me help you now. I'll lead you. There's nothing to be afraid of."

He took Ceese's hand; he didn't rush her but let her move at a comfortable pace. He even picked up her shoes and dropped them into a plastic bin for inspection. Minutes later, they stood together on the other side. "See, that wasn't so bad, was it?"

Cassie sighed with relief.

"Ow!" Rodney seethed after his head hit the overhead compartment hard. "What are you doing?"

"You said left, so I moved left," Richard answered, hitting his head, hands full with Josh's calves. The agent had announced priority boarding for passengers with wheelchairs, but already other passengers had lined up behind them. Richard tried not to draw unwarranted attention. A task doomed to fail.

"I meant *my* left, not yours," Rodney protested.

"Perhaps next time you'll be more clear."

Josh hung like a rag doll between the two of them. They'd already left the wheelchair behind blocking the aisle. "Okay, then, move left—*my* left."

Richard, desperate to be out of the aisle, pushed hard. Rodney hadn't expected such force, and already in a tight spot between the seats, stumbled, fell, and somehow managed to land squarely in the window seat. As luck would have, Josh landed on him. Richard reached in to pull him off and together they finally settled Josh in the middle seat. A flight attendant folded the wheelchair and those passengers held up by their actions moved on past.

"Well," Richard said as he settled into the aisle seat. "At least we're on the plane."

"Yes," Rodney grumbled and massaged the left side of his head. "And thanks to you, I won't be forgetting that anytime soon."

"I'm sorry, but you weren't exactly specific about which way I should move."

"Let's just drop it."

Cassie boarded ahead of Ceese and checked over her shoulder to ensure she followed. She could only hope there wouldn't be another incident like the security checkpoint. When Cassie stopped to stow her backpack in an overhead compartment, Ceese moved in to claim the seat next to the window. Cassie relaxed. At least there'd be no awkward discussion about seat choice. More importantly, this put Cassie across the aisle from Richard. She sat, her relief great.

A flight attendant overshadowed Cassie in the aisle and handed Richard several seat belt extensions. "We need him in an upright position for take off," she said.

Richard connected them at their buckles to make one long strap. He handed one end to Rodney. "Help me put this around his seat." Rodney held Josh in place so Richard could buckle it across the chest. Now his torso was upright, although his head still lolled forward.

"Oh, yes," Rodney said. "He's much safer now."

The stewardess who had supplied the belt extensions reappeared in the front of the cabin. With props and contrived hand motions she looked much like an animated mannequin as she pantomimed automated safety instructions. The plane began to taxi out and reality set in.

Ceese leaned forward and grabbed desperately for the back of the seat in front of her. For a second it looked like she might jump up and run for an exit. Rodney leaned as well and got her attention. After a tense moment, Ceese settled. With no calming words or exchange of any kind, Rodney seemed to have helped Ceese yet again. No doubt lingered in Cassie's mind now. Something was going on between the two and she promised herself to find out what it was.

Twenty minutes into the flight, Cassie saw another opportunity to learn what Rodney wouldn't tell her on the balcony of their apartment. When he stepped out of the lavatory, she got out of her seat to ambush him. When he exited the restroom she pulled him aside.

"This is really getting old," Rodney told her.

"Then tell me what I want to know and I'll leave you alone."

"There's nothing to tell other than you need to stop being so paranoid."

"Rodney, if there's something going on with Ceese then I need to know about it."

"Why?"

"So there is something going on with her."

"You're going to believe what you want to believe. Nothing I can say is going to change that."

"You could tell the truth."

"I could," Rodney said as he motioned her to move along, "but what fun would that be?"

～～

Rodney's stomach hadn't settled much since his trip to the lavatory but now that the cabin lights had dimmed, maybe he'd fall asleep and forget about how badly he wanted to throw up. He shifted around, tried to get comfortable and closed his eyes. A few hours later, his eyes sprung open—Richard had switched on his overhead reading light.

"What're you doing?" Rodney asked.

"I thought I should give Josh another injection—just to be on the safe side."

Rodney groaned inside; he felt even queasier than before he'd fallen asleep but he tried not to let it show. "So, it's like a precautionary measure."

"You could say that. Better safe than sorry." Richard swabbed the puncture site on Josh's arm. "Here, hold Josh's arm straight ahead; we are fortunate that his veins protrude so this is an easy job."

Like motorists prone to rubbernecking, Rodney couldn't take his eyes off Richard's preparations. After removing the filled syringe from his pouch, he flicked the needle to knock any air bubbles to the top of the syringe. He depressed it to expel the air and then punctured Josh's vein.

"Oh, God," Rodney cried. He grabbed for the airsick bag in the seat pocket in front of him. "I didn't need to watch that." False alarm though. He managed to hold on to what little he'd eaten before they left for the airport.

Richard returned the syringe pouch to his pocket and switched the reading light off.

"No," Rodney said and switched his light on. "Let's—talk. I need to keep my mind off getting sick."

"All right," Richard said. "What shall we talk about?"

Rodney struggled to come up with something. "I don't know. How about—all the money you seem to have? Where'd you get it?"

"Do we really have to talk about that?"

"Come on—" Rodney hugged his abdomen and gritted his

teeth until another cramp subsided. "Phew," he slumped back in his seat, "glad that one's over . . . you were saying?"

"Well, I worked for most of what I have."

"You're kidding, right? I mean, you could've hypnotized people—the way you did that guard at the airport when you guys flew into New York. You could've persuaded them to give you all their money. How boring. You're gonna have to do better than that to hold my interest."

"I did have an act at a sideshow once, as a knife thrower."

Rodney leaned forward in his seat to look around Josh. "I thought you said you earned money honestly."

"I did. There's nothing dishonest about knife throwing."

"Everybody knows knife throwing is a joke. There's no skill involved. The thrower palms the knife, pretends to throw it and a knife springs out from the target he's supposedly aiming at. If you took money for that then I'd have to say that technically—you're a thief."

"I won't deny that the technique you just described exists but the great majority of knife throwers are skilled performers."

"You mean to tell me you actually threw knives—at people—and it wasn't staged?"

"Yes."

"How long did you have this job?"

Richard's brief sour look didn't last long enough. "Until the night my usual assistant got deathly ill and I had to have a stand-in because, as you know, the show must go on. Only the young man who they sent to help out was a bit on the nervous side."

"Oh no . . . I don't think I want to hear any more."

Richard continued as if Rodney hadn't interrupted. "When I let the first knife go—well, he moved. The knife hit its mark but the blade shaved the young man's right ear completely off the side of his head. It was a bloody mess and I was hard-pressed to hold the vampire back—" Richard stopped at the sound of a retching noise.

Rodney's buried his face in the barf bag as he heaved again.

10

Impeccably dressed in standard butler attire—black suit, gray vest, black tie, with meticulously combed white hair beneath his driving cap—Geoffrey tucked his gloves away in a pocket and walked with perfect cadence toward a lower level entrance at Heathrow Airport. Had he spoken to the attendant standing just outside, flawless Queen's English would've sprung from his lips. Instead, he nodded as was more proper. And being educated at the finest butlering school in England, proper was important.

Getting Josh off the plane wasn't a big ordeal, thankfully. The group waited until the rest of the passengers had disembarked. Josh still resembled a rag doll but at least they had time—and no curious audience—to disembark him. Between Richard and Rodney, they lifted and supported the sedated Josh up the aisle and out the door. A wheelchair and attendant waited on the ramp. "We can take care of it from here," Richard told the attendant. "Thank you."

Rodney had not recovered after Richard's little knife-throwing story. His stomach continued to flip and flop, churn and cramp. A steward, concerned more for the comfort of those sitting around Rodney, offered him some kind of fizzy drink. He accepted without hesitation and did get a few hours sleep. With the unmoving ground beneath his feet, Rodney appeared much better.

Richard had closed his eyes and rested. He periodically checked on Josh. Two hours before they landed, he felt a jerk and looked down to see Josh's right hand move. It could have been the result of the plane hitting an air-pocket, but as he had told Rodney earlier, better safe than sorry. An immediate booster dose was in order.

"What's happening?" Cassie whispered from across the aisle. "Is he waking up?"

Richard held up the only syringe left then turned his face up toward the ceiling for a few seconds. As Cassie watched, he went through the syringe drill and injected Josh. After putting the supplies away, he mimicked prayer with his hands. Cassie nodded.

Ceese slept throughout most of the trip—at least it appeared to be sleep. Her dialogue with Cassie had been restricted to yes, no and an occasional thank-you when necessary. Ceese's fear of flying accounted for much of her actions—but not all. Cassie drove herself crazy trying to figure out why Ceese acted the way she did around her, constantly treating her coldly—nearly like a servant. Halfway into the trip, she decided she'd figured it out. When Richard suggested that Ceese switch places with him, Ceese grinned. However, when Richard elaborated, "That way you can talk with Rodney and I with Cassie," she promptly dropped back down into her seat. "I think I'll just sit here."

Jealous, Cassie decided. *Ceese was jealous*. It made perfect sense. She finally had Richard all to herself after being without him for years and she didn't want anything or anyone to come between them.

※

Stoic and professional, the butler strode over to Richard and his companions in the baggage claim area and stopped before the wheelchair Richard pushed. "I trust you had a pleasant trip, sir." He nodded to Richard.

Richard's head snapped up and he stared. His eyebrows met in the middle of his face and a brief smile followed. He looked behind and when he turned back the smile had left his face. Eyes narrowed, Richard's mouth slowly opened to form an O. "Geoffrey!" he gushed. "How could I fail to notice you? I—I dare say I didn't recognize you at all. Your voice and these circumstances . . . that's what finally clinched it."

"It *has* been a while." A subtle smile accompanied another nod.

"Even at that, I should've recognized you."

"Okay," Rodney piped up, "could we move this party on? Either Jeeves is here for a reason or you two need to get a room."

"Rodney," Cassie reacted.

"It's all right," Richard told her. "We really should be going." He pointed down at Josh's slumped body. "Geoffrey, man—after all this time . . ." Richard turned to his waiting friends, "I'll explain it in a minute. Right now we need to get a move on."

Warmly, Richard grasped Geoffrey by a shoulder. "I'm so very glad you were available. They told me when I called that you were presently obligated."

"I made arrangements," he said. "And now, if you have your claim tickets, I'll go secure your luggage."

"Of course."

"So you have a butler," Rodney said after Geoffrey walked off.

"He's more than a butler," Richard replied. "But then, every good butler is."

Cassie read Rodney's expressions and decided she knew what was behind his crude grin. "Keep your thoughts to yourself," she told him. "If that's possible."

Ceese, who'd been smiling since they'd landed, bubbled, "Come on Richard, tell Rodney about Geoffrey."

"Well, I'll make it a short one. I needed a servant to help with . . . things at home. It was quite the tricky ordeal and I interviewed dozens of prospects . . . you realize that finding someone who understood the whole vampire issue wasn't easy. Geoffrey sat down and recognized something within me. Once he confessed that his father was cursed as a vampire as well, I knew I had the right person. End of story."

Rodney rolled his eyes. "So, what was the deal with not recognizing him? I mean—"

"Geoffrey went on to butlering school and took another job. I called the agency before leaving New York because I anticipated needing Geoffrey in the house to help Marissa with all of you. They'd said he was otherwise engaged, but fortunately he made himself available." Richard prevented further inquiries by kicking off the wheelchair's brake and pushing it out toward the exit.

The Nissan Patrol SUV, now parked in the loading zone, idled while Geoffrey placed luggage into the back, leaving room for Josh. As Geoffrey worked, he considered, *How could we draw the least amount of attention when it comes time to load our unconscious passenger?* Finished with his task, he headed over to the attendant he'd nodded at earlier. A conversation took place and a number of British pounds exchanged. For the short time it would take to load Josh, the attendant would direct others to the next entrance. Geoffrey picked up the blankets he'd brought along and headed back to the others.

"I've arranged for a certain amount of privacy to avoid suspicion," he said.

"You've *arranged*?" Rodney questioned.

"Yes," Geoffrey replied as he draped a blanket around Josh's shoulders so it covered him.

"What do you mean by that?"

Smiling at the American lack of subtlety, Geoffrey said, "I paid the attendant off. For the time being, he's directing others to another entrance."

Rodney smiled shrewdly. "I like you. You're good."

They wheeled Josh around to the back of the vehicle but stopped short of hoisting him inside. Geoffrey had spotted a security camera. What they were about to do certainly wouldn't look good on tape. "If you'll just excuse me for one second," he said and headed back over to the attendant. A few more bills were handed over—and another deal struck.

"When the attendant returns to his post," Geoffrey shared upon returning, "we'll have five seconds to get our friend into the back before the security camera is reactivated."

They all turned to look toward the attendant's station. He had indeed left. Upon his return a few seconds later, Geoffrey said, "Starting now." Rodney jumped to gather up Josh's legs. Richard reached to grab Josh under the arms and Geoffrey pulled the wheelchair away. On two, they lifted. On three, they hoisted. On four, they quickly covered Josh and then slammed the two rear doors shut. By the time they got to five, Geoffrey had wheeled the wheelchair out of the camera's view.

The Patrol could seat seven comfortably. Richard moved into the front passenger seat, which, to Rodney's dismay, happened to be on the left side.

"Now that's just freaky." He studied the odd configuration from where he sat in the middle of the back seat.

"Before you panic," Cassie pulled the car door shut behind her, "they drive on the left side of the road as well."

"I've seen movies," Rodney protested. "I just said it was freaky, that's all."

Cassie caught Richard peeking at her in the side-view mirror. She wanted to believe he looked at her but the windows were tinted. What were the odds? Then he smiled before turning to face the front again. Perhaps he could see more than she thought.

"What are you grinnin' at?" Rodney asked.

Embarrassed and then angry, Cassie popped off. "Is it impossible for you to mind your own business?" It was childish, she knew. But he could make her so angry.

Having worked his magic, Rodney smiled and went back to staring out the front window.

Leaving Heathrow, Geoffrey caught the M25—or orbital car park as most locals called the busy freeway. Their route took them though Farnham, a lovely old market town with Georgian-fronted affluence. Had they taken a side street, they would've enjoyed the sight of large beautiful Victorian houses. Instead, they drove south where large detached houses, purposefully built by long-dead owners, had become flats of second-rate footballers.

Very soon, the view changed: rolling pastures dotted with pines, English oaks, livestock, and a slight ground fog. Richard stared with new eyes. As a vampire, he'd only ever seen any of this at night. "Everything looks so different. I never imagined that—" His voice caught. "It's just so different."

As they drove, the trees grew thicker and closer to the road. Suddenly Ceese, who'd said nothing since leaving the airport, sat up animated and alert.

"There," she said pointing. "That tree. I once marked that tree as I made my way to the castle." Then she clarified, "As the wolf."

Of all the odd things to share. Cassie drove an elbow into Rodney's side before he could have fun with it, as he undoubtedly would have.

"What?" he protested. "I wasn't gonna say anything. Besides, she was a wolf. That's what wolves do."

Richard quickly intervened. "Perhaps we could discuss the ways of the wolf at some other time when those of us who aren't as interested can go elsewhere."

Ceese took the reprimand well and went back to looking out her window. A few minutes later she spoke again, "That's where Peter Drummond lives." She pointed to a shack near the bottom of a wooded slope.

"You mean that's where he *used to* live," Richard corrected.

"He still lives there," Ceese said. "Sort of."

"But I thought—"

"—that the wolves killed him?" she cut in, her tone slightly indignant. "They came to judge him for killing Long Tail and Xavier. That's all."

"Wait a minute," Rodney said, concerned. "What's all this talk about people being killed? We were supposed to be safer here. Not in more danger."

"Xavier was my wolfhound," Richard informed. "And Long Tail was one of Ceese's wolf friends. Peter Drummond shot my wolfhound, thinking it was a wolf that was taking his sheep and—"

Rodney stopped him before he could continue. "A wolfhound doesn't exactly look like a wolf."

"It does when you're three sheets to the wind. Drummond drank heavily."

"*Drinks* heavily," Ceese corrected. "Peter is still alive. Geoffrey can tell you."

"Is that true?" Richard looked toward his butler.

Geoffrey's reply was simple. "Everyone knows about the goat herder."

11

Richard might've pushed Geoffrey for an explanation about Peter Drummond had he not been distracted by the circular brick drive and the sight of home.

Ceese drew a deep breath. "We're here, we're home." Throwing her door open, she ran past the main entrance and instead, darted down a side walkway.

"Well, someone's eager to be back," Cassie remarked as she got out behind Richard. A perfectly cared-for garden lined the long drive. The lawn itself stretched out in all directions and looked like every golf course she'd ever seen. Someone had to be working very hard to keep it manicured to the last detail. "I guess you have servants other than Geoffrey."

"A few," Richard replied. "Your grandmother hired most of them. With the odd hours I kept, I rarely saw any. Your grandmother made sure to warn them not to leave their quarters after dusk." He referred to Penelope as 'your grandmother' quite frequently now—as if he were trying to distance himself even further from her memory.

"Well, they certainly take care of things." The scent of freshly cut grass filled the air but not one clipping was visible. Cassie's eyes moved on to the house. She studied the structure before her: the intricate details of the stones, the subtle arched cornices, and although not a full-blown castle, it actually had turrets—encircled in ivy. "Wow, right out of a fairy tale."

Rodney's exposure to architecture like this was limited to low budget horror flicks. "Yeah, maybe *Grimm's* fairy tales. And for the record, it looks haunted."

"The only ghosts here," Richard said, "are the ones in your imagination."

Geoffrey came around at that moment and faked two discrete coughs. "Begging your pardon, mi Lord—"

"Me Lord?" Rodney balked at the term used for gentlemen of upper class. "A litttle over the top, isn't it?"

Richard tried to explain. "It—It's just a title of respect."

"Well, if it's *just* a title, then I want one too."

"I have a title for you," Cassie said, baring her teeth behind a tight smile.

"Perhaps you and Geoffrey can work something out," Richard offered before turning his attention back to the butler. "You had a question?"

"Your friend . . ." Geoffrey gestured toward Josh. "What shall I do with him?"

"Ah, yes. There should be a coffin in the basement—"

"You have a coffin . . . in your basement?" Rodney mumbled on, "Great. A coffin in the basement of a haunted castle."

Richard ignored him to address Geoffrey. "If you would, just put him there."

"Very good, sir."

Tiered steps led up to the main door. Richard stopped short of opening it. A hesitation marked his movements. His hands fidgeted in pockets.

"Are you all right?" Cassie asked. "You seem nervous."

"It's just—I left it in such a mess. I suppose I'm just a little embarrassed about you seeing it.

"I ransacked the place when Penelope died. Holes gouged in walls from furniture I'd tossed, torn drapes, smashed cabinets . . . It was a terrible time for Ceese and me."

"Oh, come on," Cassie prepared to open the door for him, "it'll be fine."

If he'd left a mess, it wasn't in the entry hall. Even the grandfather clock he'd toppled had been righted or replaced. He couldn't tell which until he looked at the clock closer.

"I don't understand."

"It's a clock," Rodney said. "It tells time. Get over it."

Unlike Cassie, Richard could shrug off Rodney's insolence. "No. I—I destroyed this. It was a bloody mess. I never would've thought it could be repaired."

"Maybe it wasn't as bad off as you thought," Cassie offered, eager to see more of the castle. "What's down this way?"

"Wait," Richard said, curious now. *What did the parlor look like?* "If you don't mind, I think I'd like to see what shape this room is in."

Just like the entryway, everything was in its proper place. In the center of the room, two small couches faced each other. The rug that had been burned by a lighter Ceese batted from his hand appeared mended or new. Heavy drapes, identical to the ones he'd pulled down and torn, covered three huge windows. Richard struggled to take it all in. "This place was a shambles when I left; I have to thank Marissa and Geoffrey for restoring all to its original self—but there is something not right."

"Well, it looks great now," Cassie said.

Rodney ventured to the other side of the room and pulled open the doors of a large armoire. "Oh look, a hidden computer. Now that's nifty. Does it have internet access?" Rodney searched for evidence.

As though Rodney had not spoken, Richard continued, "Something's not right. Something's very wrong."

"Hey, you *do* have internet," Rodney said from where he sat at the computer.

Ceese entered through a side door. She went directly across the room, pulled the heavy drapes closed and switched on a lamp.

"What are you doing?" Richard asked.

"You'll see, Brother." Ceese's eyes smiled as she held open the swinging door she'd just come through. "You can come in now."

Richard gawked at the man who entered—a man with hair nearly the color of his and a strong jaw line, though a bit softer than his own. The uncanny resemblance bore out suspicion when Richard finally found the breath to speak.

"Father. How—?"

"I told you he was alive." Ceese smiled at his obvious disbelief. She'd told Richard many things he'd discounted because he assumed they couldn't be true.

The man pulled Ceese under his arm and kissed the top of her head as though it were Christmas or her birthday. In return, Ceese patted his chest and turned her shining eyes to Richard. "Only, one must have a cross to be near Father now—because of his curse." Ceese pointed at the cross around her neck.

To add to the absolute mind-boggling scenario, a woman entered who appeared to be in her mid-thirties. She walked directly over to Richard, placed a gentle hand on either side of his face and kissed him lightly on the cheek. "I can't tell you how happy I am to see you. I've missed you so."

"No," he said. "It can't be."

"It can be," the woman said. "It's me, Richard. It's Penelope." Penelope turned to face Cassie, a satisfied smile gracing her lips. "I knew you'd bring them home."

The two men did favor each other in appearance—right down to the characteristic paler-than-normal skin of a vampire. Cassie could accept this. But to jump another hurdle and believe the young woman was Grandmother? Grandmother had died and this woman looked some thirty years younger. However, the voice sounded almost exactly as she remembered on the phone, that is without the quavering associated with age.

Richard looked as if a grenade had just exploded nearby, so Cassie asked, "Would someone like to explain just what's going on?"

"I know this must be confusing for the both of you," Penelope said. "But I assure you, I am Penelope, your grandmother, Cassie. And this is Merideth, Ceese and Richard's father. Perhaps it will make more sense when we can all sit down and talk about it."

She spoke as though this kind of thing happened every day. Rodney left his email account to lean close to Richard. "I thought you said the only ghosts were the ones in our imagination. Whose imagination is at work here? I know *I* didn't imagine this."

12

Dr. Clayton Henderson swung open the door of a refrigerator located near the bottom of the basement stairs and reached in for a pint bag of blood. He'd prepared for meals by raiding a blood bank after Richard had forced him to feed on that pathetic mutt. Before he could grasp the bag, he had the urge to scratch his head, certain he'd picked up a flea or two.

Itch gone, Henderson plopped the bag in the microwave. *Why would Richard care if I fed on another human anyway?* And, how interesting that Richard would know in the first place. Did it have something to do with the fact that Richard's vampire DNA had passed on the curse, even though Richard had never bitten him? Henderson had no idea what Josh, his own victim, was up to now. On the other hand, he hadn't bothered to give his former lackey the slightest thought since cursing him.

The microwave dinged, he removed the warm bag and found a dark corner. Privacy was important.

Intrigued by the letter his colleague Henderson had sent, Dr. Lucien Savine had arrived the previous day. On the other side of the room, he squinted into a microscope eyepiece. After a short examination of the specimen, he looked over to the corner where Henderson fed. "Is difficult to believe!" Savine said with a thick Russian accent. "This stem cells—you acquire this from peripheral blood?"

"Not just peripheral blood." Henderson approached. "But peripheral blood from the vampire's animal victims. Honestly, I didn't think it would amount to anything either, but you see what it does."

"Indeed!" Savine stepped over to another microscope. "And this stem cells. They are from werewolf?"

"Yes. That was after injecting her with filgrastim, the drug we use here for stem cell collection. I hoped to generate the kind of stem cell population you see in the vampire's blood but you can see there's still a significant difference."

Savine shook his head. "And such the difference!"

Henderson adjusted the eyepiece of the microscope and bent over it. "I think it must have something to do with the vampire being cursed by two. That's the story anyway." Penelope's diary had been very enlightening. He'd bribed Kyle to steal the diary from Cassie's apartment, but the two must've returned to snatch it back, along with several other items. "I can only imagine what blood drawn directly from this vampire would look like."

Confused, Savine asked, "So you never get blood directly from vampire?"

Henderson squinted his eyes. "No, he wouldn't cooperate, so I gathered animals he'd fed on. Separated his blood out. It wasn't exactly the desired method."

"And yet you have enough?"

"Quite enough. It's how I acquired the gift."

Still puzzled, Savine asked, "Vampires feed on animals?"

That sour look again. "Apparently some do. But that's another story." He moved things along to avoid any attempt to explain something he barely understood himself. "But what do you think, Lucien, about all that you see here? About what I wrote to you? You were obviously intrigued enough to come see what it was all about."

"To do the research with human-like stem cells—you have idea what this means?"

From the excitement in his voice, Henderson knew he had Savine. "It means no more working with mice stem cells. Think what that could do for your research. You could coax these stem cells into gametes."

Savine's eyes lit up, then narrowed. His American friend had gotten him into trouble before, when they had worked together. Henderson wouldn't follow rules. Their lab was shut down. Savine had to go home to Russia to continue his research.

"I know what you're thinking," Henderson said. "But the government won't be involved this time. We don't need their funding. You have all the equipment right here." He watched the man's eyes sweep around the room like he was taking inventory. "You know you want to do this."

"Is wonderful idea but why do this for me? So far, I never create mature gamete. Only immature. At least in Russia, I have make-shift environment to support zygote. Here, I don't see this."

Yet Henderson had a plan. He'd *make* things work—no matter what the cost. "*When* you are successful, I will provide you the perfect environment." To Lucien's skeptical look he added, "The werewolf is a female."

※

Richard had not been around when his father died, otherwise the situation might've struck him as odd. Aside from their mother, no one was allowed to see the body. Strangers carried the coffin—all according to what Ceese had once told Penelope. Richard knew nothing of the circumstances surrounding Father's supposed death, so he had nothing to draw from. Either way, it wouldn't have made seeing him now any less . . . disturbing. Eyes fixed on his near mirror image, Richard stood silent.

Tentatively, Merideth moved toward him. "It—it's me, Son. I swear it."

Tone expressed what his look couldn't. Cold and harsh, he replied, "You're not my father."

"I know it must be difficult for you to fathom," Merideth rationalized. "But it *is* me. And I've missed you so. I—I've missed the both of you. It's difficult for me to show you just how much—emotion of that kind is hard to come by." His voice grew softer. "Please, you have to believe me."

Before Richard could reply, he turned at the sound of footsteps. Geoffrey dragged Josh along beside him. One arm around his waist and one of Josh's arms pulled around his shoulder supported the still-sedated vampire. Geoffrey cleared his voice. "Sir, I've been to the basement. There are two coffins there. In which shall I put your friend, or does it matter?"

Two coffins meant that one belonged to Merideth. When no immediate answer came, Geoffrey added, "Some direction is required . . . m'lord."

Richard's mind remained on the stranger before him and couldn't focus long enough to provide direction.

Penelope answered. "Put him in the one furthest from the basement door."

Geoffrey nodded then left.

"Wow, two coffins," Rodney said. "Is there an old adage for that? You know, like two are better than one."

His worthless observation drew a targeted response from Merideth. "Who are *you*?"

Ceese ran over to stand next to Rodney. "This is who I told you about," she said. "This is my—my friend."

"*This* is your friend?"

Rodney bristled. "Hey, I don't like the way that sounded. You shouldn't judge people so quickly."

Ceese saw the fangs first and pulled at Rodney. "I think we should go now."

Rodney saw the fangs next and his eyes widened. "Yeah, we—we'll talk later." He allowed Ceese to tug him toward the front door.

Merideth obviously struggled with his vampyric transformation.

Penelope reached for the cross around her neck, prepared to use it, "Meri, you need me to—"

"Meri?" Richard repeated, utterly shocked. "That's what my mother called my father."

"Yes!" Merideth said hopefully, his fangs shrinking. "Julia called me that—your mother."

Eyes ablaze, tone scathing, Richard said, "Don't speak of my mother. You have no right!"

Merideth countered weakly, "I have every right. I'm her husband."

"You're a vampire."

"I only became a vampire to save you. To help you *and* Cee Cee—" He stopped short when Richard flinched at the pet name Merideth had given Ceese.

"Tell me what to say," he pleaded. "You have to believe I'm your father."

"You may believe that's who you are but you're not my father. My father was a righteous man. My father would've never stooped as low as to deny God." Richard kept right on talking despite the fact that Merideth had fallen back a step, struck by the holy reference. "My father would never consider becoming a vampire. He would've found another way."

Penelope leapt to Merideth's defense. "Richard, you have *no* right—"

Merideth reached out a hand to stop her. "No. He—he's right. The father he knew would never deny—what he suggested." Features fallen, he appeared battle-weary. "At least Cee Cee believes," he said for his own benefit.

Richard frowned. "Yes, well, about that. I don't want you going near her."

"What?" He panicked. "Richard, no—please! You can't keep me from Cee Cee."

"I can and I will. I seem to recall the process by which one can revoke an invitation made in order to un-invite—a vampire."

Cassie took a tentative step forward, between the argument's opponents.

"I'll do whatever you ask. I—I won't make any attempt to visit with Cee Cee. I *swear* it."

Richard seemed satisfied. "Then it will be in your hands."

Merideth gasped relief and turned to head to the basement; he had a very different look from when he'd entered.

Richard then turned on Penelope. "And what dark magic has you out of the grave?"

"I had no choice over what happened to me, dark or otherwise." Penelope stood firm. "And I certainly wouldn't discuss it with you even if I did understand it all, which I don't."

Mystery seemed to be the order of the day. Richard shrugged at her dismissive words. "Have it your way."

"Indeed I will," Penelope said. "And if you un-invite Meri, I'll just re-invite him all over again. I didn't allow you to bully me as a vampire and I won't allow you to bully me now." Despite the tough words, moisture filled her eyes and her voice softened. "What happened to you, Richard? Where did you go?" She shook her head and left the room.

The second she was gone, Richard grabbed the corner of a nearby sofa table for support. Cassie rushed in to help him stand, then directed him to one of the couches. He didn't look like a bully or a tormentor. He simply looked confused and disoriented. "It can't be. It just can't be."

"It's all right, Richard. You'll get through this. The hard part's over. You're no longer a vampire."

Drawing strength from her words, he took one of her hands in his. "I don't know what I'd do without you. What a disaster this would be if you hadn't come along."

Penelope had planned to go immediately to check on Meri but stopped just outside the parlor to recover. She couldn't understand the difference in Richard and needed a moment to regroup. While standing there, Penelope overheard Richard's conversation with Cassie. He used to talk to *her* like that or at least as much as he was able with the vampire holding him back. She swallowed hard, eyes stinging from the pressure of holding back tears. *Meri must feel terrible as well.* She rushed off to the basement to check on him.

13

Out the door and down the steps, Ceese pulled Rodney along—and away from Merideth's fangs. They raced across the lawn and into the surrounding woods. Rodney had never been a runner and couldn't have kept pace had it not been for Ceese. But just like that night in the alley, Ceese helped him along. She kept leading him even after the immediate danger was past. They'd gone a hundred yards into the woods before Ceese stopped and turned loose of Rodney's hand.

With the expression of someone who'd swallowed his gum, Rodney gasped. His lungs screamed for air as if he'd just exploded to the surface of a swimming pool after being pulled under. He couldn't intake fast enough.

His seal-like bark encouraged Ceese to grab his hand. "Sorry. I didn't realize you weren't ready. Are you okay now?"

"Yes." Rodney stared at his hand in hers. "How does that work anyway? How do you do that?"

"Is it important to know?"

Rodney knew Ceese's question meant she'd no idea how it worked. "I guess not," he said, wanting to ease her mind. He fell into walking with her and looked skeptically at the surrounding landscape. It wasn't every day he made it into the woods. In fact, it didn't look like he'd really missed out on anything. "Why'd we run all the way out here?"

"You upset Father. You saw his fangs."

"But he's a vampire and couldn't have come after us if he'd wanted to. We could've stopped running once we were on the front lawn. We didn't have to come all the way out here."

They walked quietly a little longer before Ceese stopped. "You don't like it here?"

"Oh, I like it." He sounded very much like someone trying to enjoy something they had no idea how to enjoy. "More trees than you can shake a stick at. Extremely mushy ground." His shoes half-buried in muck. "Or maybe it's quicksand. Not to mention bugs." He swatted aggressively at his neck with his free hand. "What's not to like?"

This time when she let go of his hand, his breathing normalized. She turned and started to walk. Rodney sighed. *Stupid mouth.* Why didn't he know when to shut up? "Ceese," he called out. "Don't be mad." He caught up with her and gently pulled her around. "I'm sorry. I—I just—I'm not used to this, that's all. Maybe it'll grow on me."

She gave him a genuine smile. "Will you kiss me then?"

"Whoa!" Rodney wondered if he'd heard right. "I'm not sure that's such a good idea."

"You don't want to?" A disappointed look replaced her smile.

"It's not that—it's just—um—one thing leads to another and uh—well, how can you even think about something like that right now after everything that's happened? I mean, you find out your dad's alive and he's a vampire. You learn Cassie's Grandma Penelope's alive and has somehow achieved reversed metamorphosis."

"Those don't bother me. I've known for some time. I've even told Cassie about my father."

"Okay, but still. It's just sort of—awkward."

"I just want to know what it's like—to kiss someone. To kiss you."

"But you already know. Remember? You 'thanked' me right on the lips in the back of Cassie's car the day she and I got you and Richard away from that hospital."

"I tried, but the wolf wouldn't let me. It was jealous and wanted to take over. It'd even started to transform."

Rodney rubbed his lip at the memory. She'd actually nipped him before pulling away completely. "I just don't know if it's a good idea, Ceese."

"Do you know how to?"

"Of course I know how to. It's just . . . I've never kissed anyone that I've—" He stopped cold, considered his next words carefully. "I've never kissed anyone that I've had feelings for." There. He'd said it. And it came out a lot easier than he thought it would.

"Then show me." Ceese leaned in closer. "Please."

⁓⁓⁓

The werewolf Zade couldn't believe Ceese had left with the vampire that night. He never believed she'd go. Yet when he'd returned to the castle to spy on her after dealing with Peter Drummond, Ceese couldn't be found. After she had strayed from the pack the first few times, he became suspicious. Then she began to spend more and more time away. She'd told him she was visiting an old friend. Zade couldn't help but suspect the vampire. What kind of hold did it have on her?

Two days, three days, still no sign of Ceese and then a car pulled up the drive. Watching from a guarded distance, he sensed her first, and then saw Ceese walk to the house. She had returned and he would have her again. She belonged to him and always would—whether she wanted it that way or not.

As a werewolf, he couldn't father his own kind—because of the emotion involved, the act itself could kill. Pain was pleasure to a werewolf and pleasure at anything other than cursing wasn't tolerated. As things went, werewolves found a way to work around this dilemma. Attacking a mother with child could affect the unborn. He'd attacked Ceese's mother shortly after he'd paid a mortal to have his way with her. Ceese belonged to him as much as if he'd fathered her himself. Now that she returned to the castle, he'd take her again. This vampire would not take Ceese from him. No one would.

⁓⁓⁓

The kiss brushed soft and timid but definitely better than the back seat kiss accompanied by Cassie's subtle warnings.

Warnings that Rodney ignored until it was almost too late. Yes, this kiss was definitely better. Ceese didn't even nip him.

"I think I'd like to try that again," Ceese said, as though she was trying to figure out if she liked it or not but not doing a very good job of sounding innocent.

"Oh, really?" Rodney smiled before he accommodated.

When Zade saw Ceese rush out the front door of the castle, he followed. But since she had company, he remained at a distance. He'd planned to take her but would wait until she was as far away from the castle as possible. When Ceese and the young man stopped, he stepped behind a tree. Would they go deeper into the woods? His patience held out until the kiss.

"Ceese belong to Zade. Zade take Ceese now!"

14

Seeing the Hulk, or at least something that closely resembled him (minus green paint), was one thing. Seeing the Hulk lumbering his way, complete with menacing fangs and in the midst of werewolf transformation, was quite another. Kiss forgotten, Ceese grabbed his hand and sprinted away. They moved at such a speed the trees and path blurred past. One close encounter with a low hanging branch proved he couldn't do it alone. Rodney's eyes trained on Ceese—he ducked when she ducked, darted when she darted. After going quite a way, the only measure of distance Rodney could come up with at the moment, Ceese stopped and pointed. "There. Hide there."

"What? I can't go with you?"

"You'll be safer here."

"How? Whatever is coming after us will just snack on me before he finds you."

Ceese shook her head. "No, he won't. Zade doesn't want you. He wants me."

The crashing and snapping close in the bush ended. Rodney trusted her instinct, darted down the bluff, shrank against the damp wall of the slope and closed his eyes tight. *Maybe it's just a bad dream and I'll open my eyes to find out it's all over.* The odd quiet led him to open his eyes.

"Hulk!" he screamed.

It breathed slow and deliberate as it stood and glared at Rodney through dark soulless eyes. Then it spoke. "Where go Ceese?"

"Ahhhhhh . . . she go . . ." He didn't tell the truth. "I mean, sh—she went that way." He pointed to the right.

A volcano about to erupt couldn't have looked more threatening. With no effort, it reached forward, picked up and lifted Rodney over its head and held him there. "You lie to Zade," it snarled.

"Does that mean if I tell you the truth that you'll put me down?"

Zade launched Rodney through the air. On the descent, Rodney's head connected with a tree. The impact, though lighter than it could've been had he hit a closer object, knocked him out.

~·~

Penelope raced down into the dark basement. She couldn't see anything but knew the way—could navigate the stairs with her eyes closed if needed. Off the landing, over to the two coffins she raced, rapped loudly on the coffin closest to her and waited for the owner to respond. The top rose up and the vampire inside slowly climbed out.

"Curse me," she said to Merideth. "Curse me, now!"

Weakly he said, "Please, do not tempt me like this, not now. You have no idea." He closed his coffin and settled onto its top.

Her eyes adjusted and slowly she made out his features. The glowing eyes meant the vampire could easily take advantage. "I'm sorry Meri. I should've known better." As if to make up for the mistake, she added, "I have my cross." She didn't need to show it. The information was enough for the vampire. The glowing of Meri's eyes subsided.

"What do you need?"

She settled down beside him. "He hates me, Meri. Richard hates me."

"Well, you won't find much sympathy here. I fear he harbors more than just hatred for me. He won't even let me near Cee Cee." Merideth shook his head slowly.

"That was too harsh. He shouldn't have gone that far. I don't care how confused he was. And as far as Ceese goes, well, if she wants to see you there's little he can do about it. She will do what she wants to do. I'll make sure she can get to you if she wants."

"No, I will honor his request."

"But for him to speak to you the way he did . . . with such resentment."

"He is his father's son. He sees evil and wants nothing to do with it."

"You're not evil, Meri. You can't help what you've become."

"Ahhh, but that's where you're wrong. I brought this on myself."

"To save your children. That doesn't make you evil."

"That's your opinion, not Richard's."

The two sat quietly for a moment. "Look at us, Meri. Richard has us both wrapped around his finger. We'll do anything for him."

"The prize is worth the challenge. I love my son." He slumped with the emotive words.

"I love him too, yet I think he may love another."

"He's quite the catch. Julia used to say he could charm the thorns off a rose—" His voice caught. He grabbed at his temple. "That was too much. Thinking of Julia always does this to me." With effort, he continued, "It's best you let Richard go anyway."

"Why would you say that? He may yet find it in his heart to forgive me."

"He was a vampire the entire time you were involved with him. You never really knew Richard as himself. You knew him as a vampire. I know you don't want to hear this, but it is true. It would never work between the two of you now, think about it: Richard would have to be a vampire again for him to be the same person you loved."

Coming from anyone else, the words would've been fodder to be dismissed. But Merideth had a way of presenting the facts. "Perhaps. I suppose I'll have to consider that." She'd kept him up too long. His shoulders slumped. He needed rest to keep control of his vampire side. She stood to dismiss herself. "I hope I—"

"Cee Cee," he hissed. Meredith leapt off the coffin and ran past her with restored energy.

"What in the—" Penelope's head spun, eyes searching. *Ceese? Where?*

Halfway up the stairs, he hollered, "Zade. Zade has Cee Cee!"

15

"There are crumpets and tea in the dining room, m'lord." Marissa, Richard's housekeeper and daughter of the couple who tended the manor after Geoffrey, stood in the parlor's doorway.

Crumpets and tea sounded very relaxing, much more relaxing than waiting for the next dead relative to arrive and surprise them all. Richard stood. He'd never been able to enjoy teatime before—the meal found him asleep in the coffin. "I think that's something we should take advantage of," he told Cassie. "Shall we?"

Happy to see him coming around, she agreed and stood. "You mean they really do have an official teatime?" she asked as they strolled into the dining room.

"Of course. After all, this is England."

The crumpets smelled delicious and tasted it too. Cassie decided they resembled an English muffin yet a hundred times better. The texture was irresistibly light and fluffy inside with a bit of crunch on the outside, enhanced by jam and rich clotted cream. "These are really good," she commented.

Just as Richard opened his mouth to answer, Merideth burst into the room, stopped abruptly at the end of the table and leaned heavily on it for support. "Cee Cee," he said, tone caustic, forehead wrinkled with worry. "Zade has found her!"

"Can't you see we're eating?" Richard said, quite unmoved by the words, or sudden appearances of both Merideth and Penelope.

Penelope stared at Richard in disbelief. "What's wrong with you? Zade has Ceese!"

Richard wiped the corners of his mouth with a napkin; he ignored Penelope but addressed his father. "Aren't you supposed to be in your coffin?" The tinkle of his silver spoon against china added to the oddness of the moment.

"I'm not making this up." Merideth bravely stepped toward the table but stopped at Richard's glaring disapproval. "You have to believe me."

"And why do I *have* to believe you? How could you possibly know what is happening with Ceese? Have you been outside? No. Did someone come tell you this? I doubt it. So you must be lying. It's not up to me to figure out why you would. It's only up to me to enjoy my tea and crumpets."

Cassie, watching the drama play out, wasn't entirely convinced. "Maybe you should listen to him."

"Listen to whom?" Richard said in an alarmingly cold tone.

Merideth turned his head to face Penelope. She addressed his worried stare. "You're going to have to tell him. I know you don't want to but you have to."

"I can't," he said, choking on the words. "I promised Julia. I *promised* her."

"I'm sure Julia would understand if she were here. Richard needs to know. If you don't tell him, I will."

Resigned, Merideth turned back to face Richard. "Ceese talks to me—in my head. She's always been able to do this—even before she was cursed."

"Well, that's a lovely story," Richard said and spooned jam onto another crumpet, "but I choose not to believe that one either."

When Merideth hesitated, Penelope prodded. "Tell him the rest, Meri."

He fumbled along. "Your mother was attacked—"

"—yes, I know," Richard said sharply, as though he resented hearing about this now, "by a wolf who scratched her on her side."

"That's not all. She was also attacked by a man—a man who forced himself on her at Zade's insistence. Forced himself on my Julia to do what the accursed could never accomplish. He took her, Richard, against her will. He took my Julia. The wolf that scratched her afterwards wasn't any ordinary wolf. It was Zade. He wants Cee Cee, Richard, and now he has her."

At some point during the recounting, Richard looked up with eyes alert.

"You can either sit there and eat crumpets or you can save her. It's up to you because I can't do anything."

Richard looked to Penelope, then back to Merideth. "You're lying. My father would've told me this. He would've."

"Julia made me promise. She didn't want anyone to know what really happened to her that day. Because of what Zade did, Cee Cee was somehow affected. I don't understand it, but she can speak to me without words and I know for a fact that Zade has her now."

Richard pushed his chair back at once and stood. "That's really something to keep from someone. How do I find Ceese and how do I stop Zade?"

Merideth put a hand to his brow, to pull the mental image back up. "They're near a lake. The young man she left with, he's still with her or at least he was at one point. And as far as Zade goes, there's a rifle behind the door in the parlor, loaded with silver bullets."

Richard, now willing to believe, stood frozen.

Merideth helped him along with one word. "Go!"

While Richard knew these woods well, things looked very different. The sunlight illuminated but he was accustomed to deciphering shadow. He'd had to turn back twice already. He struggled to sense Ceese the way he could as a vampire, but he got nothing—like flipping a light switch that no longer had power. He went through the motions, yet nothing happened.

Completely frustrated, he forged ahead, ran, turned back, ran again. He couldn't imagine anything being more difficult. As he rushed along, like a rat in a maze with no cheese to direct, he saw a path of sorts. He followed it, got too close its edge and slipped down. His footing regained, he scrambled to stand. A twig snapped and he swung the rifle toward the sound.

"Don't—don't shoot." Rodney held the back of his head with one hand and stumbled towards Richard.

Lowering the rifle, Richard asked, "What happened? Are you all right? Where's Ceese?"

"There was this really big guy. He was looking for Ceese. He threw me when I lied about which way she went."

"Which way did she go?"

"That way." Rodney pointed and they pulled each other back up the slope.

After they'd gone far enough to worry, Richard asked, "Are you sure she went this way?"

Flustered, Rodney looked around. "I'm not sure of anything, really. I thought she went this way." All at once, he placed his hand to temple. Suddenly he saw through Ceese's eyes. He focused on the little movie running in his head. "This way!" he said with confidence.

The route definitely held promise: broken limbs and footprints where the ground accommodated. They heard Ceese cry out and headed toward a clearing.

With Zade's clawed hand enclosed around her wrist, Ceese dared not pull to get away. Richard lifted the rifle and aimed. Yet, even with a clear shot, he didn't fire.

"What's wrong with you?" Rodney whispered. "Shoot him." Zade turned to look in their direction and kept his hold on Ceese. He'd seen them. "For God's sake," Rodney said, frantic and much louder this time, "shoot him."

Zade's grip weakened when Rodney said "God." Ceese took advantage and yanked her arm away. Zade reached out at once and, with one mighty sweep of his arm, tore at her side. Ceese fell to the ground.

"Ceese," Rodney called out, but she didn't move.

Zade moved to attack them then sniffed the air and darted off into the woods.

"He smelled the silver bullets," said Richard.

Rodney reached Ceese first, Richard right behind him. Ceese lay unmoving, unconscious. Rodney gently turned her head. "She must've hit this stone when she fell," he nodded toward the half-buried rock in the ground.

Richard had other concerns. "Look here, she's losing blood. Those gashes look deep and we need to stop the flow." He ripped off his shirt, tore it in long strips and wrapped it around Ceese. "That should do until we get her back to the castle."

Richard then eased his arms under Ceese and carefully lifted her off the ground. Rodney picked up the unused rifle and followed. "Does this mean she's cursed again?"

Richard shook his head. "Zade didn't bite her and he wasn't fully transformed."

"So he's a werewolf?"

"Yes."

"And you could've killed him just now."

Richard didn't respond.

Rodney continued. "So why didn't you? Why didn't you shoot him?"

"It's a sin to kill," he said matter-of-factly as though they were words that needed no further explanation. "It's one of the Ten Commandments."

Rodney was certainly confused now. "If it's a sin to kill, why did you bring the rifle?"

"It isn't a sin to protect oneself."

Rodney rushed to stand in front of Richard. He got as close to Richard's face as he could without crowding Ceese. "It may be one of the Ten Commandments but you keep this in mind, if Ceese dies, I'm gonna break that one. And it won't be Zade I'll be going after. It'll be you. You should've shot Zade. You should've killed him."

When night fell, Henderson left Lucien Savine and drove to Cassie's apartment. He didn't have a plan to capture Ceese, but he was working on one. He parked on a side road and walked around to the back side of the complex. He then levitated to the balcony and landed softly. Pressing his ear against the glass, he determined the apartment empty. He pulled the handle and found the door unlatched. He eased it open and stepped inside.

Not knowing how much time he had to explore, he moved swiftly. The refrigerator, stocked with pint bags of blood and little else, confirmed that Cassie had planned on Richard staying for a while. Henderson made a miserable face at the idea—the mutt Richard had forced him to eat earlier still a fresh picture in his mind. "You couldn't be like every other vampire, could you?" he muttered as he closed the door.

On the other side of the room, a potted plant lay in the dirt it was once anchored in. Swept up in a pile, Henderson puzzled over it. But since he couldn't understand that Rodney left it there because he couldn't find a dustpan, he refused to let it bother him further.

A pile of bills lay on the kitchen table. Someone had scribbled the word paid on each one along with a date three months in the future. Apparently, Cassie and her friends had left and didn't plan to return anytime soon. *But where had they gone?* Henderson's head turned and he spotted another piece of paper—this one listed several drugs—strong sedatives. *Why would they want sedatives and how would they get them?* Suddenly questions outnumbered answers.

A crumpled paper bag distracted him—that and small empty drug bottles that had rolled out. He picked up each one and examined it, his mouth and eyes scrunched together.

The phone rang and he froze. The answer machine picked up, "Hey, just checking to see if you guys had left yet. I guess you have."

Henderson smiled crudely as he recognized the voice of Kyle. And, he definitely knew where to find Kyle.

16

In an instant, Josh had him pinned to the bed. Kyle felt hot breath on his neck and sharp points of fangs pricked his skin. He struggled and thrashed and fought the vampire until he fell to the tile floor . . . and opened his eyes.

It was only a dream . . . just a dream. Slowly, Kyle pulled himself up and settled back on the edge of his bed.

But if it were just a dream, why did it still feel like someone was in the room?

Suddenly, a click and the desk lamp lit up. *Someone was in the room.* He slowly turned his head toward the glowing lamp and there stood Henderson. Kyle scrambled over his bed backwards and pressed himself against the cold cement wall. Henderson moved just as quickly and leaned in very close to his neck.

"Wh-what are you doing here? How'd you get in?" asked Kyle.

"Your window was open."

"But this is the third floor," Kyle's voice a nervous twitter.

Henderson pulled the list of drugs from a pocket and held it up for Kyle. "Why would Cassie need this information?"

"How would I know?" he replied with a guilty face.

"Where did Cassie and the others go?"

"What makes you think they went anywhere?"

Henderson turned his head sideways and looked disappointed. "You know I can hypnotize you," he told him. "I can make you tell me."

Kyle swallowed hard. "I don't believe in hypnosis."

"That's really not my problem but I'll give you one more chance to answer willingly. Why did you give this list of drugs to Cassie?"

"I don't know what you're talking about."

"Fine." Henderson's eyes fixed on Kyle's whose facial muscles slackened. Henderson repeated the question softly. "Why did you give this list to Cassie?

"It wasn't for Cassie; it was for Richard. I just wrote down what he asked for."

"Why did he ask for them?"

"They needed to knock Josh out."

"Why?"

"So they could get him back to England without him trying to feed on everyone on the plane."

Henderson tilted his head. "Why would they take Josh to England?"

"Because you cursed him and he's not handling being a vampire very well."

"What about Richard's own curse—and the werewolf? They left England to find a cure. Why would they go back?"

"They're not cursed anymore."

Henderson lifted a skeptical brow at that. *Was the hypnosis working?* He decided to test whether Kyle was faking it. "What's your middle name?" He knew, without hypnosis, Kyle would never answer truthfully, if at all. He hated his middle name that much.

"Frances," Kyle said, plain-faced.

"So it is," Henderson muttered. "If they're not cursed, what happened?"

"I don't know."

"Fair enough. Where did they go to in England?"

"Richard's castle."

"Which is located—?"

"Somewhere near London. I'm not sure where."

Henderson chewed at the inside of his lip. Because he no longer concentrated, the hypnosis lost its effect. "So you can do whatever you want," Kyle rallied, not nearly as bold as he'd liked to sound, but an effort nonetheless, "but I won't tell you anything."

Henderson let him believe he hadn't told him everything already. What did it matter? He already had as much information as Kyle could give him and it was enough.

~~~

Rodney held the door open and Richard rushed in with Ceese in his arms.

"She's bleeding," Penelope said, her shock revealed in her words.

"Zade scratched her." Rodney trailed Richard past Penelope and down the hall.

Geoffrey entered the bedroom just before Richard carried in Ceese. He slipped a hand under the covers on the bed and pulled them back. Gently, Richard eased her down. The bleeding looked to have subsided but the wounds needed to be cleaned. Geoffrey returned shortly with a basin of hot water and facecloths. Marissa followed with proper dressings for the scratches: bandages, medical tape, antiseptic.

Cassie took the bloody strips that Richard removed from Ceese's side. She noticed blood on him as well. "Are you hurt?" she asked.

He looked at where she stared. "No, I'm fine."

Penelope held out another shirt for Richard. He stopped long enough to slide into it. For the moment, he left it unbuttoned—the scratches needed to be cleaned. Richard had just begun to assess the damage when Merideth walked in.

"Cee Cee," he gasped.

Richard straightened and addressed his father directly. "There's too much blood. You shouldn't be here."

"I can control the vampire," he pleaded. "If you'll just let me stay—"

"Leave," Richard roared. "Otherwise I'll make good on my promise to un-invite you."

Penelope scurried to Meri and escorted him out. "I'll keep you posted," she told him. "You know I will. Go to your coffin."

Rodney asked, "Dude, you really don't like him, do you?"

"He just doesn't need to be here." Richard turned his attention back to Ceese and her wounds. He arranged the basin so that water, wrung from a rag, could cascade over them and back into the basin.

"Are you sure she's not cursed?" Cassie asked after a moment of watching.

"I'm sure. Zade hadn't fully transformed."

"Thank God he didn't catch up with her at night," Penelope added, "it's much easier to change then."

"One has to wonder why he didn't wait until night," Richard puzzled as blood-tinged water trickled into the basin. "Or why he made the attempt so close to the castle."

"We weren't near the castle," Rodney informed. "Ceese wanted to show me around."

"So you were in the woods?" Penelope asked.

"Yeah, is that a crime?" His response sounded like he might be hiding something.

"We're just trying to learn what happened," Penelope told him.

Rodney let his guard down a little. "Yeah, we were in the woods."

"So, did Zade just jump out of nowhere?" Cassie couldn't see it happening that way.

"Sort of. We were standing there talking and then, Ceese sort of asked me to kiss her—" He continued despite the fact all eyes were trained on him now, "—and that's when he came at us."

"Did you?" Richard asked. "Did you kiss her?"

"You know what? I don't think I'm going to say anything else."

Ceese stirred then. Her eyes fluttered open. She saw Richard. "Brother," she grimaced. "Zade, he—he tried to—" She took a moment to fight the pain. "I tried to run but—" Her eyes widened, then, "Rodney! Where's Rodney?"

"I'm right here." He moved so she could see him.

Relief washed over her face. "I thought I heard Father talking. Is he here? I want to see him."

"Good luck with that," Rodney told her. "Richard ran him off."

"What?" Ceese attempted to get up.

Cassie glared at Rodney. His sarcasm hadn't helped at all.

"The scratches are deep, Ceese," Richard said encouraging her to lie still. "You don't need to be moving around until we get them bandaged."

She settled but insisted, "I want to see Father."

"He's a vampire, Ceese. There's too much blood." Richard worked on the bandages.

"He wouldn't hurt me. He'd never hurt me."

"It's not something he can control."

"But he's different, Richard. He's not just any vampire. He—he's different. He told me this."

"That's the vampire talking, Ceese. They'll say anything to get to their next meal, preferably human."

Desperate tears filled her eyes. "Why do you hate Father so when all you ever wanted was to be just like him?"

The reality of that comment creased his brow. "I—I'm sure I don't hate him."

"You do. I—I sense it."

Merideth had said Zade's attack on their mother left Ceese with this ability, which didn't make things much better for Richard. He couldn't deny the truth. "I just hate what he's become."

"But he did it for us, Richard—mostly for you." She drew in air sharply wincing in pain. "He needs to know you don't hate him. He needs to know you understand. You're killing him, Richard. You're killing Father. I sense that too."

Her words were a direct hit to his soul. The last lock had been turned, the memories flooded in. Richard stood, turned towards the door and stared, motionless. Penelope studied his face—she'd seen this response before. "We'll take care of Ceese if you want to catch up with him."

Numbed by what he remembered, Richard nodded, hurriedly washed his bloodied hands, and then headed for the basement.

17

This wasn't the first time Richard had found himself running for the basement, desperate to get there—yet under quite different circumstances. Once he had rushed to his coffin before dawn. Now he ran to get to—*Father. Yes, of course it was Father. How could he not have remembered?*

He adored Father. Loved him with all his heart and would do anything for him. He'd even gone sailing with him on Swansea Bay just to make him happy. He, of course, spent the trip glued to the bottom of the boat, praying for a quick return to shore. At no point did he ever get used to the rocking and rolling.

Richard picked up the pace as he wound his way through the castle—its passages, hallways used by servants, closets that joined rooms. He knew he stood a good chance of reaching Father before he made it to the basement.

Even so, he wasn't prepared when he met him face-to-face. His jaw moved but no words came out. Richard only stared. Meredith fell back against a wall and gasped.

"No. Don't un-invite me. I swear. I'm doing what you said. I'm going to my coffin."

Devastated by his reaction, Richard reached out. He grasped him by the shoulders. "Father," he said. "I—I'm not here for that. I've not come to un-invite you."

Glassy-eyed, his father stared. Stunned, his legs buckled beneath him. Richard eased him down and knelt alongside. This time, Meredith sat silent. "Say something," Richard implored. "Please say something."

Slowly the older man exhaled as though a great burden had been lifted. "Finally."

Richard reached out with a shaky hand to touch his face. He traced remembered lines and forgotten ones. "I'm not sure how I could've ever doubted who you were," he said with tearful regret. "But the vampire made me hate you so. I fought it as best I could."

"I understand. You have to know I understand. But Richard, how did you become a vampire? If you were truly—" He flinched at what he was about to ask and reworded, "If you truly believed what you said, the curse shouldn't have touched you."

Richard looked away and then back. "I never committed my faith, Father. It was too important to be uncertain. I'd made the decision to do so on the day you were to ordain me. And if that answer isn't good enough then I should have to ask the same question of you. How is it you came to be cursed? You'll never be able to convince me you weren't a true man of—" He caught himself. "—you weren't what I knew you were. I won't believe it."

"And you shouldn't. My situation was different than yours and different from many. At the moment, that's all I can say on the matter. Perhaps one day, if everything works out, I can share."

Richard raised a brow at that. "Aren't there enough secrets being kept?"

"I'm sorry, Richard. I simply can't explain. You'll just have to trust me."

"And love you," Richard said with a steady eye to let his father know he really was back.

With emotion few vampires could show, Meredith touched his son's face. "Forever, Richard. No matter what."

"Of course," Richard assured. "You have my word."

"You look so much like your mother. But what have you done to your hair? It used to be chestnut brown, just like Julia's."

"Please don't ask me to explain things. Like you, I'm sure I can't."

"Fair enough," Meredith said, a weary edge to his voice as he took his hand away. "I think I should go to my coffin now."

"I'll help you." The two stood.

"I can make it on my own."

"Are you sure?"

"Quite certain. You've given me so much hope."

Meredith moved along then and Richard stared after him. When he came to the door of the basement, he turned. "And you'll let me visit with Cee Cee soon?"

"By all means. Perhaps this evening if she feels up to it."

"I'll look forward to that then."

⁂

Unforgiving moonlight etched shadows on shadows. Frantic, she raced down dark paths, familiar ground made unfamiliar by the moon's elusion. Branches tore and scratched at exposed skin. She had to keep moving. She had to get away.

She wasn't a creature of the darkness; *it* was. She couldn't decipher the shadows; it could. Its footfalls sounded and she moved faster. As she ran, she pictured the green-gold cast of its terrifyingly evil eyes. She recalled how they bore into her—how they'd made her feel: cold and empty. She pushed to run faster.

The ground sloped downwards. She stumbled and lost her footing—slid out of control down an embankment. Sprawled on the ground, she wondered if it had seen her. The answer came when sharp claws tore the skin on her back.

Ceese awoke with a start and leapt from the bed. The action came so unexpected that no one in the room reacted fast enough to stop her. She ran to a far corner, pressed herself against the wall there and sank to the ground, holding her side and pulling her legs close.

"Richard," she whispered, frightened tears clinging to the corner of her eyes. Then again, "Richard."

Rodney rushed over. "It's okay," he told her. "You're okay."

She shook her head back and forth, sank deeper into the corner when he reached out.

"What are we supposed to do?" he asked.
"Go get Richard," Penelope told him.

Josh forced his eyes open. He could see but couldn't tell where he was. In a box? *Rodney.* This had to be Rodney's idea of a joke. He'd find him and make him pay . . . though not at the moment. Josh sensed that the day's light had not yet dimmed. He didn't know why this mattered but neither did he question his understanding of it.

He'd find Rodney later, when the right time arrived.

18

When Rodney brought Richard up to the room, Ceese still remained huddled in the corner. Richard rushed to her at once and knelt. "You shouldn't be up," he told her gently. "You should be in the bed."

She drew her legs in closer. "I have to hide. He's here. He's come to take me."

"Zade's not here."

"He is," she insisted, "I saw him, at the window." The men looked toward the window—the drapes had been pulled—they looked at each other.

"I saw him," Ceese said. "Oh, why did Father leave me with you? I wanted to go too."

"I don't understand, Ceese."

Suddenly frustrated, she snapped her head around. "You never understand. I'm only six and I understand more than you."

"Six?"

Ceese gasped, terrified. "Did you hear that? He's in the house."

"It's not real."

"It is real, Brother. He's here," she said.

Clearly Ceese recalled something from an early age. *But what?* He hadn't had very much to do with her at age six.

She didn't respect his authority. All she ever did was cling to Father.

"Of course," he said when the memory fell on him like a rock. Father had left the two of them alone once—together. Someone had entered the house. Now he knew that someone had been— "*Zade.*"

Ceese grabbed hold of Richard. "Don't let him find me, please."

"Come on." He gathered her up in his arms. "I know where you can hide."

In the short time it took to carry her back to the bed, Ceese fell unconscious again—he hoped to sleep.

Penelope moved in to check the bandages. Satisfied, she looked up at Richard. "Zade came after her that day?"

"Night," Richard corrected. "I saw him just before he knocked me unconscious."

"Where did Ceese hide?"

"In one of the ash trees surrounding the house."

"Ash trees," Cassie said. "I'd heard of lore surrounding werewolves and ash trees. They stay away from them, I think. Sounds like your father knew a lot about werewolves early on."

"I suppose I never considered it before but I do remember the day he took me with him to go looking for ash saplings to dig up and bring back to the house. There were plenty of other trees around so it never really made sense to me. I just never thought to ask." He shook his head then, a look of wonder on his face. "It seems like it only happened yesterday, not centuries ago."

Penelope looked toward Ceese. "We should let her rest."

"I don't think we should leave her alone though," Richard added.

Rodney had already established himself in a chair by the bed. "I'm not going anywhere."

Richard excused himself to go clean up. Penelope took Cassie down the hall with her. "I'd very much like to try and explain things to you," she said as they walked. "Hopefully before it gets any more complicated." She led Cassie to a room on the back side of the castle. "This is where I e-mailed you from most of the time. There's my computer." She motioned to where a sleek monitor sat, a keyboard and mouse in front of it. "Richard bought it for me when I started spending more and more time on his."

They walked around a small tea table to the open balcony doors. Penelope and Cassie gazed over the well-manicured lawn and beyond the meticulously cared-for flower garden surrounding the balcony itself. Further out, they stared at untamed woods.

"Do you actually think you can explain everything? Wouldn't you have to understand it yourself to do that?" Cassie asked.

Penelope closed the curtains and then settled into a chair next to the table. She motioned for Cassie to take a seat. Marissa had set out tea and Penelope poured. "That's an astute observation but I wouldn't have expected anything less from you."

Her voice and words were almost exactly how Cassie recalled, except she noted again, the youthful tone. "How is it that you're alive and have your youth back? If not for the sound of your voice, I'd swear I was talking to an imposter." Cassie took her cup and sipped.

Penelope sighed. "Well, I can't really speak to the part about appearing younger, though I suspect Ceese had something to do with it. Just as she had a hand in keeping me here."

Cassie lowered her cup to her saucer. "Is that supposed to be less confusing?"

"I had cancer, Cassie. It had run its course. I was ready to die. Ready to pass on. I tried to prepare Ceese and Richard for the loss I knew they'd feel. Tried to get them to help each other. You see, I knew they were brother and sister and I knew they'd been very close at one time. My hope was that they'd remember and be able to pick up where I left off, working together to have their respective curses lifted. I so wanted to know that I was going to see them again, in Heaven.

"But working together just didn't seem to be in the cards and Ceese is horrible about not letting things go. When my time came, she kept me here. I don't know how she did it, but she did. I don't think she was aware of her success until after she reached New York. Shortly after they left, the aging process reversed. My cancer disappeared. I worried at how far my aging would regress but it's almost as if Ceese had a plan."

"But why wouldn't you let them know you hadn't died?"

"Because I needed them to work together and my being here interfered with that. It wasn't easy, I can assure you. Especially knowing Richard was leaving." Her voice caught, tears formed. "Do you love him?" she asked. "Do you love Richard?"

Cassie managed to hold in much of her tea from her last sip but it proved to be challenging. Her reaction had Penelope handing her a napkin. "I'm sorry. I suppose that was a little abrupt. I really didn't mean to blurt it out like that."

A little more composed, Cassie set her cup and saucer down. "I'm not sure I know how to answer that question. It's clear you have feelings for him."

Penelope looked away. "I do love Richard or at least Richard the vampire. I suppose I just assumed everything would be the same or better once his curse was lifted. But you can't control who people are and it seems that Richard, without his curse, favors being with you."

"I'm not sure he knows what he wants right now. He has lots to sort through."

Penelope nodded. "I think you're right."

"It must be difficult for you. You've been with him for so long. Just you and Richard."

"Richard the vampire," she corrected. Meredith was right about that.

"Nevertheless, a part of Richard was there."

"Yes, but I think the vampire kept that part well hidden. I only saw that side of Richard on rare occasion."

"Are you truly related to me or was I just a convenient way for you to get Richard back?" The bite to the remark was light but evident.

"We are related. I was married once. I had a child—a little girl whom they took away from me shortly after my husband died. We'd only been married a couple of years. He'd taken ill and died from complications. I couldn't take care of her on my own and no one around me would help. A lovely couple took her and then moved away. As I grew older, I began to resent having my child taken from me. I worked many jobs in an effort to earn enough money to go and get my child back." With painful regret, she shook her head. "It was never enough. It wasn't easy for a woman to make a living then and I was still very much a child myself."

Penelope reached for something around her neck. "Before my baby was taken from me, I gave her a locket. It was a half of a heart. It was her father's." Unclasped, she handed her locket to Cassie. "No two fit together the same way. Put this one with the one you're wearing to know the truth."

Tentative, Cassie took her necklace off. With a locket in each hand she attempted to put the two together. The fit was perfect. A tear slid down Cassie's cheek.

"My adopted mother, Nancy, said my birth mother gave me this."

"I saw you had it on earlier and wondered myself. Isn't it wonderful to have confirmation?"

"You've been doing so much research. You found me. Did you find my mother as well? Do you know anything about her?"

"A bit, but I'm not certain you need to know."

"Of course I need to know! She's my mother. Why did she give me up? Why didn't she want me? Please, tell me. You have no idea how many sleepless nights I've—well, maybe you do have an idea. So please, what do you know?"

Penelope sighed deeply. "Her visions drove her crazy, dear—literally. I found she'd been institutionalized."

Cassie gulped. "Institutionalized? Visions?"

"Yes. I believe they're hereditary."

"I don't have visions."

"You will."

"But what about my mother," Cassie said, brushing that comment off for the moment, "is she still alive?"

"I'm afraid not. But things did get better for her. She gradually came to terms with her visions, as I understand. Your father had even planned a perfect holiday for them to celebrate. As fate would have it, they were both killed in an automobile accident on the way back. They'd gone to the mountains. The brakes on their car failed on a rather steep slope. It was all in the obituary."

"Okay, so I had a mother and a father. Why did she give me up?"

"I'm not certain, Cassie. The adoption records are sealed. I have no way of knowing."

"I thought knowing more would give me closure but it's only made things more confusing."

"I'm sorry, Cassie. I truly am. I know it must be hard."

Cassie leaned to hand Penelope's locket back.

"It's yours," Penelope told her. "By your hands, two have become one. You're the rightful owner now."

Cassie took a second to look again at the two lockets before placing them back around her neck. "Back to these visions. What makes you so sure I'll have them?"

"You're already hearing voices."

The same phrase she'd heard at the hospital came to her. *Bring them home.* That was you," she said.

"And you. You'd never be able to hear me if things weren't in place for you to have visions."

"Visions sound kind of evil. I'm quite certain I won't be participating in anything dark."

"Dark?" Penelope repeated. "Visions are quite Biblical. I know I'd never participate in anything that would put me at odds with my faith. Joseph called them dreams."

Still, Cassie looked doubtful.

"Dear," Penelope said, "if you don't come to terms with it now, it's going to be difficult. Your ability to have visions is a gift, not a curse. If you look at it that way, it's so much easier."

Cassie nodded. *Perhaps.* But hiding feelings for Richard now that she knew how Penelope felt? That wouldn't be easy.

19

Henderson decided that the vampyric ability to hypnotize prey depended on experience. He'd had several successful attempts, but this one was failing horribly.

"I need you to open your bag," the cocky checkpoint agent said as he stood behind the conveyor belt.

Henderson tried harder to get through, while trying to mask his growing frustration. He had a pint of blood in his bag to hold him over. He'd not worried about getting by security because he'd assumed hypnosis would work. It had worked so well on Kyle. *What was wrong?*

"I'm sure if you think about," he said, "you'll realize I don't need to open this bag at all."

A supervisor walked over. "What's the problem?"

"This guy won't open his bag."

Henderson gave his attention to the supervisor, stared long and hard, did everything he knew to do.

"It's all right," the supervisor said. "I checked it back there. He's good to go."

"But—"

"I said, *he's good to go.*"

The supervisor then turned to apologize to Henderson, "I'm sorry about the trouble. I'll arrange for someone to escort you to your gate so you don't have any other setbacks."

"That's all right. No need for that." Henderson smiled while grabbing up his things.

※

He arrived at the airport early. It wouldn't be easy to get on a plane with a knife and a pistol-gripped sawed-off shotgun no matter how well they were hidden and he had no real plan as of yet. He had done his research and knew Sky Marshals could carry weapons on board and bypass security checkpoints. But he wasn't a Sky Marshal and couldn't readily forge ID in the amount of time he had before his flight. He could, however, impersonate one.

※

The only thing Sky Marshal Mike "Bully" Masterson could recall as he came around in his small office was the image of a large hand aimed at his forehead.

For a few moments he tried to recall more, but decided not to worry about it. He only wanted sleep, at least for a little longer, and so he did—unaware that his ID and clip-on badge had been removed from his possession.

※

After cleaning up, Richard went searching for pain medication. He had no doubt Ceese's deep scratches would cause her pain very soon. He examined each small brown plastic bottle he found in the cabinet, read labels and softened on an issue that had bothered him a lot, both when he was a vampire and even now. Penelope hadn't lied.

Perhaps she hadn't been fully honest about some things but he began to realize the cancer was real. Of course, the medicine could've been a front to help support the ultimate lie of passing on but why would she go through so much trouble? And if she hadn't lied about having cancer, she'd indeed been in a great deal of pain for a very long time. If nothing else, he owed her an apology.

But right now he wanted to make sure of Ceese's comfort. He headed off to her room with one of the bottles.

Perfect timing. The second he entered the hall he heard Ceese moaning. He hurried to her room where Rodney had moved next to the bed. His anxious, worried look indicated that he'd no idea what to do. "Can you do something?" he asked.

"Yes," Richard said. He opened a prescription bottle and shook out an appropriate number of pills into his palm. "Two of these should help her." Richard poured water from the pitcher on her nightstand into a glass. Ceese could respond to simple instructions but sitting her up to take the medicine proved difficult. Richard looked to Rodney and, without a word, communicated what he needed him to do. Being careful not to cause more pain, Rodney, an arm beneath Ceese's shoulders, helped her upright. She swallowed the pills without a problem.

After easing Ceese back down, Rodney asked, "Should she be hurting that bad?"

"I suspected she would be in pain based on what I recall."

Rodney stared hard at Richard's profile. "That sort of implies you've seen this kind of thing before. Have you?"

"Apparently Zade attacked Mother as well. All we were told at the time was that it was a wolf. Father knew differently but didn't share."

"That's sort of important information to leave out, don't you think? Maybe if he'd told everyone the truth, more could've been done to keep Zade away from Ceese."

"Possibly, but I don't think anyone would've jumped to the conclusion that Zade wanted Ceese just because he attacked Mother. I suppose we would've just thought Father crazy. After all, no one truly believes werewolves exist."

"But why would Zade want to attack your mother anyway?"

"Evidently, he had plans. According to what Father said earlier, another man had his way with Mother before Zade scratched her." Relating information so distasteful reflected on Richard's face and in his voice. "The scratches were intended to affect the unborn child should the act produce one. Apparently, it did."

"Ceese?"

Richard nodded.

"You mean, she's really not your—um, really not related—totally?"

"So it would seem."

"Whoa."

With the edge off the pain, Ceese stirred and turned toward the sound of her brother's voice. "Richard."

Richard swung around, leaned over the bed and took one of her hands in his. "You're feeling better?"

"Father—I—I don't—" The pain rallied and then subsided.

Richard pushed the hair back from Ceese's face. "You can see Father later. I've made up with him. We've worked things out. He's eager to see you and I told him he could. But once you're feeling better."

"No," she said in a very different tone than he'd expected. "I don't want to see him."

"Sure you do," Richard said, smoothing her hair. "That's just the medicine talking."

"It's not the medicine," she insisted and grabbed his arm. "Father is a liar. Zade would never plan something like that. He'd never hurt Mother."

"Now I know it's the medicine. I think you should rest."

"Only if you promise me you won't let him see me. Swear it, Richard."

Richard's mouth opened then closed. His other hand grabbed the bedpost. "Why don't we just talk about it—"

"Swear it," she repeated, desperate tears clinging to the corner of her eyes.

"All right, I—I swear it."

Her eyes closed then and she turned his arm loose.

Richard's stunned expression raised a question from Rodney: "You still certain she's not cursed?"

The awkwardness of her proclamation had yet to settle. "Something's not right."

Immediately upon deplaning, the one-armed man walked over to the FedEx drop box and placed the cardboard envelope containing "Bully" Masterson's gear inside. Without breaking stride, he peeled off the latex glove he'd worn to hide fingerprints and deposited it into a trashcan.

20

An uneasy dusk lingered and threatened. Just between the horizon and night sky, a narrow strip of daylight waned. It would be dark very soon. Inside, Richard, Penelope and Cassie sat down to dinner. Rodney remained with Ceese even though she hadn't woken up since her proclamation about her father. Penelope instructed Marissa to take him a tray.

Richard sat at the head of the table, his usual spot. He'd claimed this seat when, as a vampire, he kept Penelope company as she ate—right before his own feeding time. Cassie sat to his right and Penelope to his left. The tension in the room showed as each chose their words very carefully. No one wanted to ruin the meal by saying anything that might set someone off.

After a short time, Penelope took a chance. She interrupted the subtle noises of dinner, silver grazing china, ice gently tapping glass, to speak. She looked at Cassie. "In case you were wondering, those scratches on the table next to you are from when Ceese first came to the castle. She had a difficult time adjusting and spent much of her first days in and out of wolf form."

Cassie noticed the scratches but had reserved the question. In her mind, that fell into the area of small talk and small talk could still be quite risky. Cassie looked surprised when

Richard added, "She spent most of her first days irritating me and quite a few days after that as well."

She smiled at this attempt. He could never hate Ceese the way the vampire did. "I'm sure you weren't easy to get along with either," she said, humoring him.

Penelope looked up as though she wanted to comment further but took another bite of her meal instead.

"Please, if you have something to share, don't let me stop you." For the first time since he'd returned, Richard directed words at Penelope that weren't biting.

Penelope took a sip of tea. "That's all right. I understand my place."

"In that case, I insist."

And so Penelope did. "Richard was in fact very difficult," she said to Cassie. "I think at times he was more stubborn and irritating than Ceese. That you could bring the two of them together to actually help each other is nothing short of a miracle."

Richard cocked a brow. "I suppose I deserved that."

Penelope sized him up before speaking diplomatically, "You could hardly help yourself, being a vampire and all."

"Yes, well, I'm no longer one now and I feel I owe you an apology. A lot of things have happened that I don't understand and may never understand. Still, that doesn't give me the right to judge you. I've been incredibly harsh to you and I'm sorry. I hope you can forgive me. I now realize you weren't lying about having cancer and I—I just wanted you to know that."

Penelope accepted his words with a small smile. "I'd never lie to you, Richard. That's the last thing I'd do."

"I'd like to call a truce. I'm not exactly sure how I feel about you right now but I'm quite certain I don't *hate* you. I don't understand a lot of what's taken place today but that aside, I'd like to count you among my friends."

"I'd like that too, Richard."

"I would also like to add that I can't offer you anything but friendship. I know the vampire alluded to something much deeper—"

"That's all right," Penelope cut him off. "I understand that as well. You didn't intentionally mislead me any more than I intentionally misled you. Friends. I can live with that."

He smiled, she smiled, and Cassie smiled. Those words meant she could pursue her feeling for Richard without feeling guilty. Yet she couldn't help wondering whether she'd end up as disappointed as Penelope seemed.

Now. It's time now. His eyes snapped open and he pushed up with his hands. The lid to the coffin opened easily. He looked back as he stepped out. Rodney had really gone out of his way this time. A coffin in a basement.

"Ah, you're up."

Josh whipped around, his long dreads followed. "Who are you?"

"A friend," the voice said easily. "I had a feeling you'd be coming around. I brought you something to hold you over until the hunt."

Josh stared longingly at the bag of blood.

"Thought you might be—hungry."

Josh ignored the fact that this man knew blood appealed to him. His eyes followed the man's actions as he placed the bag of blood on one of the closed coffins. He listened intently for the moment when the man with the luminous blond hair would speak again.

"This one's for you. I've also one for myself." The need for privacy was instinctive—no explanations necessary or given. The blond stranger walked off into the shadows with his bag.

Josh rushed forward to grab his and darted off into a dark recess. He produced fangs and pierced the bag. When finished, he returned to find that his new friend awaited him, sitting atop his closed coffin.

"I'm Meri," the man said when Josh settled next to him.

Josh's brow furrowed. "Okay," he said. "I'll bite. Why are you merry?"

"Because that's my name?"

"Oh," Josh nodded slowly. "I get it." But his brow furrowed again. "Dude, are you like gay because Mary—well, that's sort of a girl's name, right?"

"Gay?"

"Yeah, gay." With no sign that Meredith understood, he dropped the matter. "Never mind."

As he checked out the basement around him, Josh tried to piece together the many missing memories. "So, what do you know about all of this? Why are we in a basement? Why are we drinking blood and why . . ." he paused to look at his clothing, ". . . am I wearing a hospital gown? Rodney's really outdone himself this time."

Merideth turned his head at the name. "You know Rodney too?"

"So you're in this with him?"

"In what?"

"Dude, is everything a question with you? By the way, I'm Josh and that's not a girl's name."

"Dude." The older vampire tried the new word out. "I can't say that I've heard that term before."

Josh put a hand on his shoulder. "And maybe you shouldn't use it. It just doesn't sound right coming from you. Maybe it's the accent. Yeah, that's probably it. Where are you from anyway?"

"I grew up in—" he stopped short. His tilted head to the side, he stared at Josh's mouth and then stuck his tongue out a little.

Josh shot up from where he sat. "Dude! You *are* gay."

"Your tongue," Merideth said as he stood up. "There's something on your tongue."

"Huh? Oh, that! Yeah, you like it? That's my tongue ring." He opened his mouth wider to reveal the ring in all its splendor.

"Is that silver?"

"Yeah, pretty cool, right?"

Merideth stared, mesmerized. "Are you sure it's silver?"

"Dude, there you go with the questions again."

"It's just that—"

"Ow," Josh said in response. Suddenly his tongue felt like it was on fire. Then again, "Ow!" His fingers flew into his mouth and worked at the ring. "Ow, ow, ow," he continued to whimper as he worked. Finally he worked the tongue ring free and pelted it across the room. For a long moment, he held tongue between tips of fingers for relief. When the throbbing subsided a bit, he attempted to speak, two fingers still holding his tongue. "Dew, 'at was f'weaky."

Merideth nodded in agreement. "Let's go upstairs and put some ice on it. It will heal soon enough."

At Marissa's shriek of terror, the three diners rushed into the kitchen. "Stay back, you devil," they heard as they entered. In front of her she held two very sharp, very silver knives, one placed over the other to form a cross.

Richard saw that neither Merideth nor Josh actually threatened her in any way and gently took the knives from her. "It's all right. We'll take care of matters here." Marissa didn't argue, but ran from the room.

Josh removed the ice cube Merideth had given him. He even grinned. "Okay. Now we're getting somewhere." He recognized Richard and Cassie. "Where's Rodney? I know he's behind this."

Richard looked at Cassie. Cassie looked at Richard and they both turned to Merideth. "I don't think he's come to terms with being a vampire."

"Oh, come on," Josh groaned. "Enough is enough."

Cassie tried her hand at an explanation. "This is real, Josh."

"Yeah, right."

Marissa's shriek had also reached Rodney's ears. Geoffrey had stopped by to check on Ceese and offered to stay with her so Rodney could go down to investigate.

"You're up," Rodney said to Josh. "Good. How're you feeling?" He, at least, acted more civilized than he did back at Cassie's apartment.

"It's about time you showed up. Now tell everybody they can quit playing along with your little joke?"

"What joke? I don't get it."

"He doesn't seem to remember anything," Cassie enlightened. "Nothing."

Rodney turned his attention back to Josh. "Dude, Henderson cursed you. Kyle went to the street to lead the police in and when he got back, Henderson's body was gone and you were—on the ground—with bite marks on your neck and very little blood. He cursed you, dude."

Josh put a hand to his neck. He realized the puzzle pieces had been there all along but he hadn't bothered to put them in place. "Y-yeah. He snuck up on me. And Kyle, *man*, I wanted to curse him. Where is he anyway?"

"He decided not to come. You're in England, Josh. Richard thought it might be easier for you here."

With a dumbstruck look, Josh said, "Okay. I guess I'd like some more blood then."

Merideth eased up beside him. "We can go hunt now."

"Sure." He stared down at the hospital gown. "I guess I'd sort of like a shirt, too."

Rodney pulled off one of the two shirts he wore. Josh tore at the knots that had formed and slid the gown off. He turned at Cassie's gasp. With a bare torso, all could see the scars and welts along with skin discoloration that marked him as Mulatto. The texture of Josh's hair, which easily accommodated dreads, his large almond-colored eyes and the full lips—he was the product of a mixed union and apparently, not a very happy one.

"Go ahead," Josh said. "Take your best shot. Everybody else has." He assumed her gasp and stare equaled racism.

"It's not what you think. I'm not—it's just—I can't imagine what you've been through."

Her words and intentions did little to mollify. "No. You can't. So don't try."

"Your jacket's over there." Rodney pointed.

Josh actually smiled before heading over to get it. "Cool."

Merideth followed after him but stopped short of going out the door. Hand on the doorknob, he looked back and said, "You promised I could visit with Cee Cee tonight."

Richard had in fact, but before Ceese had made her proclamation. "Yes, about that—"

"She's in no condition," Rodney blurted.

Richard hadn't planned to be so blunt. "She's still resting, Father. If you could just be patient."

"Patient?" Rodney said after Merideth left. "Ceese said *never*. I don't think anybody is *that* patient."

"What's he talking about?" Penelope asked.

Richard struggled to play it off. "I'm afraid Ceese heard me talking to Rodney about what Father said earlier. About what happened to Mother."

"Merideth didn't want Ceese to know."

"Yes, well, it wasn't exactly intentional. I thought she was resting."

"But what did she say?" Cassie asked.

Richard made a dismal face. "That Father was a liar and she never wanted to see him again."

"Oh, my," Penelope said. "That's not good."

"Honestly, I'd just given her some pain medication. I'm sure she didn't mean it."

"I hope you're right," Penelope told him. "Because I'm not sure Meri can handle hearing that Ceese considers him a liar and doesn't want to see him."

What did that mean? Before he could voice his question, Richard decided he didn't really want to know.

21

Phew, I just dodged a bullet—at least for the present. Richard had convinced his father that Ceese needed more healing time. The wait also gave time for his sister to reconsider. *What a tight rope.*

"I didn't think he was going to believe you," Cassie said, as she and Richard walked down the hall toward her room. Richard had recommended the room with a view of the night garden. "He looked so disappointed."

Hands in pockets, his hair pulled back and tied, Richard nodded. "It wasn't an easy thing to tell him, I assure you. And I'm at a loss for what to tell him in the morning. I know he'll ask again."

They stopped just outside Cassie's door. She smiled. "You'll think of something."

Richard returned the smile. "Perhaps Ceese will come to her senses before I have to."

"On another note, Josh seems to be taking everything in stride."

"Judging from his scars, I'd say he's probably used to things not going his way."

"I just feel terrible about staring. But when I saw—I know he thought I was being racist, but I wasn't," Cassie insisted.

"He doesn't know you, that's all."

She smiled at his efforts to make her feel better. "No, he doesn't." She opened her door and stepped inside. "I suppose I'll see you in the morning then."

"Indeed," he told her. "Sleep well."

Richard walked down two doors to his room. There he found Geoffrey turning his sheets back. "Geoffrey," Richard beamed. "You're still here."

Geoffrey kept his smile in check though he did offer a little more than he would've given any other client. After all, this was Richard. "I was just finishing up for the day."

Richard eased his door shut almost as if to prevent Geoffrey from leaving. "But couldn't we talk first? You know, like we used to."

Geoffrey had been a real find. It's not easy to find a son of a vampire as one's manservant. *That* was priceless.

"Lord—"

"No," Richard said. He pulled the band from his hair. "Don't you remember? When we'd have our chats, you'd call me Richard—just Richard, right?" His smile wasn't anything Geoffrey could ignore.

"I remember. So what shall we chat about . . . Richard?"

"Yes," Richard said as he settled back in an armchair. "There's something I really need to talk to someone about. And please," he said while assessing Geoffrey's attire, "do something to look less like a butler." Richard rose and helped Geoffrey out of his coat. "And unfasten some shirt buttons." Geoffrey did so. Richard motioned an invitation to sit. "Much better."

Richard opened their chat, "I think I'm in love, Geoffrey."

Geoffrey's look was a mixture of emotion. Confusion's angled brows won out. "I'm not sure I understand. I have very deep respect and emotion for you—"

Richard stopped him at once. "Oh for heaven's sake. It's not you! I won't deny a feeling of complete adoration at times, but you know me better, man! It's Cassie."

"Ah, I thought I saw something there."

"Really?"

"Yes."

"Well, what do you think I should do?"

Geoffrey shook his head. "I'm sorry, Richard. I just don't feel comfortable advising you in this matter. Ask me anything else."

Richard slid to the edge of his chair. "But you understand about being a vampire. You often commented on your father's lack of emotion. I've been without mine for so long. How can I trust my feelings?"

Geoffrey moved closer and he leaned to take Richard's right hand between both of his. "I've known you as a vampire and now I see you as a mortal. I've never witnessed a bigger change in anyone. I don't see someone who isn't in charge of his emotions. I see someone who is entertaining a long lost friend. You are who you used to be. I don't have to know you to know this. Trust your emotions, Richard."

The night garden shone breathtakingly beautiful. Cassie now understood why Richard chose this room for her. The garden, just off the bedroom balcony, wasn't all that impressive in the day, but what a nocturnal difference. Blooms opened and basked in the moon's glow. Sweet aroma filled the night air. She'd never seen anything like it . . . a fairy-tale garden. She inhaled deep and suddenly her legs weakened beneath her. *What in the world's happening?* She reached out to steady her dizziness and grabbed the balcony railing. Everything went dark.

"Cassie." Penelope knelt next to the figure on the floor.

Cassie opened her eyes. "What happened?" she asked, groggy and confused.

"I—I don't know. I came to talk with you and found you here. You don't remember?"

Cassie pulled herself to lean against the railing, her strength restored. "I'd just come out here to look at the garden. I took a deep breath and then—I guess I passed out. I do recall my legs weakening."

"And you were lightheaded, as if all your energy was drained from you."

"Yes."

"And there was a very sweet aroma."

Cassie became suddenly guarded but answered nonetheless. "Yes. I assumed it to have been the flowers." She took a deep breath again and realized the scent had not been floral. She turned back to Penelope. "What do you know about this?"

"I think you had a vision. But don't worry. You'll learn to recognize the signs and you'll become stronger so that you won't pass out every time one presents itself to you."

"I'm quite certain I didn't have a vision." Cassie rose and stepped back into her room.

"What makes you say that?" Penelope asked, following.

"Because I don't remember anything—like a dream."

"You will."

Cassie stopped at the foot of the bed and turned. "When?"

Penelope fixed her with a deliberate gaze. "Now."

Cassie dropped to a seat on the bed and grabbed at her temples. She squinted.

"What do you see?" Penelope asked quietly.

"A man. He has one arm. His left arm is missing from just above the elbow. There's something significant about him but I'm not sure what." She squinted harder. "He's at an airport and he's coming. He's coming here."

22

Rodney stretched out on the pallet he'd made from the blankets Geoffrey brought in earlier. He wouldn't leave Ceese until he knew more about what was going on. She hadn't come around since Richard had given her the pain medication that afternoon—hours ago, now.

It wasn't the lack of verbal communication that bothered him. He no longer felt Ceese in his head. Every time he missed the sensation, Rodney frowned. He'd always felt her presence and now he had nothing. Could the pain medication affect that? He didn't know and not knowing made him frown too.

"Why won't you talk to me, Ceese?" he whispered. "Why won't you let me know what's going on?"

With Penelope gone, Cassie got ready for bed. After pulling her favorite blue nightshirt over her head, a light knock sounded on the door. "Who is it?" she asked while rummaging through her open suitcase for a bathrobe.

"It's me. It's Richard," came his timid voice.

She cinched the bathrobe's belt into a simple knot and walked to the door. "Richard?" she whispered and opened the door a crack.

"I know it's late," he said, his longer hair framing that face Cassie now had difficulty ignoring. "May I come in?"

Cassie couldn't resist. "Sure." She opened the door wider. "I'm not disturbing you?"

"Not at all." Cassie immediately wondered how she'd said that without giving anything away. Her heart raced and her palms felt damp.

"I couldn't sleep," Richard said walking onto the balcony. "And I just wanted someone to talk to."

"Sure." Cassie followed him.

"Isn't it beautiful?" he said taking in the moonlit garden.

Cassie stood next to him and pushed a strand of hair behind her ear. "It certainly is."

Awkward silence followed. Perhaps he just needed to be prodded. Cassie broke it. "Did you—want something?"

Richard's expression sank. "I've made you uncomfortable. I'm sorry. That wasn't my intention."

"No," Cassie rushed. "I'm fine; why would you think otherwise?"

"You pushed that lock of hair behind your ear," he said, touching the strand. "You always do that when you're uncertain about something. You always push that lock of hair back and sometimes—twist it."

Cassie stopped twisting it at once and crossed her arms. "I do not." She laughed lightly. "Okay, so maybe I do." Did he have any idea how his presence affected her? Why wouldn't he come out and say what he wanted so she could shift gears and calm down? "Are you going to tell me why you're here or should I start guessing?"

He took a moment to gaze at the garden. "I suppose I just wanted to talk."

Of course that's what he wanted to do.

Yet he stood silent.

Her gut lurched. "I'm curious. I've not seen you smoke since your curse was lifted. Was it that easy for you to break the habit?" There. That was an innocent subject. How could anyone read anything into that?

"It wasn't really a habit as such. I could've stopped whenever I wanted to. Smoking irritated people and the vampire loved to irritate."

"So you weren't addicted?"

"A vampire is only addicted to one thing and that's blood. Nothing else matters. Nothing."

Silence followed, but this time Richard filled it. "The object is to curse and no distraction is tolerated. All one's energy is focused on that task. It isn't easy at first. You have to adjust. You still want to have control of your emotions but the vampire doesn't allow it. It demands that you focus on one thing and one thing only."

"That must've been frustrating for both you and Penelope. Especially after her curse was lifted."

He gave her a sideways glance. "It was frustrating for her, I'm sure. But I was incapable of feeling her frustration."

"I don't believe that, Richard. You can't tell me you had no feelings for Penelope."

"I suppose I had respect for her. Great respect. But beyond that, nothing truly emotional." Richard saw Cassie squint an eye and he explained further, "If I were to tell you that in order for you to survive you had to bite and take in the blood of another living being—very likely causing their death—would you do it?"

She didn't have to think about her answer. "No."

"The vampire knows this. It knows what it's asking you to do is unnatural and something most would never consider. And so it channels all thoughts and emotions into feeding. No other pastime or activity can bestow what feeding affords a vampire. Nothing comes close. It's my understanding that feeding on another human, rather than animals, offers you the ultimate satisfaction. Absolutely nothing on this earth compares or satisfies so completely."

Cassie could hear in his voice and see on his face just how difficult it had been to resist. "It must've been torture for you."

"It does make me appreciate what has been taken from me and what has been given back."

What was that look? Was he actually leaning in closer? Why did she suddenly feel like she was going to melt into the floor? "Richard I—"

"Yes?" he said, his lips nearly touching hers; his intoxicating breath washing over her.

"I—"

"Yes?"

"Nothing," she said breathless. The kiss came next—so much more than the kiss outside of Ceese's room in ICU that night when Richard thanked her. This was so unbelievably sensual that she couldn't speak. She didn't say anything when he lifted her up and carried her back into the bedroom. Didn't say anything when he picked up where he'd left off. This kiss was both gentle and strong—and incredible! She'd never experienced anything like it. She knew she didn't want it to stop, but then he pulled away.

Richard traced the features of her face with the tips of his fingers. Seconds later, he returned to trail kisses down her neck. *I should stop this. I shouldn't allow this to happen.* Then, just like that, she didn't have to. With a sharp intake of breath, Richard jumped up. Grabbed at his temples.

"Cyn," he said, with an absolute look of horror.

"I'm sorry." Cassie gathered her robe together and stood as well. "I'm so sorry," she whispered. According to Penelope's diary, Richard had studied the Word closely with his father. He had once wanted to be a minister. Certainly he had strong views on things such as this. "I—I suppose it is a sin," she stuttered. "Or at least I—I guess it could've been."

"No," said Richard and rushed back to her. "Not that kind of sin. Cyn as in 'Cynthia.' One of the two who cursed me. I saw her. You were her."

"I don't understand."

"I don't either," he hushed.

"Did I do something to remind you of her? I won't do it again. Tell me what it was."

"I just can't believe, after all this time, that she could have this effect." His tone had pain.

"You knew her before she cursed you?"

"She tricked me. We were to be married." Scowling, he explained, "She led me to believe she was . . . something other than what she was."

"Richard, how? She was a vampire. You had to know that."

His look was telling. "She's a very good liar."

"You mean *was*."

Richard shook his head back and forth. "I wish I did mean *was*." His sigh was deep. "Do you remember when I sensed that Henderson was about to curse a man?"

Cassie nodded and recalled Richard bleeding from the cut made by his razor, staring hard into her bathroom mirror. "I sensed Cyn in the same way. It seems, after all this time, she too, is still around."

Cassie struggled to take that in. "She goes by Cyn?"

"It isn't her real name. In fact, I don't know for sure what her given name was. She'd get bored and pick a new name. She always went back to Cyn, though."

"So you stayed with her after you were cursed?"

"Eventually, I got away. But I assure you, it was no easy task."

Cassie shivered and pulled her robe tighter.

"I'm sorry," Richard rubbed the backs of her upper arms. "I shouldn't have come here. I've ruined everything. I so wanted this to be a special moment."

"It's all right, Richard." Cassie tried to sound convincing. "Go now. We'll have other moments."

"But I've upset you and that wasn't my intention." He reached out toward her again.

She retreated a step back. She didn't trust herself at all right now. "I—It's fine, Richard. I'm not upset. I just really need some time to think about things."

He reached for her hand and she allowed him to take it. "Until the morning then?"

"Yes," she promised. "I'll see you in the morning."

She watched him leave, returning his smile when he looked back. When the door closed behind him, she sank onto her bed, physically worn and prepared for sleep. Her mind, however, had its own ideas.

23

Under the canopy of densely thicketed forest and under the darkness' cloak, Henderson both levitated and walked. His flight had been relatively uneventful as was the taxi ride to the forest's edge. Cabbie Stephen Martin asked no questions and had him out of London in short order. Henderson paid him for his trouble and bought the driver's silence with a little more. With the information the cabbie provided along the way, he'd easily find Richard's castle.

With what he had learned before coming to the UK, plus Martin's helpful words, he knew Richard's castle was close by. Levitated, he spied what looked like the very top of a turret. *Finally.* He dropped down to search for a place to hide so he'd be in a safe spot well before dawn arrived.

Red slitted eyes watched the form descend to the ground. Silently, hands bent branches. A hunched figure stalked slowly forward. Zade timed the collision pinning the man to the ground. Roughly, he flipped the vampire onto his back, straddled him and glared. Zade's open shirt revealed a well-muscled chest.

Henderson knew he needed to be careful.

"Zade *hate* vampires. Zade kill vampires." Canine-like incisors broke through and the werewolf drew back to strike.

Henderson's eyes widened. A werewolf—this close to Richard's castle . . . and *his* neck? What were the odds? His mind raced and searched . . . "I'm looking for a werewolf. She calls herself Ceese."

Zade whipped his head close. "Vampire know Ceese?"

Henderson risked the wrong answer. "I might."

The werewolf grabbed hold of Henderson's shirt collar and stood, pulling the man up with him. "Tell Zade what you know."

"I know Ceese isn't a werewolf anymore."

This brought an angry snarl. "Ceese still belong to Zade."

Henderson pulled his head back to avoid those fangs. "I'm not here to question that. In fact, I think Ceese needs to be a werewolf again. That's why I'm here."

Zade quirked his head to the side. "Why?"

He had the werewolf's attention. "If you let go of me, I'll explain."

Stars in the eastern sky started to fade. Josh didn't have a good feeling about it but he had to find Merideth. A few minutes later, his friend sprinted over a hill.

"What are you waiting for?" the older vampire shouted as he drew nearer. "Go!"

Josh fell in beside him. "Why are we running?"

"Ashes to ashes, dust to dust—the sun shows no mercy."

Together they cleared a downed log and leapt over a small ditch. The castle in sight, they ran even faster and darted inside just as the sun breached the distant horizon. They reached the basement door and Meri stopped. "Richard said I could visit with Cee Cee," he panted.

Josh raised a brow.

"She's still resting," said Richard as he stepped from a shadow. "I was waiting for you. I knew you'd want to know."

"Could I look in on her? Can I just see her?"

"In good time, Father. I promise."

"Come on," Josh encouraged, already a few steps into the basement.

Merideth sighed and followed.

24

Richard had risen early to catch his father and felt surprised he wasn't more tired. After all, over the course of the past few days, he'd had very little rest. Richard decided it was nothing to worry about and headed for his study. Certainly, there would be some catching up to be done, bills to be paid.

When he entered the room, he was pleased to find the drapes open. His smile was telling. How nice not to have to worry about the sun's rays turning him into a pile of dust! He even went out of his way to walk past one of the windows—just because now he could. That's when he saw Cassie. Out one of the three windows, Richard saw her walking. He forgot the bills. Now he just wanted to go see her.

She headed toward a larger garden on the eastern side of the lawn. *Why was she up so early?* Had she not slept well? Did she hate him after last night? Would she speak to him? Something told him he should give her more time to think and then just as quickly something else made him ignore his own advice.

She was indeed headed toward the larger garden. He followed but stayed back between shrubs, out of sight. He had yet to figure out what he'd tell her. What if coming to talk to her was a mistake? Richard slid behind a shrub, and then ventured a look. He didn't see her anywhere.

"Richard?" Cassie came around the shrub from the other side.

Richard jumped and turned to face her.

"I thought I heard something. Are you following me?" she asked.

"No," he sputtered and drove his hands into the front pockets of his pants. "I was just up and thought I'd come out for an early morning stroll. It is quite peaceful, isn't it?"

Her silence told him she wasn't buying it.

"All right, I confess. I came out here because I saw you. Please tell me you're not angry."

"Why would I be angry?"

"Well, you said last night you needed some time to think. And I've hardly given you that."

"I've had enough time," she said.

Encouraged, he shifted his weight. "If you've come to visit the garden, I'd love to walk with you."

"I'd like that," she said.

Crushed stone cushioned their steps as they strolled. Morning dew clung to the very edge of leaves and petals. "So, this Cyn, she was one of the two that cursed you?" asked Cassie.

So much for enjoying the garden. "Yes."

"Is it really that hard for you to talk about her?" Cassie asked. "It was so long ago."

"I suppose it might be easier had I not experienced what I did last night. But it was like she was right there. As if she'd stepped right into your body."

"That would be eerie. Was she really that horrible?"

"You have no idea. She deceived me. She lied to me and took advantage just so she could have me for herself."

"I wasn't aware vampires stalked their prey."

Richard stopped walking. "They don't usually, but the temptation was too great. Nothing is more tantalizing or satisfying than the blood of someone who is one phase away from being off limits." To her look of confusion he added, "I had no assurance of salvation at that point, but planned to commit my soul the very next day before Father was to ordain me into the ministry. She knew this and planned to share me with her friend."

"I'm sorry, Richard. I didn't mean to pry."

"It's all right. It's over now."

"I am curious, however, about something you just mentioned."

"What's that?" Richard said.

"You said that you planned to commit your soul the next day . . . before your father ordained you. Did he not know you hadn't done it yet?"

Richard shook his head.

She nodded and extended her hand to him. "Okay, just curious. Come on," she said. "I'm supposed to show you something."

25

Richard stared at her extended hand. "It's all right," Cassie told him. "Last night was just as much my fault as it was yours." She then reached over and took his hand. "Now come on."

She led him out of the garden and onto the lawn. When she didn't turn back toward the castle, Richard spoke up. "Aren't you going the wrong way?" They were headed toward the woods.

"No."

Had she turned around to look, she would've seen his worried expression. "Why don't I feel better about this?"

They left the well-manicured yard and Cassie forged ahead. A low branch she'd pushed out of her way swung back at Richard. He dodged it but just barely. The near-hit reminded him of just how outdoorsy he wasn't. As a vampire, he'd made concessions. He no longer had to do that.

"I had a vision last night, before your visit," Cassie said as they walked. "One of the things I learned from it was that I'm supposed to take you somewhere."

Near the edge of the forest, dead leaves littered the ground. It was easy going for a very short while, but that didn't last long. Cassie stepped over a log she'd seen on the ground but didn't think to warn Richard. He tripped and tumbled to his knees. "Are you all right?" she asked after his awkward fall.

There was no real look of pain on Richard's face until he seemed to consider his situation. "I think I twisted my ankle. Yes, indeed I have. Perhaps we should go back." He looked over his shoulder back the way they'd just come. "It may take a while, but I think I could limp back with help."

"I watched you fall, Richard. If you truly twisted your ankle, it should've been the one you're not holding."

"Okay, you caught me. I suppose I'm fine." He pushed up and stood.

"You really should leave the lying to Rodney. You're horrible at it. And besides, aren't you the least bit curious about what it is I'm supposed to show you?"

"I suppose."

He allowed her to pull him along—this time they picked their steps carefully. "There," Cassie said finally. "I distinctly remember seeing that in my vision."

"A bush?"

"No," she said as she headed over. "There's supposed to be an entrance to a cave behind it." She walked over and went around. "And there is."

"Does that mean we can go back now?" Richard said from where he stood.

Cassie ignored his comment and searched the ground around her. "Here's the lantern. And the matches—just like in the vision." She set the lantern on the ground and lit it. Then she stood back up. "Come on, Richard. Let's go see what's inside."

"Don't you know?" It certainly made sense that she should. "I mean, so far your vision seems to have been quite detailed and accurate."

"I'm afraid I don't know. We're going to have to go in. That's why I was supposed to bring you here. That's what we're supposed to do."

Richard took the few steps over to her. "I know this may sound odd but believe it or not I'm not a big fan of caves. As a vampire I favored them, but without the curse, I can honestly say I've always stayed away." He looked over his shoulder and stared uncomfortably.

She took his hand again. "You're supposed to go in here, Richard. We'll go together."

They both had to stoop to enter the cave. Once inside the high ceiling loomed three to four feet above their heads and they could stand straight. The lantern sufficiently illuminated the area around them. All walls could be seen and they couldn't make out another exit or entrance. Cassie slowly swung the lantern around.

"There's something over there," Richard said, moving toward an odd shape.

"A box." She knelt beside him. The large wooden box had five-inch-thick sides and a hinged bowed lid.

"Oh . . . my," Richard crouched to sigh. "I've not seen one of these in quite some time. It—It's a Bible box." Richard placed the lantern on the ground to shed more light. He didn't touch it at first, but examined it respectfully.

"Is it locked?" she asked when he didn't make a move to open it.

"Not exactly." Richard manipulated the locking mechanism as though he'd done it many times before.

"You've seen one of these then."

"They were quite common—back in the day." Unlatched, the box opened easily. Both bent closer to look.

Richard gasped. Cassie snapped her head to look at him and then back to the box contents: An animal pelt—definitely not overwhelming. Still, Richard stared, glassy-eyed. He lifted out the pelt and handled it like a precious treasure. With deliberate and cautious movements, he folded back layers until he revealed what the animal pelt covered. "It can't be—it simply can't be."

A book. Cassie assumed a Bible. The gold-embossed letters on the cover weren't English. "Do you know what language that is?"

"Yes. It's Gaelic and very old Gaelic at that." He sounded it out. "Bib-la New-eeva. That's how you say it and of course, that means Holy Bible."

"So it's a Gaelic Bible."

"It's not just any Gaelic Bible." Richard opened it and turned a few pages. "It belongs to Father. It's the very one he used to preach from. He had several Bibles but this one he treasured.

His friend, Reverend Robert Kirk, a seventh son of a seventh son, gave it to him."

"Seventh son . . . Is that significant?"

"Well, yes. These individuals are said to be gifted with second sight. Father was also the seventh son of a seventh son."

"Second sight?"

Richard leaned toward her. "It means they can see and talk to faeries and the like. Reverend Kirk was called the Faery Minister."

"Okay, Richard," Cassie said uncertainly. "I can honestly say I don't know as much about fairies *and the like*, as I do about vampires and werewolves but I do know they're often discussed in a very dark light, if you know what I mean. I hardly see a minister, a man of God, speaking of such things."

"Well, Father can certainly tell you more about that than I can. I hardly put much stock in fairies. Father did take me to Doon Hill once. I can't say it did much to bolster my belief."

"Why would it? What is Doon Hill?"

"It's in Ireland. Reverend Kirk would often go to visit and talk with his fairy friends. According to legend, he died there, his ear pressed to the ground, listening to the fairies. Many say the fairies took him."

"What do you say, Richard?" Cassie asked carefully.

"I say it's time to head back to the castle." He put the pelt back around the Bible. "I don't believe in fairies, Cassie. But I won't judge Father if he chooses to."

As they ducked out of the cave, Richard lugging the box, Cassie continued with her questions. "Do you know why your father would treasure this Bible over any of the others he had? You said he had quite a few."

"It has to do with his heritage, I suppose. He loves the Gaelic language."

Once outside, she made another observation. "If that's your father's Bible as you say it is, how did it get here? As a vampire, he wouldn't be able to carry it. It's a Bible."

Richard studied the box he carried. "Perhaps Father can tell us."

Cassie stopped. She cocked one ear and stared out to the trees. Then turned and walked back to the entrance where she extinguished and replaced the lantern as it sat earlier. "I'm supposed to leave this here," she said.

"Of course," Richard said. "Now let's take what we found back to the castle."

After they were out of sight, the one responsible for Cassie's vision walked to the cave to retrieve what she'd left behind.

26

Rodney heard the large front door of the castle open and then close. Frantic and frustrated, he raced from Ceese's room and down the hall. Downstairs, he ran toward the voices, slid to a stop before the parlor doors and stared hard at both Richard and Cassie.

"Where is she?" he demanded.

"Where's who?" Cassie asked.

Determined to get the truth, Rodney strode over. "Don't play dumb with me. I know you know where she is."

Richard placed the Bible box on a nearby stool then turned to Rodney. "Perhaps if you explained—"

At once, Rodney took Richard by the collar of his shirt, forced him over and up against a nearby wall. "You've got no right to keep me from being with Ceese," he said through clenched teeth. "No right at all!"

"And why would I try?" Richard tried to be patient despite being manhandled.

Confused and now a little frustrated as well, Cassie attempted to intervene. "Let him go. He's been with me all morning. He doesn't know what you're talking about and neither do I."

Rodney tightened his hold on Richard's collar. "Right. You're probably in on it too."

"In on what?" Cassie protested. "You're not making any sense."

"The two of you took Ceese somewhere while I was asleep because you don't want me around her. You've taken her and plan on turning her against me."

"I don't think you have anything to worry about there," Cassie said. "Ceese seems quite determined to like you no matter what anyone else thinks about it."

Richard didn't bother to address Rodney's paranoia. "Are you saying Ceese isn't in her room?"

"What part of 'where is she' did you fail to understand?"

With one quick motion, Richard brought his arms up between Rodney's, pushed out hard and broke Rodney's grip.

Stunned, Rodney fell back a few steps. "Hey," he said as Richard and Cassie charged out of the parlor. "Wait."

When Rodney arrived at Ceese's room, the search was already underway: in closets, clothes on hangers pushed aside and boxes shifted, curtains pulled aside. Penelope arrived from the kitchen to address the commotion. "What's going on?"

"Ceese isn't with you?" Richard asked, hopeful.

"I'm afraid not." Penelope looked at the empty bed then to Rodney. "Weren't you with her?"

"Apparently he didn't hear her leave," Cassie said, bringing to light the mystery that drove him into the parlor a moment ago.

"Well, where in the world do you think she's gotten off to?"

With the worried look of a parent who'd lost sight of their child, Richard scanned the room once again. "I don't . . . know?"

The last word hung in the air as they all saw the same thing at about the same time. A corner of the bed skirt hung at an awkward angle. Richard went over, knelt down and lifted it up.

"Ceese," he sighed with relief. "What are you doing?"

She stared out but said nothing.

Rodney moved to the other side of the bed and looked under as well. "What do you think is wrong?" Clearly something was.

"I'm not sure," Richard said. "But we need to get her out. Since she doesn't seem to be responding, we'll have to move her ourselves. If you can gently pull her, I'll ease her toward you."

Ceese lay limp—her eyes open but unseeing. "I don't understand," Richard said as they placed her back on the bed. "She should be better." Penelope brought him an old medical bag and he prepared to take her blood pressure.

Rodney reached out and carefully slid her lids shut. When he moved his hand, she reopened her eyes. "Ceese, can you hear me?"

No response—worry etched lines in Rodney's face. "Why do you suppose she was under the bed? I know she spent a lot of time there as a werewolf."

"She may have spent a lot of time there as a werewolf but it had nothing to do with her curse." It was clear what Rodney was worried about. "Apparently when she was very young, she decided that beds had too much to do with death. She even told me once, when I tried to explain otherwise, that most people die in bed. She feels safer under the bed. Where, she said, not many die."

Richard moved to take off the blood pressure cuff he'd secured to Ceese's upper-arm, returned it to the old-fashioned medical bag he'd brought in the day before. "Her vital signs are all normal," he reported.

"So you don't think we need to get her to a hospital?" Cassie said.

"I think all they would do is what we can do. Watch for any changes."

The implication wasn't good. "This has something to do with Zade, doesn't it?" Rodney said.

Ceese exhaled, "Zade."

Richard placed a hand on Ceese's forehead. "Sister," he whispered, "can you hear me? Can you tell me what's wrong?"

"Zade," she repeated before falling back into silence.

They took shifts sitting with Ceese so she was never alone. Except for an occasional blinking, her eyes never shut. The day seemed to drag on until finally night fell and all but Rodney gathered. That Merideth wanted to visit with Ceese had been completely forgotten, otherwise Richard might've been better prepared with an answer.

Rodney chose the wrong moment to step into the dining room. A sturdy chair sailed through the air and smashed against the dining room wall . . . right above Rodney's head. He hit the floor.

"What are you doing here?" Cassie hissed from under the table where she and the others had taken cover. "You're supposed to be watching Ceese."

"Geoffrey's with her. I came to get something to eat. Why is Merideth throwing furniture—" A plate broke nearby. "—and china?"

Richard spoke up. "He didn't like it when I told him he still couldn't visit with Ceese. He didn't even give me a chance to explain."

"You said I could see her," Merideth bellowed, now fully transformed and fully enraged. "I'm tired of waiting."

Rodney started to back out from under the table with plans of crawling out of the room. "Looks like you have your hands full here. I'll come back later." But, in his desperation, he hadn't considered Merideth's location. The last sound placed him at the other end of the table. Before he knew it, Rodney was pulled to his feet. He managed a pitiful "help" so that the others knew he'd been caught. The others scrambled out from under cover in time to see Merideth levitating off the floor with Rodney in tow—and fangs that neared his neck.

"You will let me visit Ceese or I will curse him."

"Do something," Rodney whimpered.

"He won't curse you," Richard challenged. The vampire reached its fangs closer.

"Oh, God," Rodney muttered and the vampire held its victim tighter. Not even Rodney's simple prayer moved him.

"Do you have your cross?" Richard asked Penelope.

"I'm fairly certain it's going to take more than that to get his attention now."

Rodney's panic grew. "That's all you can come up with?"

"If you have a better idea," Richard said, frustrated himself.

Josh had waited outside for Merideth but he had been gone far too long. He decided to go and fetch the older vampire.

He knew something was wrong the second he entered the kitchen. Instead of tending to her duties, Marissa huddled against a far wall.

"Where is he?"

"There." Marissa directed with a shaky hand toward the dining room. When Josh saw the dangling Rodney and the vampire ready to strike, he raced over and tackled Merideth mid-air. The three tumbled to the floor.

"Let him go," he said. "We'll go hunting. You'll be fine." Josh locked an arm around his neck to assure cooperation. He pulled back and wrestled him away. Finally free, Rodney scampered out of reach.

"Come on." Josh pulled Merideth along. No one moved until the kitchen door closed.

"A cross you say?" Rodney rubbed his neck and stared at Richard.

"It always worked for me," Richard replied.

27

As he worked with Zade, Henderson tried to forget how the werewolf made fun of him the night before, tried to ignore how Zade kept him guessing. Was he leading him to safety or to certain death? Sunrise threatened and Henderson needed to find a place of refuge. Zade never volunteered to help him but there was no other reason for the werewolf to have taken off running, crudely motioning for Henderson to follow. But to stop in the clearing and to stare with that furtive grin—while the sun's rays eased closer to breaking over the horizon? Zade waited until the very last second to shove Henderson toward the mouth of the hidden cave.

"The word is please," he repeated once again, trying hard to hide his satisfaction at getting back at the werewolf.
"Zade not say that. Zade *never* say that."
"Yes. But if Zade want Ceese," Henderson explained in stilted werewolf grammar, "then Zade will listen—"
"Zade listen only to Zade. Zade do what Zade want and Zade *take* what Zade want."
"I'm sorry," Henderson politely challenged. "I thought Zade want help. I thought Zade want Ceese to come to him. To not be frightened." Henderson took a cautious step toward him. "Zade take what Zade want and Zade will end up with

nothing. Ceese will run from Zade. Never stop running. Zade understand that?" Henderson took the lack of response as an affirmative. "Now try again, won't you? The word is please."

Zade's eyes narrowed, his chest heaved as if summoning the breath to say the word was more than he could bear. With great effort, Zade spit the word out. "*Please.*"

Henderson tried to appear satisfied even though he knew it meant little to the werewolf. Wiping werewolf spittle from his cheek he said, "That's fine. We'll work on delivery later."

Josh wrestled with Merideth out onto the lawn and didn't let up until it was clear Merideth had control of the vampire. He still couldn't believe what he'd seen in the dining room. "What's wrong with you? You were about to curse Rodney."

Merideth staggered to a nearby tree and fell against it. "I just—I don't know. I just want to visit with Cee Cee—and Richard promised."

"Okay, I get that, but you can't go around threatening to curse people, right? Isn't that what you've been telling me this whole time? That cursing others is—bad. So you want to visit with Ceese but she doesn't want to see you. You're just going to have to be patient."

"What?" a dazed Merideth asked.

"I said you're going to have to be patient."

"Cee Cee doesn't want to see me?"

"Yeah, dude. That's what Rodney said. Something about her mom not being attacked by Zade and you lying. I don't remember exactly. I was ready for my coffin. And right now, I'm ready to go hunting. So what do you say? Aren't you ready to feed?"

"You go on," Merideth told him. "I'll catch up later." He pushed away from the tree. "We can meet back here."

"Sure thing," Josh replied.

Merideth maintained the façade of resolve until he could no longer see Josh. He then broke down and staggered off into the woods. "It can't be," he muttered. "My Cee Cee hates me."

The dining room was in shambles and Penelope suggested the three of them move to the small kitchen table.

"Perhaps you can have Geoffrey call in the morning to get things back in order," Penelope said to Richard. "He's quite the wonder. It was nothing short of a miracle the way he pulled things together after he arrived. He even knew of a man who was able to repair that clock you toppled in the foyer."

"Yes," Richard said. "Geoffrey is quite the butler."

"You looked so surprised to see that clock," Cassie said. "Geoffrey must've had his hands full then—working to get things repaired I mean. You couldn't tell anything was out of place when we got here."

"Oh, my," Penelope said. "There were holes in walls, large furniture had been thrown. The bulk of the damage was in the parlor though. That made it a little easier, I suppose."

Cassie watched Richard's expression. "You were quite destructive as the vampire."

"I'm better now," he smiled. "Thanks to you."

Marissa came over and placed plates of salad before them. "Thank you, Marissa. Actually, he wasn't all that horrid," Penelope said. "The vampire could actually be very caring in an odd sort of way. Much like Meri." Richard frowned down into his salad. "Excuse me, I meant Merideth."

"Well, all I know," Cassie said, "is that Merideth is very angry. What are we going to tell him the next time he asks to visit with Ceese? If Ceese doesn't change her mind about seeing him, that is."

"I only hope she comes around soon so she can at least discuss the matter," Richard replied.

"Does Zade have some hold on her?"

Richard nodded. "I do believe he does and I think she's trying to fight that hold. I just don't know if she's strong enough."

"She's strong," Penelope confirmed. "We just need to give her time." Penelope passed out plates from the cart Marissa pushed over before she left to take a tray up to Rodney. For the next few minutes, the concerned group ate. They all stopped, however, when they heard the thunderous knock at the front door—three solid raps that echoed down the main hallway. Penelope and Cassie exchanged glances.

"Are the two of you expecting someone?"

"Not exactly," Cassie replied.

Richard arched a brow. "What exactly does 'not exactly' mean?"

Cassie looked to Penelope for help.

"The vision that led the two of you to the cave this morning also suggested that someone would be coming to the castle."

"The knock didn't *exactly* sound friendly," Richard commented. "Was there anything to suggest this vision was a warning?"

Before either woman could answer, Geoffrey came to stand in the doorway. Richard anticipated he would announce the guest, but the guest appeared before Geoffrey could say a word.

Richard stood.

"I'll take it from here." The large bearded man placed his open right palm on Geoffrey's forehead and then caught the butler when he slumped unconscious.

"What did you do to him?" Richard yelled.

"The same thing I'll do to ye if ye don't cooperate."

"Is he dead?"

"There's always life in a living man. Does he look dead to ye?"

"What? Who are you? What do you want?" Richard glanced at the empty left sleeve of the man's long duster. *Is there no arm beneath it?*

The stranger moved on into the kitchen. "I willna be wasting my time answering questions though it would be in your best interest to answer mine."

He was being far too cocky, Richard decided. "You can't just waltz into my home and demand—"

The stranger drew a sawed-off shotgun from a leg holster beneath his long coat and aimed before Richard could finish. "Ye were saying?" the man snarled.

Richard remained calm. "There's no need for aggression."

"We'll see about that." The man didn't holster his gun but he did lower it to his side. "Ye keep seers around you? Soothsayers?" he said of Cassie and Penelope. Then to Richard's puzzled look, "Clairvoyants, if ye will."

"Why would you call them that? You don't know anything about them."

Cassie, who'd been staring from where she sat, chose that moment to speak. "You're the one," she said eyes wide. "—the one I saw in my vision."

The large man responded to Richard. "It seems I know them better than ye think."

Richard ignored his words and faced Cassie. "He's the one?"

"Exactly the one."

All at once, the large man lost patience. "All right, enough of this." He pointed his shotgun's barrel at them as he spoke, "I'm ready for answers. And since I dinnae come here for trouble, I won't expect any in return."

"Didn't come here for trouble?" Richard rallied. "Then why do you have a gun and why do you keep waving it around?"

"In case ye didn't notice, I've got but one arm. That puts me at a slight disadvantage."

"Why would that matter if you didn't come here for trouble?"

"I'm outnumbered."

Richard looked around. "Even at that, I hardly see the threat."

The large man narrowed his eyes. "All right. I'll put the weapon away."

A surprise attack seemed appropriate. Richard charged the second he had the advantage—*before* the stranger could finish holstering his shotgun.

28

Richard charged but the larger man wasn't surprised. "Do ye think I was born yesterday?" He picked up Richard and hurled him across the room. He crashed into the wall, fell to the floor and lay too stunned to move. With very few strides the stranger closed on him again. He effortlessly flipped Richard, who slammed to the ground. Then the stranger straddled him and drew back a solid fist.

"Richard!" Cassie gasped. She turned to his captor. "Please, don't!"

"What did ye say?" asked the man.

"Don't," Cassie repeated as she rushed over. "I said—don't."

"Nay. What did ye call him?"

"Richard. That's his name."

"Richard what?"

"Bastóne—"

"—Porter," Penelope corrected immediately. She stood next to Cassie. "His name was originally Porter."

The arm drawn back like a rubber band ready to snap, slackened. Richard might've sighed with relief had he enough breath. Instead, he lay gasping for air, and stared up, hopeful that all the words being tossed about might result in removal of the weight pressing down on his chest—*before* he suffocated.

The man did move but not to get up. Instead, he forced Richard's head to the side and pushed his long hair out of the way. "Well, knock me over with a feather," he pointed at the heart-shaped birthmark on his temple. "If I dinnae see it for myself, I'd nae believe it."

Richard did manage to get some air into his lungs and with it he heaved his desperate demand. "Get—off—me!"

In a rush, the stranger did just that; he even helped Richard to his feet. "Ye have certainly changed since I last saw ye. And who'd have thought ye'd still be around."

"I'm sorry. I didn't get your name," Richard oozed sarcasm.

A broad smile formed beneath the thick beard and a hearty laugh erupted. "Aye, ye dinnae know, do ye? Ye haven't figured it out. How about this?" the man offered. "Ye used to get your dander up something fierce when I'd call ye Father's 'good' son. Does that stir something in ye? Does that ring a bell?"

Seeing his father alive was one thing but this—this was quite another thing. "Brendan? No. It isn't you. That's impossible."

"What's that? After all this time, ye are still pig-headedly stubborn. I guess it's a good thing for little Dalia I dinna let that bother me the day ye nearly let her drown."

What is he talking about?

"That's right," Brendan continued. "Ye wanted to go back to the mission for help, but there was nae time."

"Dalia?" Richard repeated. "Drowned?" There was something familiar about the words but not enough for him to piece anything together.

"She fell in the river and ye left me to do all the work of saving her."

Being hit with a brick might have had the same affect. Memory drew Richard's eyes wide. "You tied a knot in the end of the rope. I was supposed to lower you into the river. You weighed more than I did and I was pulled into the river myself and nearly drowned."

"That's how *ye* choose to see it. Like I said: Pig-headed."

"How I choose to see it? Brother, I—" Richard stopped short, realized what he'd just said. "Brother," he gasped. "It *is* you."

No one else could elicit that kind of strong emotion from him with such ease. "But how?" he asked after initiating a bear hug that he had to beg to be released from. "Are you cursed? It is night. Are you a vampire?"

"I had a run-in with a werewolf. I'm nae cursed, but it did affect me. That's how I lost the arm."

"But you've got a bloody Scots accent! I have to say, that throws one."

"Aye, a Scot by the grace of God." Then to Richard's obvious disenchantment with his accent, "And what are ye to say of that? A bloody Englishman, though I do hear a smidgen of Father's Gaelic influence coming through every now and again. I suppose if I'd been listening closer this morning when ye were at the cave—"

"You were at the cave? Was it you who put Father's Gaelic Bible there?"

"Why would I do that? I've no need to go lugging something that old around. And why would I want to? I doubt it still exists."

"Oh, it exists. Cassie and I found it. The vision she'd had the night before led us to it."

"Aye, one of the seers."

Cassie stood behind Richard. He reached around and pulled her next to him. "Cassie helped Ceese and I. Because of her efforts, we're no longer cursed. And this," he motioned toward the silent blonde, "is Penelope Cromwell. I spent many years with her in this very castle when I was cursed. And now that you know all of us and our purpose, what's yours?"

"A certain werewolf offered me information which proved Ceese was still alive." Brendan presented the locket Tobias had given him. "It led me here. I've been looking for Ceese ever since I learned."

"Yes," Penelope said when the locket was handed to her. "It has a very strong aura."

"I'd say," Richard confirmed. "Especially if it led you here."

Brendan swallowed hard. "So she is here." His eyes teared.

"I don't remember the two of you being as close as your tears certainly suggest."

"After ye left, Brother, much changed. Ceese came to depend on me much the way she depended on ye and Father. Then Father died and—"

"—um, not exactly," Richard said cutting him off.

Wary eyes met Richard's cautious ones. "If ye know something, then share."

"He's not exactly dead. Father's a vampire. He—he's here too. Well, he's not here right now. He's out hunting. But he'll be back before sun-up."

"Father . . . a-a vampire? That's preposterous. He's a man of God. The curse would nae take hold. Besides, I buried him myself."

"Did you now?" Penelope said. "Ceese told me that strangers carried his coffin."

Brendan looked away. "Well, I should have. I wanted to carry the coffin but Mother would nae hear of it. She was worried about infection. That whatever took Father would take one of us." Brendan recovered a little from the bitter memory. "But how, Richard? Ye know as well as I do that Father should nae have been able to acquire the curse of the vampire. If what ye say is true, then how?"

"I've talked with Father about it. It seems he worked some sort of deal that he can't talk about. Perhaps you can get more out of him."

"I'd love to see him."

"Yes, well. He isn't quite so easy to talk to right now. He wants to visit with Ceese but Ceese has insisted that we keep him away from her. I'm running out of lies to tell him."

"That does nae sound like Ceese. All she ever wanted after ye left was for Father to dote on her the way he used to."

"What do you mean? My leaving and vampire curse changed how Father treated Ceese?"

Brendan drew a deep, heavy breath. "Ye were Father's life, Richard. Nothing anyone could do would change that. God help us, we tried. Your leaving destroyed Father. He nae recovered."

Richard numbed to the core. Tears formed. "I wanted to spare him more pain. I thought he'd get over my leaving."

"He dinnae know why ye left, Richard. How could he get over it? Nae of us knew."

"Ceese knew," Richard muttered. "But the vampire swore her to silence."

"Aye, he did at that and Ceese kept her promise. She dinnae even tell me, and she told me everything. But again I ask, why do ye suppose she avoids Father now?"

"It seems she overheard something Father didn't intend for her to hear."

"And what would that be?"

"That mother was attacked by a werewolf—not just a wolf. That Mother was also taken advantage of by another man, at the werewolf's insistence." Richard braced for what he knew was sure to follow.

"I knew it!" Brendan charged. "That day at the river—I knew it."

"I know, Brother—"

"I tried to tell ye but ye swore *me* to silence!"

"You can't blame me. You were always one to twist the truth."

"Joachim told me everything and he told me to tell Father. That's what I tried to tell ye the day Dalia nearly drowned, but ye would nae listen."

"Joachim," Penelope repeated. "Ceese spoke of him often. He's the werewolf that helped her along after Zade cursed her."

Brendan whipped around his head. "What did you say? Zade dinnae curse Ceese."

"He most assuredly did," Richard replied. "And he tried again yesterday morning. He left scratches on her side."

"I cannae believe I dinnae sense he lied when he said another cursed her. I had a chance to kill him, but I dinnae," Brendan said.

"Yes, well, don't feel bad. I had the chance to kill him as well. Looks like we're all subject to making mistakes. As a result of my bad choice, Ceese is lying in a coma, more or less. She isn't responding to anything."

"Take me to her," Brendan said. "Perhaps I can help."

29

Rodney lifted his head off his pillow and listened. The high ceilings in the main hallway amplified the smallest noise and the sound of a small group drawing closer intrigued Rodney—in particular, an unfamiliar voice. He opened the door to Ceese's room as the group approached. He stepped out and pulled the door closed behind him.

"What's up?" Rodney asked Richard who'd stopped before him. "Your dad hasn't come back to throw more furniture, has he—or maybe he'd like a snack? You can tell him I'm not available."

"We've come to help Ceese."

"She's—resting." He looked at the stranger. "Who's he?"

"If ye could just step aside," Brendan said abruptly.

Rodney moved to block him. "I said, she's resting."

Rodney stiffened when the stranger took a step closer. "I'll tell ye what, lad. We can do this the easy way or we can do it—another way."

Cassie gave it her best effort to avoid things going downhill fast. "Rodney, this is Richard's brother, Brendan. Of course, that would mean he's Ceese's brother too. He's here to help her. You need to let him help her."

"He's your brother?" Rodney said with drooping shoulders.

"Yes."

"He doesn't look like you. He doesn't even sound like you. He's got that whole Scottie-from-Star-Trek thing going on."

To that Cassie said, "I've never known you to watch Star Trek."

"I'm a closet Trekkie." He presented the Vulcan "V" sign with the fingers of his left hand. "Live long and prosper. But you two," he said of Richard and Brendan, "you two have taken the entire 'live long' thing a little too far, haven't you?"

"I know it's difficult—" started Richard.

"Difficult," Rodney spat out. "Balancing a peanut on your nose and attempting to walk a straight line *after* a couple of beers is difficult. Believing he's your brother, that's something else. Unless, of course, you plan on telling me he's cursed."

"Well in a way, he is."

Rodney spread his arms. "You're kidding, right? You don't expect me to buy that." He looked around for any break in the alliance. "Oh, come on. Is there anyone in your family who isn't cursed?"

"Rodney, move," pled Cassie.

"No can do."

Before Rodney could protest further, Brendan's palm found his forehead.

Richard caught Rodney as he slumped, unconscious. "That's certainly a handy little gift you have there—uh, no pun intended."

Ceese lay on the bed, eyes open wide with an empty blankness. Brendan approached cautiously as though he might wake her. He lightly touched her face with the back of his hand. Tears formed in his eyes; one broke free and ran down into his beard. "How long as she been like this . . ."

"Since this morning," Richard said.

"She did wake up once yesterday," Cassie added. "She seemed to have had a bad dream. She ended up under the bed."

Brendan nodded. "Aye, he's got quite a hold on her."

"Do you still think you can help her?" Richard asked.

Brendan walked to a nearby window. He threw open the half-closed drapes and stared out. The big man stood for a good two minutes without a word to anyone.

Finally Richard repeated, "You didn't answer my question. Do you think you can help her?"

"He is helping her," Penelope said gently. "Let him work."

~~~

The etiquette lessons were going well, Henderson thought, until Zade jumped up for no reason and let out a deafening canine howl.

"Brendan," Zade snarled and stared off toward the castle. "Brendan with Ceese."

"Who is Brendan? Another werewolf?" Henderson certainly hoped not. Two people who spoke like Tarzan would drive him mad.

"Brendan not werewolf," Zade said, a belligerent edge to his words. "Brendan not cursed."

"Sorry, I didn't know. And I'd have to add that I don't get it. If Brendan isn't cursed, then why are you so bothered? What's the problem?"

"Brendan want Ceese too. Brendan big problem."

~~~

The howl carried all the way to the castle. Ceese responded. "Zade," she whispered.

Brendan shut the drapes at once. "She's calling to him. She's leading him here." He ran to the balcony doors, pulled the drapes there as well, and secured the lock.

"What?" Richard said. "How is what you're doing going to stop Zade? This is how you help Ceese?"

Brendan stopped long enough to shout at Richard. "At least I'm doing something."

Rodney rushed into the room. "You stay away from her," he said to Brendan.

"Zade," whispered Ceese.

Rodney stood guard over her. "Why does she keep saying Zade's name?"

Brendan leaned against a long dresser and pushed it toward the balcony doors. "She's calling to him. She's leading him here."

"So get the rifle with the silver bullets."

"Willna do anything but slow him down. He's too powerful. Ye cannae kill him in the traditional manner."

"Well, then make her stop calling him."

"Aye, that would be the thing to do but the question would be how do we do that?"

"Knock her out," Rodney said without flinching. "The same way you knocked me out."

Richard looked toward Brendan. "What do you think?"

"It's certainly worth a try."

With a gentler touch than he'd used with Geoffrey and Rodney, Brendan placed his palm over Ceese's forehead and closed his eyes. Within seconds, Ceese grew quiet and a few seconds after that, her eyes closed.

Zade took off. "Ceese lead Zade."

"What?" Henderson was certain he hadn't heard right. "Ceese lead Zade where?"

"Ceese call Zade," the werewolf said, charged ahead in the direction of the castle. "Zade take Ceese now."

"But you aren't ready. My plan—*our* plan won't work." Henderson tried to keep up. He flew over some of the rougher terrain. Zade suddenly stopped. Eyes fixed on the distant horizon, his hands curled into fists of rage. His face bore an angry scowl. A dead stump felt his fury and his kick launched it into the night air. "Zade not hear Ceese. Ceese not lead Zade."

"So Ceese was calling you?" Henderson said calmly. "And why is that important? It isn't like you don't know where she is."

"Brendan try to take Ceese from Zade. Brendan will pay."

"And by pay you mean—"

"Die. Brendan will die."

Henderson noticed a trend. There was no common ground with Zade. It was his way or no way. The trick, Henderson gathered, was to make everything seem like Zade's idea. So far it had worked for him.

"What are you doing now?" Henderson asked as the werewolf eagerly sniffed at the air.

"Minister," Zade said as though he couldn't believe his luck. "Minister here."

Zade ran. Henderson never got the chance to ask why the werewolf needed a minister.

༺༻

Every muscle in Merideth's slight frame fought against the vampire's force. He didn't want to feed. Didn't want to continue on. Josh's comment about Ceese took him down that low. Ceese hated him and he no longer cared about anything. As he hunted, then fed, his thoughts became clearer. He couldn't break his promise with the vampire. He had to think about Richard too. He buried the corpse of the deer and stood.

At the very top of the ridge, Zade saw Merideth's moonlit form against the dark backdrop of forest and sky. "Minister," he seethed, before climbing the craggy slope.

Henderson lost sight of Zade; he turned back at least twice before realizing his mistake. He raced to catch up again. He couldn't risk the werewolf doing something stupid and jeopardizing his plan. He wanted Ceese and he wanted her as a werewolf. Henderson followed the dry creek bed until he found Zade again. *But who is that with him?*

Merideth hadn't been expecting company and judging by his noncommittal look, he wasn't sure how to take this one. "Why are you here? What do you want?"

Zade's hot breath formed smoke in the cool night air. "Minister should've left," he growled, his upper lip curling, "but Minister stay."

"They needed me. They needed the mission—"

"Zade there first!"

"It was my calling. I couldn't leave—"

"And now Minister die," Zade said, violently lifting him, forcing him close to those canine-like fangs.

"Yes," Merideth said with a throaty plea. "Kill me."

"Stop," Henderson shouted as he dropped to the earth. "It's a trap. He's tricking you."

"Vampire leave," Zade demanded. "Zade take Minister now."

"Do it." Merideth's listless gray-blue eyes begged as well. "Take me now."

"Listen to him," Henderson said. "He wants you to kill him. What kind of sense does that make?"

"Zade not care. Minister die." He drew his head back to plunge.

"I'm telling you," Henderson pointed out, "if you kill him, you will die as well." Neither Zade nor Merideth had seen the deer carcass Henderson dragged along with him. "He's a vampire. He fed on this not over five minutes ago." Henderson dropped the carcass at Zade's feet and went about checking Merideth's forearms. "See," he said holding the right one so Zade could get a good look. "He wiped his mouth clean after he fed." Zade considered the arm with a slight interest. There was blood on it. "Do I have to tell you what will happen if you try to curse a vampire?"

The cursed knew. Any cursed being who killed another undead would be taken as well. The trick was to bring them as close to death as possible but to let them die on their own.

"Minister can't be vampire. Minister man of G—God!" Zade flinched at the mention. Henderson made a horrid face as Merideth cried out.

"Minister cursed?" Zade questioned. "Minister vampire? Can't be."

"It—it isn't true. I swear, it. Kill me now. It's what you want."

Zade met his eyes with an icy stare. "Who does Minister serve?"

"You know who."

"Name him."

"You already said it."

"Name him!" Zade blared.

Merideth shook his head, defeated. "I can't."

Muscles tense with pent up anger, Zade lifted Merideth high and hurled him. Merideth hit a tree and never felt it when he hit the ground.

Josh's search ended at the sight of his friend flying through the air—and from the way he slapped and slid down the tree, he assumed Merideth had help. Josh flew directly overhead. At the very top of the ridge, stood a strange sight. "Henderson?" The professor seemed to spot him as well and scampered off down the other side of the ridge. "Weird," Josh rationalized. He landed and knelt to check on his friend.

"Meri," he said shaking him until he spoke. "Dude, are you okay? Why'd that guy throw you?"

The older man pushed himself up and stood. "Just a territory issue, that's all. I'm fine."

"We better get back to the castle then." The eastern night-blue sky had started to lighten.

"You go on. I'll be there shortly. I need to bury the carcass I fed on."

"I'll help you—"

"No," he said abruptly before finishing in a less caustic tone. "I just really need to do this alone."

Josh shrugged. "Okay. But you better hurry."

With Josh out of sight, Merideth headed away from the ridge and the deer.

30

Brendan determined Ceese no longer summoned Zade, and Penelope reassured them. There seemed no need to stand guard beyond leaving Rodney on his pallet next to her bed.

The night did indeed pass uneventfully. With morning's sun Rodney awoke to Ceese's empty bed. He smiled. *She must be with the others.* What a difference a day made or rather, a night. With no urgency whatsoever, he walked downstairs and into the parlor, certain one of the voices he heard belonged to Ceese. His facial muscles tightened when he realized he was wrong.

"She's not here." It wasn't a question. They didn't wait for Rodney's explanation but hurried past him to Ceese's room: Richard, Brendan, and then Penelope.

"Good work," Cassie threw out as she trailed the group.

"I'd thought she'd be *here.*" Rodney followed.

Yesterday when Ceese disappeared, they panicked. This time Richard headed straight for the bed and knelt down. "Ceese." Relieved to see life in her eyes, he continued, "You're up." She nodded, another good sign. "Are you going to talk to me today?"

"I had a nightmare," she started. "Zade was calling me—no made me call him. He was coming after me. He was going to take me."

"Yes," Richard confirmed. "But you're all right now. You're safe."

"There's more," she told him. "I dreamed I heard Brendan or at least, it sounded a bit like Brendan yet his voice was different. But he helped me, Richard. I felt his hand on my forehead. I know it was him."

Brendan knelt next to Richard and bent to look at Ceese. "And some dream that must've been. Here I am, little one."

Giving little thought to her scratches or the pain she felt when she moved, Ceese scrambled out, grabbed hold of Brendan and wrapped both arms around his thick neck. "It was you, Brother," she said and buried her head against him. "I knew it was. I just knew it!"

Brendan hoisted himself up by the bed to stand, Ceese dangling from his neck.

"Well it seems the two of you are a lot closer than I recall," said Richard.

Brendan settled with Ceese on the edge of her bed. "Let me take a good long look at ye." He smiled. "Aye, ye are a sight for sore eyes. But with short hair like that, ye put me in mind of Christian."

Richard's jaw tensed. "I don't suppose I can comment on that, as when I left, Christian was ten. From what I recall of him at that age, I'd have to say no, I don't see all that much of a resemblance."

"Sorry," Brendan said, though it was unclear whether he really was. "Guess ye wouldna know."

"You really think I look like a boy?" Ceese pouted.

"I said ye favored Christian. I dinnae say ye looked like a boy. There's a difference."

"Is Christian cursed too?" Rodney piped up.

Though the question was completely rhetorical and sarcastic, it made Ceese consider Brendan with new sympathetic eyes. "You're cursed, Brother?"

"Aye, but it's nae as bad as ye think." He brushed a wayward tear from her cheek. "I donnae carry the full curse like ye did once. Just some pesky side effects. I age slowly and cannae seem to die."

Ceese stared, puzzled. "I've heard one could be affected but not cursed."

"Well, I guess ye have," Brendan laughed. The rest eyed each other. How far would Brendan take this?

"What do you mean?" Ceese asked.

Richard shifted his weight and crossed his arms, but Brendan missed the subtle body language.

"Well, when Zade scratched Mother, ye were affected."

"Zade didn't scratch Mother."

"Sure he did. He—"

"No, he didn't," Ceese interrupted but kept her voice level. "That's a lie that Father made up. Zade would never do that."

"Ye defend him . . . ye defend Zade?"

"Perhaps we could talk about something else," Penelope suggested.

"Yes," Richard seconded. "Anything else would be nice."

Stunned, Brendan looked from Penelope to Richard like they'd lost their minds.

"How'd you lose your arm?" Ceese asked before Brendan could voice his thoughts on the matter.

"I lost it to—" He stopped short. He'd lost it to Zade but did he dare say that now? "I lost it in a battle."

"It must've hurt," Ceese said, sounding sad.

Silence fell and Cassie filled it. "Maybe you should check those scratches, Richard."

"Yes. It wouldn't be good if infection set in."

"I can save ye the time," Brendan said, turning to Ceese. "If ye allow, I can heal your wounds. I've learned how to reverse the werewolves' self-healing process."

"I'd like that," Ceese said. "It hurts something awful." She'd not had any pain medication since the day before.

"Then just relax." Brendan placed his palm lightly over her bandages. "Ye will feel warmth under my hand, perhaps discomfort. But it shouldna last long. Ye will have to let me finish though, in order for it to work. If my concentration is broken, I have to start over. Ye understand?"

She nodded. "I understand."

Brendan put his hand on the bandages and closed his eyes. Ceese bit at her bottom lip and shut her eyes tight. "It can't be any worse than being scratched."

The area did become warm and even stung—Ceese bit hard on her lip.

Then, Brendan stood. "That's it," he told her.

Richard sat down to remove the bandages. "That's amazing," he said of the smooth flawless skin beneath.

When Brendan slumped against the wall near the head of Ceese's bed, Richard turned to look—then jumped up to reach and steady him as his brother teetered. "There's blood soaking through your shirt." Richard carefully pulled up the side.

Brendan now bore the scratches. "Powerful evil," Brendan said, inhaling sharply.

Richard lowered the shirt and helped him along. "Come on. I'll help you to your room."

"I'm fine," Brendan said but dropped to one knee with his first step.

Richard didn't wait for permission. "Like it or not, I'm helping you to your room."

Once Brendan lay flat on his back, he noted, "They really shouldn't take long to heal."

Richard checked the room. "You'll need a clean shirt. Do you have one packed in your duster—"

"Nay! Stay away from my coat."

"All right. Then I'll have Geoffrey find something you can wear until he can wash that shirt."

Brendan settled. "Richard, why do ye suppose Ceese feels the way she does about Zade? Why does she speak so harshly of Father?"

"I'm not sure but we can talk about it later. Now I'm off to find you a shirt."

With Richard gone, Brendan stared at his duster. He wondered if or when he should tell Richard about the knife.

31

With her brothers gone, and her scratches with them, Ceese announced, "I'd like to go outside."

"Wouldn't you like some breakfast first?" Penelope asked. "It's been a while since you've eaten."

"And, is going outside really safe?" Cassie added.

Ceese smiled at Penelope then turned to sneer at Cassie. "Of course, I wouldn't go far."

"I'm sure Cassie is only concerned for your health," Penelope said.

"Well, she shouldn't think I'd not be careful. Rodney's going with me, aren't you Rodney?"

Rodney shrugged. "Sure."

Ceese hopped up, took Rodney's hand and they headed out.

"Did I really deserve that?" Cassie asked.

"Certainly not," Penelope said. "I've noticed Ceese isn't exactly cordial to you."

"Thank you for noticing. At least I know I'm not going crazy. I just can't seem to figure her out."

"It doesn't sound like she's making it very easy for you either. But that's Ceese. It took some time before she warmed up to me. She was horrible in the beginning. But she's had such a rough time of it. Nevertheless, I suspect something else is going on here," she said looking at the doorway. "And I intend to find out what."

※※※

Walking next to Ceese, hand in hand, had Rodney smiling. "You're sure you're okay?" he asked as they strolled around the castle to the front lawn.

She grinned and swung their arms. "I'm fine."

Her tone of voice made him wonder if this walk had been a good idea. Rodney hadn't forgotten the kiss and he hadn't had a chance to discuss it because of Zade. Now that she had his hand and that look, he wondered if he should say something. "Ceese, we need to talk."

"We *are* talking."

She always looks at things so simplistically. "Yeah, right. Well, we need to talk about what happened in the woods—*before* you were scratched."

Ceese pulled him toward a large shade tree where they sat. "You mean when you kissed me," she said.

"Uh, if I'm not mistaken, you asked me to kiss you."

"I didn't ask you the second time."

"Yeah, right." He looked down. "You didn't."

"So is that what you wanted to talk about?"

"Well, not exactly."

Ceese furrowed her brow.

"I just don't want you reading too much into what happened. I kissed you because you asked me to. I kissed you the second time because you let me."

"You didn't kiss me because you like me?"

"Ceese, I'm not sure I know how to like people and so far in life, I haven't had to worry about it too much. People pretty much stay away from me. I'm a creep, okay? I hurt people and I don't care. And it doesn't really bother me that I'm like that except . . ." He paused to draw a deep breath. "I don't want to hurt you. You've been hurt too much already."

"You would never hurt me, Rodney. I know that."

"Still, Ceese. You deserve better. I'm never going to change. I'm not any good for you."

"Please d-don't say th-that," she said. "You are all I've got, Rodney."

"That's not true. You've got Richard and now Brendan. Then there's your dad—"

"—he isn't my father."

"Well, whoever he is, he certainly cares a lot for you. He destroyed the dining room last night because Richard told him he couldn't see you." Renovations already underway, workers traipsed up and down the terraced front steps, fetching tools and supplies from their trucks. "If Josh hadn't come along when he did, he would've cursed me."

"But he isn't my father."

He realized how important it was for her to be certain. "So you've said but you don't know that for sure."

"He's not even sure."

Rodney sat quietly for a moment. "If you could be sure, would it matter? Would it make a difference?"

"Yes." Her faint voice made Rodney's heart sink.

A moment later, Rodney stuck out his tongue.

"What's that for?"

"Tag, you're it." Rodney jumped up and ran.

Ceese grinned as she gave chase.

<hr />

Josh slipped into a deep vampyric slumber. However, he could not stay that way. Something kept disturbing him. He didn't need to feed, so he didn't understand the weird feeling. It felt like a heavy weight bore down on him and he couldn't get it off. No matter how many times he rolled over or opened his eyes in the absolute black, he couldn't shake it. Maybe someone with more experience would know. *I'll ask Meri.*

Standing over his friend's closed coffin, he rapped lightly. "Dude, I need to ask you something."

No response. Knowing first-hand how deeply a vampire could sleep, Josh lifted the lid. "Meri?"

Mouth dropped open, Josh gaped at Merideth's absence. He had to tell somebody. They had to find him.

<hr />

"How long has she known him?" Brendan asked as he stared out the parlor's front window.

"Not very long . . . and too long," Richard answered as he carefully turned antique pages of his father's Bible. "Are you sure you should be up? You only rested for an hour. It's hard to believe those scratches healed that quickly."

"I'm fine." Brendan grunted as he continued to watch the pair. "They're playing chase now."

"Yes, well, you'd best get used to seeing that sort of thing. I don't think Rodney's going anywhere anytime soon and I'm very certain he isn't going to lose favor with her."

"What could she see in him and why is his hair two different colors?"

"Oh, do ask him. He always has such fun answers."

Brendan turned at the sarcasm. "Why haven't ye done something about him already?"

"And what would you suggest I do?"

"Run the *eejit* off."

"I've tried that. Even threatened to suck the very life out of him when I was a vampire. Didn't work. Ceese wants him near and so near is where he'll stay."

"Well, I dinnae like him."

"His fan club is growing then."

The servant door swung open. Josh cried out then fell back.

"What was that?" Brendan asked.

"It looked vaguely like Rodney's vampire friend, Josh. Only what's he doing up, I wonder?"

Both Richard and Brendan went to investigate. When they entered, Josh cried out again. "Close it."

They did.

He huddled in a dark corner.

Richard asked, "Why aren't you in your coffin?"

"Meri's gone," he blurted. "I couldn't rest. I got up to ask Meri about it. I looked inside his coffin but he wasn't there. He's gone and you have to find him. I don't have a good feeling about him. I have a very bad feeling."

Geoffrey appeared out of nowhere and spoke up. "I'm having the carpet in the dining room replaced. The workers just carried the old carpet outside. Perhaps you could use it when you find your father. Roll him up in it to protect against the sun's rays."

"And I'll get my gun," Brendan said. "Meet me out back."

Not only did Brendan have his weapon strapped to his leg, he also wore his duster.

Richard picked up one end of the rolled carpet. "It's a bit hot for that coat, don't you think?"

"Is it nae clear what I think?" Brendan picked up his end. "I'm wearing it."

"Yes, I suppose you are." Richard glanced around then. Josh had told them where he last saw Merideth and they started off in that direction. They hoped their father had found shelter somewhere in that general area. They chose not to entertain the fear that he hadn't.

"What do ye suppose happened to him?" Brendan asked.

"I don't know but it certainly doesn't make sense. Josh said Father had fed. The vampire was surely strong enough to prevent him from trying to stay out on purpose."

"Ye vampires are an odd lot," said Brendan.

"I'm not a vampire anymore."

"In some small way, ye will always be a vampire."

"There," Richard pointed. "There's a cave. A fine place for a vampire to hide."

"I rest my case."

32

The ability to see in the dark often proved to be useful and Brendan dropped his end of the rolled carpet to search for his father in the cave before them. Both brothers knew the cave well—the Bible box had rested here until yesterday. Irony or coincidence?

"He's here," Brendan called out. "Saints be praised, he's here."

Meredith moaned and Richard ran in. "Did you forget he's a vampire? You can't speak like that in front of him unless you want to kill him . . . which is entirely possible if a vampire is weak enough." Merideth lay flat out and still.

"I just canna believe it's him. After all this time." He reached out to touch him, to make certain he was real when a hand reached up and grabbed his arm.

"Bren? Son, is that you?"

"Aye, Father it is," he said as he and Richard each held an arm to help Merideth to his knees.

"I hardly recognize you with that beard."

"And I'd shave it if I could but it grows faster than I can keep up with."

"I assume then, that you're cursed."

Richard answered, "Well, it does seem to be the question of the day."

"I'm not cursed, Father. Not entirely anyway."

"And I'd let him explain further," Richard said, "if I didn't sense you were stalling."

"Why would you say that?"

"For the same reason you didn't return to your coffin last night."

"I just got caught out," their father said, his eyes wide and innocent. "How did you know I wasn't there?"

"Josh told us. It seems he was looking for conversation and found you were gone," Richard replied. "What are you doing, Father? What's really going on? Does it have something to do with seeing Zade? Josh told us about that too."

"What did he tell you?"

Richard looked to Brendan before he answered. "He said he saw him throw you—a very great distance."

Merideth let his head fall forward. "I tried to get him to kill me but that other man, that other vampire, he convinced Zade not to."

"Other vampire? What other vampire?" Richard asked.

"I don't know. He sounded American though. He found the deer I'd fed on. Told Zade about it. That's how Zade knew I was a vampire. That's how he knew he'd die too if he killed me."

"Kill you? Why would you want him to do that, Father?"

"Because Josh told me that Cee Cee doesn't want to see me. He told me what you wouldn't."

"And you wonder why I didn't tell you? Even at that, I never thought you'd do something as rash as trying to end it all."

"I don't want to exist knowing Cee Cee hates me."

"She wasn't herself, Father. But Brendan has helped her. He even healed the scratches Zade left. Before we left to find you, she was running around the front lawn with Rodney."

Merideth's voice lifted. "So . . . so you think she might . . . change her mind?"

Richard didn't want to give him too much hope. Ceese was still angry that her father had lied. "All I'm saying is that you have to at least consider she might."

"All right, but how do you plan to get me back to my coffin?"

Richard went to the cave entrance and dragged in the rolled up carpet. *Father'd fit nicely.* At least they didn't have to worry about him breathing—vampires did so only for appearances. They survived just fine without taking a breath at all.

~·~·~

Josh jumped up from his seat on the casket when the door to the basement creaked open. "You found him! That's great." They unrolled Merideth; he sat up and took hold of the hand Josh offered.

"Dude," Josh said. "I was worried about you. Don't ever do that again. I had this really bad feeling and I couldn't rest. I wanted to talk to you about it but—"

Josh closed his mouth and placed a hand to his chest. "Hey, the pressure's gone now. You're back and it's gone."

"That was the vampire sensing another of its kind was gone," Richard told him. "Pain is the only strong emotion the vampire will let you feel."

Josh turned to see Merideth's forearm then hand disappear into the coffin as the lid closed. "So, since the pressure in my chest is gone, does that mean he's going to be okay?"

"For now it seems he is." They turned to leave when Richard remembered to ask, "Did you see another man standing with Zade, before he threw Father?"

"Oh yeah. How could I forget? Henderson was with him."

"Henderson? You know this for certain?"

"Dude, he cursed me. I know who I saw."

~·~·~

After learning of the brothers' success, Cassie and Penelope settled down to morning tea. But before they began, the front door opened and shut and laughter rang down the hall. Penelope seized the opportunity. "Run along," she told Cassie, "and let me see if I can persuade Ceese to come and chat."

Cassie nodded and smiled, "Great idea."

"The back door. She won't see you if you go that way. Follow the path around the back of the house."

Rodney huffed from the game of chase while Ceese looked as fresh as the moment she'd awoken. "Why don't you sit down and have tea with me? We've had so little time to chat since you've been back," Penelope said as they entered the kitchen.

Her eyes bright, Cassie said, "Yes, Rodney let's do that."

Rodney put his hands up at once. "Count me out," he managed in between breaths. "I'm just . . . gonna go . . . pass out."

Ceese took the chair across from Penelope and stirred a spoonful of sugar into her teacup. "You must feel so much better without those scratches," Penelope started.

"Yes," Ceese beamed. "I'm very happy Brendan came along and could do what he did."

"And what an interesting character he is. I remember you telling me how he let you go after Richard the night the vampires came for him. The two of you seem much closer than I would've imagined based on that story." Ceese had threatened Brendan—told him that she'd tell Father that she'd seen him with the neighbor's daughter if he tried to stop her.

The spoon tinkled against the china saucer as Ceese set down her spoon. "Brendan changed a lot after Richard left."

Penelope abandoned the subject for the moment. "I never got to thank you, Ceese, for what you did for me."

"I didn't do anything."

"Ceese, I know you're the reason I'm still here. I know it was you who wouldn't let me go the night my cancer tried to take me."

"I didn't want you to leave," Ceese confessed. "I didn't want you to go."

"How did you do it, dear?"

"I don't know. I just gave you some of your youth back. Back to when you were healthy."

"Ceese," Penelope said carefully. "How did you determine how young I needed to be?"

Ceese shrugged. "I guessed."

Penelope took a sip of her tea. "Are you sure there isn't more to it than that?"

"Yes, why?"

Penelope set her cup down. "I'd only had my cancer for seven years. You took me back some twenty years before that. One has to wonder."

Ceese's beguiling look confirmed her words. "I know how much you love Richard. Now you can have him."

"You didn't exactly count on Cassie, did you?"

"No. But Richard doesn't love Cassie. You wait. You'll see."

Penelope sighed. "Is that why you've been so indifferent to her? Because you see her as interfering with your plans?"

Ceese stared blankly out the window.

"You have to let Richard make his own decisions, Ceese. And you have to accept that he might actually love someone other than me. Just as I have."

Ceese looked up at the older woman. "I know you still love him. I can sense it."

"I loved Richard as a vampire. He isn't that anymore. Furthermore, you should stop being so hard on Cassie. If not for her, you would most likely still be cursed."

Ceese pushed her chair back and stood, hands on hips. "So tell me, cursed or not, are things really that different for me?"

Speechless, Penelope watched her troubled friend stomp out of the room. *Not being cursed has to be better than being cursed . . . doesn't it? What's the problem now?*

33

Penelope rounded the corner in time to see a pant leg and shoe disappear into the bedroom. The door closed with a whump. She knew so few specifics about Brendan but she could tell he didn't feel at peace with himself and perhaps she could help—*no time like the present*. Her light knock was answered by a gruff, "It's open."

Penelope headed over to where he stood leaning against the balcony railing.

"What do ye want?" Brendan barked. He closed his eyes and set his jaw.

She placed a gentle hand on his left shoulder. "What does Brendan want?"

He opened his eyes and looked at her. "Werewolf third-person. Clever."

"It got your attention. So tell me what it is Brendan needs?"

"Ye have to ask? What kind of seer are ye?"

"I wish you wouldn't call me that."

His look mellowed. "What would ye have me call ye?"

"Penny. Now give me your hand. I want to know more about you."

He hesitated.

"You've nothing to fear from me." At the touch, she sensed an overwhelming heaviness.

"You suffered a great loss. What was her name?"

"Gwen. Gwendolyn."

"Something happened to her."

He surrendered to emotion. "I watched her grow old. I had to bury her. She wanted me there when she passed on and I promised her I would be. But I had to take a trip and she passed before I returned. I couldna fulfill my promise. She died alone."

"You've carried this burden for so long. It's time to bury the dead. Time to bury your grief."

"I've tried and I canna do it. I'll never forgive myself for not being there for her."

After a moment of silence, she spoke. "There's something you need to know. Gwen thought you were there. She spoke with you and your words helped her along. She never knew any different."

"I thought ye said ye weren't a seer. Ye sound very confident; how do ye know this?"

"Do you not believe in angels, ministering sprits that are focused on Him and what He wants for us, His children? Gwen was one of His, was she not?"

"Aye, an ardent believer. She kept me focused."

"That's who I'm hearing from now, those who were with her, those who are with you and I at this very moment. They're saying that Gwen went in peace, believing you'd fulfilled your promise. She wasn't alone, Brendan. She wasn't frightened. She heard your voice. They want me to tell you this." She enunciated as best she could. "Ha gool akam orst."

"Tha gràdh agam ort?" Brendan repeated. "Ye know this language. Ye speak Scottish Gaelic?"

"I've never spoken any form of Gaelic. What does it mean?"

"It means 'I love ye.' Those were the last words I heard Gwen speak—the day I left for battle."

Penny placed a hand on the side of his face. "And those were the last words she heard you speak on the day of her passing."

"Aye," he said, accepting the peace she offered. "I thank ye, Penny."

Penelope left the room satisfied. Next she would locate her granddaughter and share what she'd learned from Ceese. Perhaps she could help Cassie as well this morning.

Peter Drummond's small, one-room cottage sat unoccupied by anything other than occasional vermin. A missing front door meant easy access—Drummond hadn't made a move to fix it since the werewolf ripped the door from its hinges. In fact, he'd not stayed in the cottage after the werewolf and its pack had visited. His new shelter was a lean-to just behind the house; the place where he slept . . . and drank—heavily. Seeing a wolf change into a man right before his eyes had done it for him. He never wanted to see that again. But neither did he want to explain to the curious why he chose not to live in his house anymore. So he herded his goats by night to avoid questions and drank away his waking hours to keep out the memories.

Josh and Merideth always left the basement together but rarely hunted as a pair. They'd even set up separate territories to keep from getting in each other's way—especially after that first night when they had targeted the same meal. Josh sniffed at the cool night air. As usual, several possibilities existed and after a quick study of scents, he turned to face one that had his immediate and undivided attention. No other scent mattered and he took off after it.

Peter Drummond staggered among the brush and trees in a drunken stupor. He turned the bottle in his hand upside down and grumbled. *Empty.* He tossed it and turned to head back to his lean-to. If memory served, he had stashed at least one other bottle.

Josh came at him fast and knocked him to the ground hard. Stunned, Peter groaned then slowly rolled his head to look up. No one stood over him.

A rustle of leaves in the tree drew his gaze up the trunk and into the eyes of his assailant. Horror stricken, he rubbed his eyes and reopened them slowly. Peter gasped at the fully transformed vampire staring down . . . at him.

Territory or not, Merideth found himself drawn to that same scent, the unmistakable scent of a human. *But what fool would be out at this hour?* Most heeded the warnings, or rather the rumors, Richard had started to protect the locals from his vampyric ways.

Merideth followed the alluring human scent and as he neared it, shadows parted to reveal familiar shapes.

"No," he shouted before leaping, tackling and knocking Josh from his perch.

Josh jumped to his feet and yelled at the one that stood between him and his meal. "What are you doing?"

"What are *you* doing? You don't want this. You don't."

"How do you know what I want?"

"Because I am what you are."

From the ground behind Merideth, Drummond slurred in his Cockney accent, "Bastóne?"

The vampire turned. "What did you call me?"

"Bastóne. You're that bloody vampire what lives in that bloody castle."

Bastóne: the name of the heretics who'd murdered his parents—in the name of religion. "What're you talking about?"

"Richard Bastóne. You're 'im." Peter staggered to his feet and swayed before reaching at the tree trunk for support.

Merideth felt a sudden rush of adrenaline, that irresistible lure, and took a hungry step toward the human. Josh ran at him, and from behind flung his large arms around the other vampire. "If I can't have him, neither can you."

The goat herder just stood there, frozen against the tree.

"Run, fool," Merideth screamed, "run while—" The rest of his warning was drowned out by the scream of the panicked Drummond as he stumbled his way to freedom.

Josh turned Merideth loose and patted his back. "You're not setting a good example," he said.

Clearly the lightheartedness of Josh's words didn't reach his friend's ears.

"He took on the name Bastóne?" Merideth's cried as he stumbled off the way he'd come. "Richard took on the name Bastóne."

Because Ceese had recovered nicely, Rodney no longer slept on a pallet by her bed. The first night back in his assigned room, across the hall from her, he received a visitor. The curtains in front of the open balcony doors billowed in the breeze. "Hey," Josh said as he nudged Rodney awake.

Rodney rolled over, saw Josh standing above him and immediately formed a cross with two of his fingers. "Okay, okay now . . . slowly step away from the bed."

Josh sighed and walked to a chair piled with Rodney's clothes. He tossed them over. "Get dressed and meet me outside. I need you to come with me."

Josh moved easily through the dark forest but Rodney had a hard time keeping up. Already, Josh had to circle back a couple of times. "Can't you just tell me where you're taking me?" Rodney asked again.

"We're almost there. Come on."

Josh had propped Merideth up against the tree next to where he had fallen. He'd not fed and had rejected all Josh's encouragements.

"He doesn't look so well," Rodney said.

"I know. He needs to feed but he won't."

Josh dangled a rabbit. The vampire's head remained slumped, his eyes shut.

"You brought me here to show me . . . this?"

The experience with Drummond fresh on his mind, Josh replied. "He needs something more tempting."

Rodney jumped up from where they'd both come to kneel. "No way, dude. I ain't letting him curse me."

"He doesn't need to curse you. I just need to get him interested. I need to get the vampire's attention."

"I said no, all right. What part of that don't you understand? Besides, how'd you make me bleed without biting me?"

Rodney had forgotten that Josh was once a self-cutter to escape the pain in his life. He also forgot that Josh had a cocaine habit and therefore always had a razor blade nearby.

The silver glint in Josh's hand reminded him. "Oh, no . . . you . . . don't. You're not using that on me."

"You don't have to worry," Josh said, "I won't let him bite you."

"Forget about him! What about you?"

"If I'd wanted you, I'd already have taken you. Come on, dude. It's just a little blood."

"And I think I'll keep mine, thank you. *All* of it."

Josh lowered his hand with the razor blade. "Yeah. Sure. Whatever."

Rodney stared at him, his eyebrows met. As many times as he'd sat with Josh at rehab in therapy sessions, he'd never detected that Josh worried about anything other than where and when he'd get his next fix. "Dude, you really care about what happens to him?"

"Yeah. Yes. I guess I do."

Rodney stared at the rabbit on the ground for several seconds. He looked up at Josh and said, "I'll tell you what. I'll help you out *if* I can have that rabbit once Merideth's done with it. Provided we can get him to take it at all."

Josh became animated. "Roll your sleeve up."

Rodney barely felt the cut on his wrist though it did sting a little when Josh squeezed to get the blood flowing. "So what's the big thrill with cutting anyway?" he asked. "I could never figure out why you did it for so long. Just look at all the scars that will never go away."

"It's not a big deal. It's just a way to cope, I guess."

"You guess?"

"When I was in rehab they said it had something to do with dwarfs and sex."

"Dwarfs . . . and sex?"

"Yeah, something like that."

"Did it ever occur to you that you got something wrong, dude? That dwarfs and sex is kind of, well, a stu—?" Rodney stopped. "Snap. Endorphins, Josh! They were talking about endorphins. They regulate pain and hunger and they have something to do with the release of sex hormones. I learned that at Templeton."

"Yeah, like I said, dwarfs and sex."

With the blood flowing freely now, Josh eased Rodney's arm toward Merideth but Rodney snatched it back.

"You sure he won't try and curse me?"

"I'm going to give him the rabbit as soon as he's interested enough."

Rodney sighed and slowly extended his arm. "I can't believe I'm letting you do this."

At first Rodney watched but turned away the second it looked like the vampire might respond. He felt something warm and moist on his wrist and curled his lip in disgust. "Please, tell me that's not him."

"Okay, I won't tell you."

The sensation felt—interesting and Rodney relaxed, a little. *Maybe there is something to the whole endorphin theory.*

"I think I see fangs." Josh grabbed the rabbit. "He's coming around."

"Just whenever," Rodney said.

"Now." With one motion, Josh shoved Rodney aside and substituted the rabbit. Merideth sank his fangs in deep.

Rodney, landed hard on the ground, looked at his wrist and then over at Merideth. "I feel so rejected."

"He's going to need more." Josh stood, darted off after a new scent and returned in less than a minute.

"Here," Josh switched out the drained rabbit for the fresh one and Rodney grabbed it from where it had landed.

Once he saw Merideth feeding, Josh asked, "What do you want it for anyway?"

He'd explain things if Josh didn't present such a challenge—"Dwarfs and sex," he muttered and shook his head. "Let's just say I want to remember the moment."

34

Geoffrey secured his robe and opened the bedroom door. Every hair sat in place. Rodney stared in mock surprise. "Do you ever *not* look like a butler? It's three o'clock in the morning and you look like you could just throw on your butler suit and go."

Indeed it was early morning, yet Geoffrey did not comment; instead he stated, "You have a rabbit."

"Oh, yeah. I need a favor, G-man."

Geoffrey raised his eyebrows at the new moniker but said, "I don't have any rabbit food."

Rodney stared at the lifeless form in his hand. "It isn't exactly hungry. I need you to put him on ice."

"Mightn't he get cold?"

"No, I think he'll be just fine. Oh, and *mightn't* I use your phone?" Rodney brushed by before Geoffrey could answer.

"Shall I see to your wound? It seems you are bleeding."

Rodney glanced at his wrist. It was a bloody mess. "Just show me where the bandages are. I'll take care of it. After I make my phone call, that is."

Henderson slumbered in the deep recesses of the cave as he waited for nightfall. The time came to rise but he found it difficult to move. His arms felt heavy—his legs too. He opened his eyes to discover his entire body covered with vampire bats, hundreds of gargoylic creatures, none bigger than his thumb. They'd bite then lick. Presently all licked their way to a nutritious meal.

No vampire could easily avoid vampire bats.

Henderson swatted at a few of them as he struggled to stand. When that didn't faze them, he flailed his arms about in an attempt to get the damned things off. They'd just flap in the air for a few seconds and then settle on another part of his body. Henderson tried the flail-and-run-about method. Bats scattered and flew out ahead of him. Having some success, he ran faster and exited the cave at top speed. He almost hit lift-off when he stumbled over an unfortunately placed obstruction. With a solid thud, he hit the ground, stomach first.

Momentarily stunned, he shook his head, rolled on side, pushed up and turned.

"Zade kill Tobias."

Henderson gaped at the body he'd tripped over. "And a fine job you did. But did you have to turn him inside out?"

The mangled mess moaned and Henderson gasped. "He's not dead."

"Tobias dead soon."

"But what did you do to him? It looks like you stripped him of his skin."

"Tobias not need skin."

Judging from the overall condition of what resembled a body, Tobias didn't need a lot of things. "I'm not a very caring person myself, but nobody deserves that."

"Tobias not man. Tobias werewolf."

All right, so now he understood why Zade didn't finish the job, but still. "Don't you think you went a bit overboard?"

"Zade is what Zade does."

Henderson stared a little longer. What on earth had he gotten himself into?

Josh followed Merideth back to the castle and along the way did his best to ignore the bitter words.

"I can find my own way," Meredith complained. "I don't

need you tagging along after me."

He looked up to see both Brendan and Richard standing at the steps. "You had to get up early to make sure I made it in? Well, I don't need to be coddled." He nodded at Richard. "Especially by *you*."

When Josh walked up behind him, Merideth grumbled his way up the steps and into the house.

"What happened out there?" Richard asked.

Josh sank hands in the front pockets of his jeans. He avoided both pairs of staring eyes. "He—uh, he didn't want to feed."

"Why, lad? Did something happen?" asked Brendan.

Richard translated for Josh. "He means 'dude' not lad."

"Oh. Right. No, nothing happened. Well, except that Meri took it pretty hard when that goat herder called him Bastóne. He even tried to curse him."

"Why would he call him Bastóne?" Richard asked.

"I don't know. That's just what he called him—that bloody vampire, Richard Bastóne. Or something like that."

Brendan cut his eyes to Richard. "That's what you get for calling yourself that name. I wondered about it myself when Penny introduced you as such."

Richard sighed with regret. "I suppose I should go try and explain. Could you wait a few minutes before you go down to your coffin?" he said to Josh. "I'll try to keep my talk with Father brief."

Josh glanced out through the window behind him. From the look of the eastern sky, he had about ten minutes before he had to start worrying.

Richard called out to his father as he descended the stairs. At the bottom step he jumped when the unseen Merideth shouted, "What am I to think of you taking on that name? You know what that family did to your *Daideo* and *Mamó*."

Richard inhaled sharply at his grandparent's pet names.

"Murdered for what they believed. Executed because they stood firm."

Richard closed his eyes against the assault. "It wasn't by choice, Father. I swear it." Anguished tears filled his eyes. "You have no idea how much it affected me. No idea. But the vampire insisted—no, *demanded*."

Richard's eyes adjusted to the darkness as his father walked toward his coffin. *Did my words made any difference?* "You do believe me?"

"I believe you," Meredith said as he sat. "I was wrong to assume you'd taken the name by choice. I suppose just hearing it—after not hearing it for so long . . ."

"Then you forgive me?"

"As much as I can."

"Yes, of course. Forgiveness doesn't come easily to a vampire," said Richard. "I just feel horrible that you almost didn't feed based on hearing what the vampire made me call myself."

Merideth looked up and reached out a hand to touch his son's face. "I'll try to be stronger. It did hit me hard though."

"Well, if there's ever anything I can help you with, you know I will."

"There is one thing," Merideth pulled his hand away. "I would like you to promise me something."

"Anything."

"I need you to promise that, when the time comes, you'll do whatever you have to do to make things right—no matter what."

"So dramatic," Richard said. "Especially for a vampire."

"Promise, Richard," he insisted. "I need your word."

"If it's important to you, of course, I'll promise."

The sound of Josh lumbering down the stairs brought their conversation to an end. "Sun's up." He opened his coffin and climbed in.

"I should rest too."

"Goodnight, Father. And thank you for understanding . . . and forgiving."

Richard climbed the stairs and sighed. *What in the world did I just promise?*

35

This time Kyle picked up on the third ring. "Dude, did you get it?" Rodney blurted before Kyle could say anything.

"And hello to you, too, dude. Yes, I am well, thank you for asking . . . you ungrateful—"

"Did you get him to say he'd do it and do you have an address?" Rodney asked.

"Hey, everybody has their price."

"Okay so what's it gonna cost me?"

"He said he'd do it for fifteen hundred dollars—cash."

"Okay, how does he want me to get the money to him?"

Rodney jerked the phone away from his ear.

"Dude," he heard Kyle ask when it was safe to listen again, "where are you gonna get fifteen-hundred dollars?"

"Fine. I'll just put it in the package. Were you able to get what I asked you to get from Henderson's place?"

"If you're talking about the vial of Ceese's blood from the refrigerator in Henderson's basement, yeah, I got it. But you owe me. Getting it wasn't as easy as you said."

"Why? Don't you have a key to Henderson's place?" Kyle did grunt work for Henderson on occasion, which warranted him the privilege of a key.

"Yeah, but there was someone there. I had to wait until they left."

"Someone there? What are you talking about?"

"Some guy has set up shop. Looks like Henderson's lab is back in operation. Oh, and I got Josh's cell back too."

"Cool. At least he won't be able to use it to trick me again. But whatever, just tell me you got the blood."

"Do I have to tell you twice? What part of 'yeah' don't you understand?"

Rodney ignored Kyle's irritated tone. "Okay. So if you could just tell your friend to be on the look out for the package and the money, that'd be great."

Rodney hung up before Kyle could ask questions about the source of the money . . . *though, it is a good question.*

He stepped into the hall, turned and pulled the door shut—and jumped when he backed into . . . Cassie. "Do you always stand just outside other people's doors?"

"I was just walking down the hall. Why so jumpy?"

"I told you. You scare me—I mean scared me."

"Yes, well I was just passing by. Were you talking to someone? I thought I heard voices."

"Sounds like a personal problem. Don't you always hear voices?"

"So you weren't talking to anyone?"

Rodney threw the door to his room open. "Do you see anyone?"

Cassie crossed her arms in front of her. "You could've been on the phone."

"And you could be nuts. Shall we take a vote? You might think before you answer that. I'm not so sure you'd fare very well."

Exasperated, Cassie moved on. Rodney watched until she'd made the turn into the parlor. He turned and hurried out the back way. He caught Geoffrey, clad in driving gloves and cap, just as he stepped out of his quarters.

"Perfect." Rodney guided him back inside while glancing around furtively. "You're going somewhere, right?"

"Not at the moment, it seems."

"I mean you're about to go somewhere."

"I do have some errands to run."

"Good." Rodney took a deep anticipatory breath. "You know that rabbit?"

"Your cold pet."

"Yes. Exactly. I need you to mail it for me." Rodney pulled a small piece of paper from a pocket. "Here's an address. You need to keep it cold—the rabbit, not the address—and mail it in some sort of refrigerated container. It's got to stay cold though. That's very important. I know it's an odd request but I really need you to do this for me."

Geoffrey took the slip of paper. "Certainly. What shall I use for payment?"

"Payment?"

"Yes."

"Money?"

"You don't have any money, do you?"

"No, and the worst part about it is I need fifteen hundred dollars over and above the postage. I planned on asking Richard for it but I really don't want to explain what I need it for. Besides, I don't think he'd understand."

"Sending a cold rabbit and fifteen hundred dollars express mail could make one wonder."

Dismal, Rodney stared at the ground.

"Perhaps I could help you out."

"Would you, G-man? That'd be so great. I'll pay you back as soon as I can, dude."

"As well, may I suggest special packaging, along with the refrigeration?" Geoffrey asked.

"What? You talking a bow or something? Get real."

"Young man, I refer to the fact that you are attempting to send a dead animal through two borders—two sets of customs officials with all their experience, electronic equipment and trained sniffer dogs."

"Oh yeah, I see how that could be a problem."

Geoffrey drew a breath. "I will see to the package and ensure its . . . ahem . . . safe passage."

"Dude, thanks; you're the best," said Rodney.

"However, I have one condition."

"Sure. You name it."

"If you would, please don't bring me any more rabbits to keep for you."

"Done. I won't. I promise." Rodney shook Geoffrey's gloved right hand and hurried off.

"Stockholm Syndrome," Cassie said to Brendan. "Ceese defended Zade because she has Stockholm Syndrome; it's when a victim identifies with their captor. It's the only way some can deal with their situation. Especially when they realize there's no escape."

Brendan paced the parlor floor like a caged tiger. "But she seems to hate Father now. I dinnae understand that. It doesn't make any sense. Father meant everything to her, always has." He looked over to Richard. "Ye know this to be true. Even after ye left, that dinnae change."

"Well, it's certainly different now," Penelope offered. "And, I have to agree with Cassie. It does sound like Ceese feels trapped because she sees no escape. It must be terrifying for her. When she'd visit me the way she did so many years ago, I knew it was to try and get help. She wanted someone to tell her she could get away from Zade—yet he was the only family she had. Everyone else was gone. Or so she thought. However, I've always thought it interesting that without any proof, she wanted to believe you still existed, Richard. It was as if believing kept her sane."

Brendan stopped pacing. "And a lot of good it's done her to know that he does exist. She still defends Zade."

"She's still scared of him," Cassie said. "Fear doesn't just go away."

Brendan stared out the window at Ceese and Rodney seated on the front lawn. Richard followed his eyes, then back to watch Brendan walk away. "Where are you going?"

"I don't remember having to answer to ye."

As soon as Brendan left, Cassie said, "I don't think it will be good if he tries to talk to Ceese about her situation."

"I agree," Penelope said. "But if that's what he wants to do, I don't see how we can stop him. It appears Brendan does what Brendan wants."

"Welcome to my nightmare," Richard sighed. "Do you have any idea what it was like growing up with someone like that? Even Father had a time with him."

"I think he means well."

Richard turned his attention to Penelope and quirked a brow. "Really?"

"Yes, why?"

"Nothing. It's just that for a moment it sounded as though you were worried about him. Perhaps even cared a little."

"I can't care about him?" she asked.

Richard shrugged. "I suppose you can care about whomever you please though I'm certain you don't know Brendan well enough . . . just how well do you think you know him?"

"I think I'll not answer that question," Penelope said. "Now if you'll excuse me."

Richard stared after her. "I hope she doesn't plan to fall for Brendan's pitiful act," Richard said to Cassie.

"Would it bother you if she did?"

"No—no, of course not." Richard's hesitation didn't reflect his words.

Brendan locked his door behind him and walked to where his duster lay draped over a chair. He held it up and pulled out the dagger-like knife from a specially-made inner pocket. He hadn't mentioned the knife to his brother and wasn't sure he should. He certainly wouldn't tell him about the rumors that it could kill vampires and werewolves—nor that he believed the rumors. He heard footfalls in the hall and quickly tucked the knife away.

36

"Let go of my arm," Cassie protested. Rodney pulled her down the hall toward his room.

"Then quit asking questions and come on."

"Fine, just let go of my arm."

Cassie followed Rodney into his room and stopped at the closet door. "You've lost your mind. No way I'm going in that closet with you." She stretched her arms out in front with palms up.

But Rodney reached out, yanked her in, and then pulled the door closed. The light produced by a bare bulb overhead showed her eyes wide. "I swear, if you touch me again—"

"I'm worried about Ceese," Rodney said as he guarded the closed door.

"You're worried about Ceese?"

"Yes."

"That's rich," Cassie smirked. "I've been worried about Ceese for some time but did you bother to care? No, you just blew me off."

"Sh—shut up. Would you just shut up and listen?" His abruptness stunned her. "She's scared of Zade, okay? I mean she's *really* scared of him. She told me so when we were out on the lawn. Not in so many words, but I could tell."

Cassie let him finish. Rodney wasn't exactly himself and she *was* alone in a closet with him. Her eyes moved from her feet, to Rodney, then to the door—the only way out. "Okay, so are you worried about anything else?"

"Yeah. She also said as long as she's here, at the castle, that no one is safe. Do you understand what that means?"

"All I understand," Cassie said carefully, "is that I have been asking for you to talk to me about Ceese for some time now and you haven't. You just look at me like I'm crazy. Now you drag me into a closet and want my opinion? That isn't the way it works, Rodney. I have opinions but I hardly feel like sharing them with someone who doesn't really care."

"What?"

"You heard me. You don't care. How can you? You don't care about anything. You came along as a freeloader because you knew Ceese wouldn't have it any other way. You've taken advantage of her, me, Richard—"

"—Geoffrey," he added. "Though I'm not sure that situation qualifies as taking advantage of someone since Geoffrey volunteered."

"The butler?" Cassie said in amazement. "Have you no shame? Never mind. The point is I'm through with you. I'm tired of trying to make you feel better about always choosing to do the wrong thing."

"But this is different."

"You always say that."

"But it *is* different. I—I care about Ceese. I care what happens to her."

Cassie shook her head in disappointment. "Ever heard the story of the boy who cried wolf, Rodney? If you haven't, just go back and look at your life. You don't even have to go back that far. It will be a long time before I believe anything you say."

Cassie pushed past Rodney and opened the door. As she walked out she said, "And furthermore, I don't think it's possible for you to care about anyone but yourself."

Alone, Rodney fell back against a wall and slid down to the floor. "You're wrong," he said. "You're so wrong."

Tobias died, finally. Henderson covered his nose as he stepped around the body. On the upside, unlike the previous night, Tobias made no sound. The scientist looked up and saw that Zade stood a few feet from the cave entrance staring off at something . . . or possibly nothing.

"Are you just going to leave him here?"

"No. Zade have plan."

"Well, I'd like you to do something with the mess before we get started with your lessons."

"Zade finished with lessons."

"Really?" Henderson came to stand behind the werewolf. "Can Zade say please without frothing at the mouth? Can Zade speak nicely and actually come off sounding sincere? I don't think so."

"Zade's plan better."

"I thought we'd already discussed which plan was better and we both agreed—"

Zade turned at once. He pulled Henderson toward him. "Zade's plan better."

"On the other hand," Henderson said looking back at the corpse. "I'm open to any new ideas you might have."

Zade let go. "Vampire feed, come back. Zade tell plan then."

Visitors to the castle were rare. Visitors after dark were quite rare indeed. It was no surprise that the heavy thud, followed by a quick knock, at the main door brought the curious down the stairs and into the hall.

"Who could it be?" Penelope asked.

Richard cocked a brow. "I don't suppose either of you have had any visions concerning the matter?"

"I've just had the one," Cassie replied, "about Brendan."

"Don't look at me," Penelope said. "I've not had any recent visions."

Geoffrey, still on duty despite the hour, walked past the group to answer the door.

Brendan stepped out into the hall last. "Did I hear someone knock?"

They all grew silent when Geoffrey pulled open the door. Instead of the expected greeting, Geoffrey gasped in horror and shut the door. "It appears to be a dead body, sir."

Richard strode to the door, yanked it open and became the second to gasp at the sight. "God have mercy."

Wearing his duster and now armed with his shotgun, Brendan walked past Richard and around the mangled mess on the stoop. The others peered to get a glimpse.

"Is it human?" Richard asked.

"I don't think I want to look long enough to find out," Cassie replied.

Brendan kicked at it with his foot and it rolled down the last step. "Aye, would ye look at that."

"Do you think there was a reason behind leaving the face untouched?" Penelope asked.

"I'd say," Brendan replied. "That's Tobias."

"Tobias?" Richard said. "You know him?"

"It's the werewolf that gave me Ceese's necklace—the pendant that told me Ceese was still alive."

Cassie stole a quick glance. "What kind of accident leaves you in that sort of shape?"

"This was nae accident. It's Zade's work. Tobias broke rank quite a while ago. Left the pack. That's why I was after him. I had a feeling he knew something."

"Why would Tobias come back?" Richard asked. "He had to know Zade would kill him."

"Tobias wasn't the brightest werewolf around. I suspect he got tired of being on the run and decided to confront Zade. Perhaps he wanted to take over."

"Yet one has to wonder," Penelope said, "how he ended up here on the castle steps. The smell alone suggests he's been dead for at least a day, so he clearly didn't crawl here."

Rodney arrived at the doorway with Ceese behind him. "Take her back inside," Richard ordered. "She doesn't need to see this."

"No," Brendan said. "She does need to see this. She needs to know what Zade can do."

Penelope shook her head. "Go back inside, dear."

"Why do ye coddle her?" Brendan asked.

"We can talk about it later."

Seconds later there was nothing to debate. Ceese had gone back upstairs.

"Zade did that?" Rodney lingered a little longer.

"Aye, and he's done far worse as well. Ye can count on it."

Rodney backed away before going after Ceese. His voice echoed in the entry way as he called to her.

"I'm not so sure Ceese needed to see that either," Cassie said. "Rodney cornered me earlier to say how frightened Ceese was of Zade. This only stands to make that fear worse."

"Indeed," Penelope said.

"And what if ye are wrong?" Brendan asked.

"Three of us." Richard closed in on his brother. "I feel the same way."

"Do you now?" Brendan drew his weapon, chambered it and aimed.

"Brother, if I—" The shotgun blast both silenced and deafened him. When he noticed the others staring past, Richard looked over his shoulder. He stiffened as he looked down at the wolf, half its chest blown away. Richard looked back to his brother's gun and followed the line of sight to the dead creature. Judging from where it landed, had Richard moved, he would've been in trouble. Even at that, Richard had a difficult time sounding grateful. "You couldn't have warned me?"

"There was nae time."

"Yet you had time to use my shoulder to steady your aim."

"Next time I'll just let the wolf attack."

"Maybe we should just go inside," Penelope suggested, "before Zade sends more hunters."

Rodney met them coming in and gunned for Brendan. "You bastard," he shouted.

He shoved Richard who stepped in front of him. "Get out of my way. Ceese is gone and it's his fault."

"I'm sure Ceese isn't gone," Richard rationalized.

"Yeah," Rodney fired back. "Well, she's not under the bed. She's not anywhere. You can go look for yourself. She left because of what *he* said."

"I'll look upstairs," Penelope said, her tone urgent. "The rest of you spread out and search down here."

"I'm sure she's around here somewhere," Brendan pointed out. "I'm sure we'll find her."

Rodney shoved harder against Richard. "You better hope we do."

Richard held Rodney until Brendan had moved along. "He wouldn't do anything to hurt Ceese," Richard told him. "Not on purpose anyway."

Rodney pulled away. "Does it really matter if it's intentional or not? If Ceese is gone, it's his fault."

37

Ceese raced into the night, desperate to get away. Desperate that Zade not catch her. Desperate that she not be cursed again. The body on the stoop proved that she needed to protect those she loved. Zade would do anything to have her for his own again.

She ran faster, harder . . . then stopped suddenly. "Father."

Merideth dropped down from where he hung in the air. "Cee Cee. Why are you out here? Zade's out here. You know it's dangerous. Go back. Go back to Richard and the others."

How she wanted to go to him, to feel his protective arms around her, to know how much she was loved. "Father, I—"

A wolf howl came from close by.

"No." She backed away. "I can't."

Josh landed just as Ceese darted away. "What's she doing out here?"

Merideth stared off toward the castle, opposite to the direction Ceese had run. "I don't know," he said with concern. "But I'm going to find out."

≈≈≈

They searched the castle several times, to no avail. Ceese had indeed left. Cassie flopped on a couch in the parlor, bent over and covered her head. "I should've seen this coming. Rodney finally offers to tell me something about Ceese and I don't even listen to him."

"Why would ye listen to him? Why would anybody?" Brendan huffed. "Why is he even here?"

"He's here," Richard said with a heavy sigh, "because Ceese needs him. He's here because he helps Ceese cope. Clearly, he's not the easiest person to get along with but the rest of us have all found some common ground with him. Perhaps you should as well. He's in her room."

"I'll not be wasting my time talking to that *eejit*."

"Am I to take that to mean you won't be helping Ceese then? Because, like it or not, she's chosen Rodney to depend on. Not you, not me, not even Father. Cut him out of the equation if you like, but rest assured, you'll likely be cutting Ceese out as well."

"He's right," Penelope added. "She seems to depend on him that much."

A slow frown gathered on Brendan's face and he shut his eyes tight.

"Like I said, he's in her room."

Rodney sat staring at the floor. He raised his head slightly when Brendan entered without knocking. Cautiously, he peered out from behind bangs that covered one eye.

"Mind if I join ye?" Brendan asked. He settled before Rodney could answer. "I think we got off on the wrong foot."

With a quick snap of his head, the long bangs flew out of the way for the moment. "Hand," Rodney cut his eyes at Brendan. He'd not forgotten the night Brendan arrived. The palm to his forehead. "I think you mean hand."

"Aye," Brendan said. Tight-lipped, he attempted a smile. "But I dinnae come in here to cause trouble. I just thought we should try harder to get along."

"I'm sorry. Did I say or do something to make you think I was interested in that?"

Brendan drew a tense breath and tried again. "Richard tells me we need to get along in order to help Ceese."

"Fair enough."

"So maybe we can do our best to nae get on each others' nerves."

"As long as we don't have to shake on it."

"Aye," Brendan said, terse. *This isn't going to be easy.*

Rodney sat for a quiet moment then asked, "How do you do that anyway, that palm thing?"

Or maybe it'll be easier than I thought. "It's a wee bit hard to explain but—"

"Why are you here?"

"Excuse me?"

"Why are you here? Everybody's here for one reason or another. Why are you here?"

Brendan stood, went over and closed the door, then reclaimed his seat. He reached inside the duster he still wore and took out the knife. "Do ye know what this is?"

Rodney's eyes widened and he threw his hands up to ward off an attack. "Forget what I said. I—I don't wanna know why you're here. Forget I asked—"

"Not so loud. I'd like to keep this just between us."

Rodney gulped. "Oh, I'm sure you would. But how are you going to kill me quietly? I can scream pretty loud."

"Would ye calm down. I'm nae going to kill ye."

Rodney slumped; his jaw still tense. "I think you should put that back in your coat."

"I just wanted to show it to ye. It's the knife of the Akedah. The very one Abraham used on Mount Moriah." He lowered his voice to a whisper. "I understand it has the power to kill vampires and werewolves. I really dinnae want anyone else to know about it."

"Oh sh—sure," Rodney said. "Of . . . of course."

At a nearby noise in the hall, Brendan slipped the knife back inside his coat. When the footsteps stopped outside the door, Brendan put his arm around Rodney's shoulders. "Nae a word."

Brendan responded to a knock on the door, "It's open."

"So you made it," Richard said. "I just wondered if you'd had a talk with Rodney." Brendan's wide-eyed stare didn't seem to bother Richard at all.

"We were just—talking. Weren't we, Rodney?"

Rodney's stiff posture, his bugged eyes and bloodless pallor refuted Brendan's words.

"Are you all right?" Richard asked.

Rodney shot to his feet. Ran to Richard, grabbed his shoulders, and pulled Richard in front to shield himself. "Brendan has a knife," he blurted.

Brendan jumped up. "Why ye wee—ye promised."

"Didn't promise anything," Rodney said from behind Richard. "Brendan has a knife and it's big and it's ugly and he plans on killing with it."

Brendan forced a laugh. "Ah, he's making that up."

"And it's there," he pointed, "inside his coat."

Brendan lunged at Rodney and Richard blocked him. Taking no chances, Rodney zipped out of the room.

"I'm so very curious," Richard said. "Let's see it."

"There's nothing to see."

"Brother," he said, holding his hand out. "Let's see it."

"Ye are going to believe him? He lies about everything."

"Oddly enough, I've grown to trust some of what he says."

"Over your own brother?"

"In this instance, yes."

Brendan muttered then reached inside his duster and pulled out the knife. Richard took it by its blade, then grasped its hilt. He turned it and studied it. "Is this Aramaic writing?"

"Aye, that it is. It's the knife of the Akedah." Brendan watched Richard's face.

"You're suggesting this is the very knife Abraham used on Mount Moriah to perform one of the most significant sacrificial acts known to man?"

"Ye see the writing."

Richard scrutinized the knife. "Aramaic writing on the hilt doesn't exactly mean it's the knife of the Akedah."

"It was the language of the day or so I've heard."

"Where did you find it?"

"An antique dealer."

"*Where* exactly did you get it?" Richard prodded.

"How am I to know exactly where he got it?"

"No, not him. You. Where exactly did you get it?"

"I don't see how that's important."

"Then why won't you tell me?"

Brendan blurted, "eBay, all right. I found it on eBay."

Richard cupped his lips between his teeth and pressed—hard.

"And despite what ye think, there are legitimate traders on the site."

"Did I suggest otherwise? I dare say, I'd wonder how that search went, though."

"Have your little fun. I don't care. The knife is what it is."

Richard balanced it on the end of the forefinger of his right hand. "It is a fine knife to be sure. A nice weight and balance to it. I tell you what. Go over there and pick a spot on the wall. Any spot."

"Why?"

"Humor me and be specific," Richard told him. "Point out one particular spot."

Brendan did and in a flash, Richard flipped the dagger in the air, caught the end of the blade and launched the knife across the room. *Woosh!* It stuck exactly where Brendan had pointed.

"That was for shooting over my shoulder without warning," Richard said to the stunned look on his brother's face.

Brendan charged Richard and successfully pinned him against a wall. "I've got but one arm," he growled loudly, "and ye risk taking it by trying to get even?"

With an arm across his throat, Richard opened his mouth but not a sound escaped. He could barely breathe.

"Let him go," came the voice of their father. "There are important matters to deal with. And why are you two going at it anyway? You're grown men, not children."

Brendan released Richard and turned. "He threw a knife and nearly took my arm off."

"Only because you unloaded your weapon next to my ear."

"This knife?" Merideth asked as he tugged it out of the wall.

"Yes," Richard confirmed. "Brendan thinks it's the knife of the Akedah."

Merideth drew back. The reference to one of the most prominent events in Biblical history affected him but he had no problem handling the knife itself.

"So there you have it," Richard said. "Father isn't affected so it can't be the relic."

Merideth handed the knife to Brendan. "It could very well be what he says it is. I told you. My situation is different than that of any other vampire."

Brendan returned the knife to his pocket and gave Richard an I-told-you-so look behind their father's back.

"But why aren't you out hunting?" Richard asked. "What brings you back to the castle?"

"Cee Cee," he said. "I ran into her racing through the woods, Richard. Why?"

Brendan spoke before Richard could. "Ye saw her?"

"I did. And when I questioned her and told her to go back to the castle, she ran in the opposite direction."

That settled it. Ceese had left of her own free will. "Come with me," Richard said. "I have something to show you that might help you understand."

They headed off toward the main entrance and the werewolf, Tobias' remains.

38

Ceese stopped running and knelt on the forest floor. It had been half an hour distance since she left the castle and now time to make a decision. *But what? Everything is such a jumble.* A twig lay at her side; aimlessly she picked it up and began to dig at a mossy patch. As confused as Ceese felt, two things stood clear: she wouldn't put the others at risk and she couldn't return to the castle.

One glimpse at the dead werewolf told the story. Of course, she remembered Tobias—Joachim had introduced them long ago. Ceese dropped the twig and ran a hand lightly over the top of the moss, so soft and springy. Brendan had said Zade was responsible. She'd always defended Zade—even as she feared him. But, until she knew for sure, she wouldn't feel safe with him.

But what should I do, right now? Where will—the skin on her nape erupted in goose bumps. Fingers froze on the moss. Frightened, she looked to the side. There stood Zade.

Like a sprinter at the block, Ceese sprung up to her feet, stumbled backwards up against a tree and froze.

"Zade want Ceese."

"I—I know."

"Zade want Ceese come with him." He held his hand out for her to take. "Zade want Ceese please come with him."

"This has to be a trick," Ceese whispered.

"Zade want Ceese please come with him."

"You're asking?"

"Please."

"Wh-why don't you just curse me now? Get it over with. I won't fight you."

"Zade not hurt Ceese. Zade sorry he hurt Ceese before."

"You're *sorry*?"

"Yes."

Zade didn't say anymore. He didn't rush her; in fact, he gave her a minute to mull it over.

Tentative, she took his hand and allowed him to lead her off.

When they were out of sight, Henderson stepped out from his hiding place—his eyes almost as wide as his open mouth. The student had surpassed the teacher's expectations; Zade had delivered a flawless, spectacular performance. Henderson had nearly given his hiding place away when Zade said the "P" word with so little effort . . . and no spittle. By all accounts Henderson should have felt pride. This teacher, however, closed his gaping jaw and his eyes narrowed. He padded off behind the pair.

At Richard's request, Cassie explained Stockholm's Syndrome to Merideth.

"It does make sense," he said from his seat at the small kitchen table. "And it does help explain Cee Cee acting the way she's acting. But it doesn't help to know she's out there with that monster looking for her. At least I have the satisfaction of knowing he can't get her this time."

Brendan, sitting across from his father asked, "What do ye mean?"

"Certainly one of you led her to—has gotten a commitment from her."

"Oh, that," Brendan sighed.

"Commitment?" Rodney said, clueless.

But how could they explain without causing Meredith undue duress? "It has to do with her faith," Richard said, then to his father, who'd flinched a little, "Sorry."

"Did she come to either one of you?" Merideth asked.

"She dinnae speak to me about it," Brendan told him.

"Nor did she come to me," Richard added.

Merideth sighed deeply. "So she's at his mercy once again. Richard, how could you not broach the subject with her? How could you not see this was important?"

"You're right, Father," Richard said, fully chastised. "I have no defense. I should've asked her about it straight away."

"What makes any of you think she wanted to talk about it?" Penelope asked. "Many make the commitment of their own accord. I see no reason to ride Richard or Brendan about it. Let's just assume she did make it and move on."

"Yeah," Rodney said from where he stood. "What do we do next? I'm all for going after her and I don't care what the rest of you think. She doesn't want to be with Zade. She doesn't want to be cursed again."

"I wouldn't be so sure about that." Josh's silent entry alarmed all and they jumped. "I saw her with that werewolf dude—what's his name again—Zade?"

"What'd you see?" Rodney asked alarmed.

"Chill out. The two of them were just talking and then they left together. Walking hand in hand."

"Yeah, right. What do you know?" Rodney said.

"I know what I saw, dude. And I know what I heard. She went with him and without a fight too. Hand in hand. You know, like boyfriend and girlfriend."

"Now I know you're crazy. Ceese wouldn't go with him willingly. Sh-she wouldn't. She nearly broke her neck to get away from him when he was after her the first time. She's scared of him."

"Whatever. I'm just telling you what I saw. And why do you care anyway? If I didn't know better, I'd say you liked her. But what are the odds of that? You don't care about anybody but yourself."

"Yeah." Rodney added a dry laugh. "What're the odds?"

"Can we stick to the subject," Brendan said. "Ceese is out there and we need to bring her back."

"It won't do any good to bring her back if she doesn't want to come back," Richard pointed out again.

They both stopped talking when Rodney started out of the room.

"Where are you going?" Cassie asked. "Certainly you have some input on going after Ceese. You were all for it a minute ago."

"Yeah, well Josh made a very good point."

"I did?" Josh said.

"Yes, you and Cassie both. It seems the two of you know me better than I know myself."

"What are you talking about?" Cassie asked, confounded.

"The boy who cried wolf, remember? I can't care about Ceese because I can't care about anyone. Thank you for showing me the error of my ways—again. Go find Ceese yourself. Do whatever you want. Clearly you don't expect me to help. Why should I disappoint you by trying?"

Rodney left the room and Cassie took a step in his direction. Brendan said, "Ye'd go after him? I say good riddance. We dinnae need him to find Ceese."

"Who said anything about finding Ceese?" Richard said. "I think we're still debating whether that's a good idea."

Brendan stared hard. "Why do ye insist on crossing me?"

"I don't think he's crossing you, Brendan," Penny said. "I think he's just being realistic. If Josh really saw what he said, then Ceese isn't in any immediate danger. Like you, I want to go after her. Deep down, however, I know it won't do any good. We just need to think about this a little more. Perhaps even sleep on it."

Brendan turned his attention to Josh. "Are ye sure about what ye saw? Ceese went with Zade willingly? There was nae struggle?"

"Yeah, you know, like a kid going with somebody they knew."

Cassie's brow creased. "But you told Rodney it was more like boyfriend and a girlfriend. Which is it?"

"What's the difference? She went along with him. Okay?"

"Because of the way Ceese feels about Rodney, we need him on our side even if we don't want him. Thanks to your description, he most likely isn't going to help us at all."

Josh made a curt noise with his mouth. "You don't know nothing about Rodney, do you? You think he's helping you? He's helping himself. He always said you were a pushover."

Richard stepped in. "I think Penny's right. It seems Ceese is safe for the moment. We should just sleep on it."

~~~

Rodney stopped just outside the door and thumped his back against the wall. He'd spent his entire life not caring what happened to others. In the end, it was always about him. Life was just easier that way. He'd never met anyone who made him question how he operated—until Ceese came along. Caring about anyone else was new territory for him.

Rodney recalled his childhood, his alcoholic father who barely acknowledged he existed unless Rodney happened to be near something he wanted. Even then he'd call him *Boy* instead of by his name. Rodney often wondered if his father even *knew* his name.

He stayed in that situation for years knowing there was something better, more normal. Social Services offered several times to place him with another family but he always chose to stay where he was. It wasn't until he made the decision that they could officially help. Ceese would have to make that decision too. *Please Ceese, make it soon.*

He stayed just outside the door to hear what the others were going to do. When he learned they'd decided to sleep on it, he was forced to comply. He still wanted to go after Ceese but he'd hardly be able to face Zade alone. He wasn't even sure how they could face him together—but they'd have to eventually unless Ceese escaped.

Until she did, they wouldn't be able to help her.

39

His hand completely surrounded hers yet he didn't grasp tightly. Despite the illusion, Ceese didn't feel bold enough to break and run. Zade would come after her and maybe he wouldn't be as nice. For that reason alone, she went along.

He walked her into the cave and motioned to lie next to him. Ceese complied but noted that he'd never worried about where she slept before. But then, she'd never run off with plans to stay away.

"Ceese safe here," Zade said. "Zade protect Ceese."

And so the charade continued. Perhaps she wasn't safe but as long she stayed with Zade, everyone else would be.

Tears formed as she lay with her back to her captor. *I'm sorry, Rodney.*

Quiet spread through the castle. The group had decided to meet in the morning to make plans to find Ceese and then they settled for the night. Penelope alone remained in the kitchen.

As she waited for water to boil she stared, expressionless, at the wall above. The tea kettle whistled and sputtered. With a start, she shook her head and prepared the pot for tea. One spoonful of tea made for a weak brew but strong enough to calm nerves.

"So I'm nae the only one who finds rest difficult," Brendan said as he entered the room and settled at the small kitchen table.

"I don't think anyone's going to be resting tonight. Let me get you some tea."

"Nay," he said, "I'm fine, thank you."

Penelope sat down, pulled her chair back in. With a sigh, she slumped her elbows on the table and cupped her face.

Brendan watched steam swirl from her cup before asking, "Why do ye keep your feelings for Richard a secret?"

"I beg your pardon?"

"It's hard to ignore how strongly ye defend him."

"Your father was being too hard on him. I don't care if he is a vampire, he should work to show a little more symp—" She caught herself. "I did it again, didn't I?"

"Nay worry," he said. "Maybe I alone see it."

"I'm trying, Brendan, really I am. But it's not easy. The Richard I loved is gone. Some of what I loved about him is still there but not enough. I just wish I could convince myself."

"I can help ye," he said, showing his palm. "After all, ye were there for me."

She gave an accommodating nod.

Gently, he touched her forehead and settled into what he did best.

After a moment, he took his hand away. "That's for helping me with Gwen," he told her as he rose from his seat. "I never thanked ye properly."

"Thank you, Brendan. I feel much better." Penelope smiled; the lines on her face softened. "Are you going to try to sleep now?"

"Aye. I'll try."

Penelope watched him leave then carried her tea over to the window. As she stared, her face reflected in the glass. Eyebrows met and frown lines reappeared. The china tea cup and saucer rattled in her hand. She whispered, "I love him. I'm doomed to love Richard forever."

The meeting at dawn didn't bring any new answers. Rodney stalked out, grumbling, and headed for the front lawn. Halfway down the entrance stairs he stopped and stared ahead at the woods. He walked slowly at first, then picked up the pace until he ran—full out in amongst the trees and brush.

Panting, he slowed to a canter and after a minute's rest, he ran full-out once more until he gained more distance from the castle. Without warning, Rodney slowed and then stopped. He bent over and with hands on knees, looked from side to side. Ceese had asked for a kiss at this very spot. *That's crazy. I couldn't find this place with a map.*

Startled by a noise behind him, he turned. "Ceese."

"No, stay back," she said when he moved closer.

He did as she asked. "Are you okay? You're not hurt?"

She shook her head, lips pressed together.

"I'm glad you're okay," he added. "Don't you want to come back to the castle?"

She shook her head again and stepped back. "No. I can't."

"Sure you can. You can go back with me—" He tried another step and she backed up two. He stopped where he was.

"Rodney," she said just above a whisper.

"What, Ceese? What is it?"

"Help . . . me."

Yes. It was what she wanted. "Okay. I will."

～～～

Rodney needed to call Kyle but somewhere in private. *Geoffrey's quarters.* He looked about and spotted the butler near the formal garden, overseeing workers.

"Is there any way I can use your phone?" Rodney asked as he approached.

Geoffrey reached into a pocket. "Will this do?"

"A cell phone? That's even better. Sure. I'll get it right back to you. But please don't tell anyone I asked you for it."

Geoffrey held up a freshly cut flower, "Mum's the word," he said.

"That's good, Geoffrey—a mum. You should take your act on the road, you and your gardeners. Speaking of gardens, which one will give me the most privacy?"

Geoffrey pointed off to his left and Rodney could see tall trestles wrapped with vines. He easily found a spot where no one would see him.

"Hey," he said when Kyle answered. "Did your friend get everything I sent?"

"Yeah, he got it. Dude, why'd you send him a dead rabbit?"

"Did he ask you that?"

"No. He just told me to let you know he got it. Oh, and he said thanks for the money—but there was more in the package than the fifteen hundred he asked for. Dude, where're you getting all that cash?"

"Never mind."

"Well, he figured you messed up and gave me the rest. By the way, what am I supposed to do with what's left?"

Rodney took a moment to think. "Get a pen and a piece of paper and I'll tell you."

⁓⁓

"All right," Brendan sighed deep. "It's been an entire day and we cannae think of new ideas. It's hard to believe she's still out there with him."

"Not by choice," Rodney said.

"What do you mean?" Cassie asked.

"I mean, I saw her and she asked me to help her."

"Where?" Brendan came chest to chest with Rodney.

"Back off." Rodney stepped back. "I went into the woods and she found me."

"What exactly did she say?"

Rodney smirked. "Let me see if I can make this easy for you. Two words. First word: *help*; second word: *me*."

Richard jumped between them before Brendan could react. Brendan pushed against him anyway. "Let's not do this tonight," Richard said. Then to Rodney, "If you continue to irritate him, I'll stop protecting you."

"Yeah, whatever," Rodney said and moved away from Brendan.

"How do we know he's right about Ceese?" Brendan asked. "How do we know she really wants help?"

"She does," Merideth said, entering the room with Josh. "She allowed me to sense this as well. It seems she's seen through Zade's little game."

"Aye," Brendan said, "it's good she's come to her senses or

at least has nae completely lost hope . . . but does any plan jump to mind?"

"Henderson would probably just botch it up anyway."

Cassie turned to face Josh, her mouth spilling questions, "What? Henderson?"

Richard rushed to explain. "Yes. It seems he's with Zade. Josh saw him the other night. Honestly, I meant to tell you. It just slipped my mind."

"But how? Henderson shouldn't even know who Zade is."

"He shouldn't know a lot of things," Richard replied. "But it seems he does."

"There's more," Rodney said. "There's someone staying at Henderson's house and working in his lab."

Cassie's confusion blossomed into irritation. "Should I ask how you came across this information?"

"You can but I won't tell you. I will say that word on the street is that the guy is a short bald man with a Russian accent."

"Savine," stated Cassie.

"Who is Savine?" Richard asked.

"The Russian scientist in the newspaper clippings in Henderson's files, the files I have in my backpack. His forté is creating male gametes from stem cells."

Penelope looked worried now. "Didn't Henderson hold Ceese captive?"

"Yes," Cassie said. "She thought she could give him what he wanted so he'd leave Richard alone. She didn't understand how dangerous he was. None of us did until it was almost too late . . . and now he's here."

All eyes shared heavy-browed answerless glances. Zade alone was dangerous. Zade and Henderson together, working with Savine . . .

"Things weren't good to begin with," Cassie said. "And now they've gotten worse."

40

Werewolves hated fire, yet Zade had built one for Ceese. She sat in front of it on the large stone Zade had carried over and dropped. Ceese ignored Henderson who sat on a log across the fire.

"I know you don't like me," he said. "And you've got the right. But I'd like to make things up to you." Ceese knew vampires weren't particularly fond of fire either. Henderson forced an amicable smile nonetheless.

"Why wouldn't you leave Richard alone in New York?" Ceese asked, "Why wouldn't you leave *me* alone? You planned to do terrible things to Richard and me; I knew your thoughts."

"I'm a scientist, Ceese. Research. It's what I do. I step over the line sometimes, I know that, but I'm working to change things."

Ceese lowered her voice to a whisper. "Why is Zade acting the way he's acting? What lie did you tell him?"

"I told him no lie. I have no control over what he does."

Ceese sat back and pulled her arms around herself. She didn't believe Henderson and never would.

"Couldn't we just let bygones be bygones? I'd like to be your friend."

Her upper lip curled. Her hands balled into fists as she stood. "I'd sooner go to Hell than side with you!" She kicked at the fire hard and then stomped away.

Hot ash sprayed Henderson and he jumped to his feet howling and brushing at the burning embers on his clothes. Smoke wafted from his jacket and with a pop, burst into flames. He ripped it off and then dropped and rolled. Zade saw Henderson's panic and howled as well—with laughter.

Henderson stood and brushed ash off his clothes. "Oh, you think that's funny? Well, I'm glad you enjoyed it. After all, it seems we're all here for *your* pleasure." He twisted around to check his back. "When can we get this little game over with? When do you plan on cursing her?"

Zade stopped laughing. "When time right."

"Lovely. I don't suppose you have any real idea when that might be?"

Zade looked up at the night sky and nodded toward it. "Tomorrow."

"Good. Excellent. I'll look forward to that then."

The two men didn't seem concerned about whether she'd heard them or not but they did turn to look when she stood and walked to the cave. Ceese's arms hung limp at her sides, her neck bent as though her head was too heavy to hold up. Zade was going to curse her . . . at tomorrow night's full moon . . . and no one could stop him.

Richard slumped back against his chair and Brendan leaned against a wall. Neither had any more to say, nor did Merideth who sat across from the desk, eyes trailing along the ceiling and around the room. They'd thrashed out plans, and ideas for new plans, and discarded all as unworkable.

Unable to let the brainstorming session stop, Richard sat forward, leaned elbows on the desk and sighed. "Rodney has that connection with Ceese, perhaps we—"

"Where'd you get that?" Merideth pointed. His sons followed the direction of Merideth's finger—to the bookcase's knickknack laden top shelf behind Richard's desk. He pushed himself out of the chair and headed over.

"Father," Brendan yelled, "I cannae believe this! Ceese is in the hands of a monster and ye choose this time to check out trinkets?"

Meredith reached up over his head and took down an antique. "I used to have a balancing piece just like this."

"Well, I'm sure this isn't it." Richard grabbed it from his father and returned it to the shelf.

"If you don't mind, I'd like to look at it."

"Why? It has nothing to do with what we're talking about."

But Meredith had already taken it back down. Carefully, he held it up so he could see the base's bottom plate. "Richard, this has my initials carved in it. The very ones I put there."

"I'm sure it's just a coincidence." His lies weren't holding up very well. With a defeated sigh, he conceded, "Yes, I know."

"You took it?"

"You had several. Why would you care?"

"Why? Because this one was very important to me."

"I didn't want to take it," Richard finally admitted how the vampire had manipulated him. "It made me. I knew this one was your favorite, though I never understood why, and the vampire sensed this. But I took good care of it. That's got to stand for something."

Brendan had turned his back in disgust with his father but now even he was curious. "What was so special about that one, Father? Ye did have several."

"This one's hollow," he said and carefully unscrewed the balancing arm. "I kept my sailing charts in here to keep your mother from worrying. She never minded if I sailed. She just didn't want to know about it. She considered it a very unsafe hobby. But I do so love the sea."

Brendan stared at the charts Merideth laid out. "Ye can make sense of these?"

"Certainly. You can determine many things. High tide and low tide."

Something else caught Brendan's interest. "Look at this. It looks like the different phases of the moon."

"Yes. The moon's gravitational pull controls the tide. It's helpful for a sailor to know what phase will be next."

Richard was losing interest quickly. "That's all very nice but it hardly helps us—"

Brendan interrupted, "Can ye tell when the next lunar eclipse occurs?"

"Let's see." He traced a finger around the chart. "There's a spring tide coming up, when the sun, moon and earth are all aligned and . . ."

"Again," Richard said, "fascinating but—"

". . . and form a lunar eclipse," Brendan sighed.

"Indeed. I've seen quite a few and have always marveled at the coppery red hue of the moon." Merideth chuckled.

"When? When exactly is the next occurence?" Brendan asked, his eyes penetrating.

"Tomorrow night, I think."

"All right," Richard intervened. "If you two astronomers could please shed some light on why we're having this discussion?"

"The gravitational pull will be strong."

Richard raised his voice. "And how does knowing this help us with finding Ceese?"

"It won't help us but it will help Zade and it explains why he hasn't cursed Ceese already. He's waiting for his best opportunity—the time when it's easiest for him to transform—and be at his strongest. He's waited because tomorrow night offers him that chance."

"Am I to feel better about knowing when Zade plans to curse Ceese . . . again? I was sort of hoping you had more than that."

Brendan glared. "A werewolf is weakest when the moon is not there to influence. For a werewolf, a lunar eclipse is both a blessing and a curse. Yes, he'll have access to as much power as he can summon, but for that brief moment, when the moon is completely blocked, he'll have nae power. Absolutely none. I submit that we take Zade then."

"Just a minute. Since I am not a werewolf I suppose I'll have to take your word for it. But, before we go off and make plans, I'd feel better with some sort of confirmation."

Brendan snorted. "Aye, what a surprise ye cannae take my word for it. Has there ever been a time that ye—"

"It's not a matter of trusting your word. You're basing all this on maps and navigational charts all a few hundred years old . . . all I'm saying is let's at least check the accuracy."

"Aye, big brother always knows best and—"

"Boys!" Meredith interrupted. "I am getting rather weary of your bickering. Richard has a good point . . ." He paused to glare at his oldest son. "No need for smirks from you. And, as I was saying, I agree that we need to confirm this lunar eclipse. What about the computer? Why don't one of you do a little research to verify things?"

"Well, little brother is skilled at using eBay, so . . ."

Brendan rolled his eyes. "I can check the NASA site . . . unless someone," he jerked a thumb Richard's way, "has a better idea."

After two minutes of one-fingered typing, mouse clicks, and beeps, Brendan pointed at the screen. "Bingo! tomorrow night's the night indeed."

The men looked up and at each other in turn. Smiles spread on their faces and Richard clapped Brendan on the back.

"That's good Brendan, very good indeed. Now all we have to do is figure a way to draw Zade out of hiding, and time it perfectly with the eclipse. What could be simpler?"

41

"Oh, Looo-cy, I'm home!"

In disbelief, Cassie stared. *No way. That is not Kyle.* Then Kyle stepped into the parlor with Rodney. Hands on her hips, she asked, "What's he doing here?"

Rodney shrugged. "A really good Ricky Ricardo impression?"

"Oh, good one," Kyle said and high-fived Rodney.

"You know what I mean."

"I needed moral support," Rodney told her. "I wasn't getting it from you or anyone else, for that matter."

"Your bags." Geoffrey placed two suitcases just inside the door.

"I'm not finished, Rodney." Cassie said. "You have a few questions to answer."

Before she could continue, Richard had a question of his own . . . for Geoffrey. He walked over to the butler and asked, "You've been to the airport? I don't remember sending you."

"Begging your pardon, Sir, but Saturday is my day off."

"Ah, yes. I suppose it is. Sorry."

Geoffrey nodded politely and turned to go.

Rodney picked up one of the bags, Kyle, the other. "Kyle needs to settle in. He's had a long flight." Rodney grinned at Cassie's searing glare that followed them out.

"I liked it better when he was moping about Ceese running off," Cassie said. "Even if it was short-lived."

Rodney dropped the suitcase inside his room. "You can go to your own room later." He closed the door behind him and locked it. "So, do you have it?"

Kyle plopped the suitcase on Rodney's bed, reached a hand behind him and pulled a sealed and folded envelope out of his pocket. "Right here."

Rodney studied the envelope. "So this is what I paid for."

"That's it."

Rodney folded it in half and tucked it away in a pocket of his own.

"You're not gonna look at it?"

"Not right now. Maybe later. It's not for me anyway."

"Whatever." Kyle looked around the room. "Is he . . . here?" Kyle checked the closet and looked behind drapes. "Wh-where's . . . Josh?"

Rodney's eyes widened. "Dude, he's behind you!"

Kyle spun around so suddenly he lost his balance.

Rodney laughed. "Use your head. He's a vampire. You don't have to worry until night falls."

Henderson forced himself out of his vampyric sleep and walked toward the front of the cave to get a signal on his cell. He stopped when the bars indicated he had one. He dialed but got no answer. He flipped the phone shut and shoved it back into a pocket. He'd try again later.

As the day wore on, the parlor began to look more and more like headquarters. People huddled around the map now spread on a table. Bursts of nervous laughter and chatter filled the room. Marissa bustled in and out carrying trays of beverages and snacks. While the lunar eclipse information gave everyone hope, it soon became a source of frustration. The plan to rescue Ceese was far from complete.

"Look," Richard said, "I'm not debating your knowledge of werewolves and the lunar eclipse, Brother. I just don't know how we're supposed to help Ceese and kill Zade if we don't know where they are."

Kyle nearly choked on the sandwich he'd just bitten into. "Kill?" He looked over at Rodney. "What's this about killing? You didn't say anything about killing."

"A mere technicality; don't worry about it." Rodney waved his hand.

"Technicality? I already have Josh gunning for my throat—or neck, whatever. I've been lured to some foreign country where I don't get most of what's going on. Now I find out I'm a co-conspirator to a premeditated murder." Kyle's voice passed crescendo point, "And all you can say is don't worry? Don't *worry*?"

"Lookout," Rodney said, "he's gonna explode."

"We certainly aren't going to come up with anything unless we all calm down," Penelope interrupted.

"Okay Kyle, I'll explain it, again, slowly. Zade has Ceese and he's going to curse her tonight. We need to kill him before he does curse her. Our best chance, according to what I'm hearing, will be when the lunar eclipse is in full swing and every werewolf is cut off from the moon and at their weakest."

"Well," Cassie said, "no one has to ask if you've been paying attention. I wonder if you could put as much thought into coming up with a solution?"

Just as she finished, a ring tone version of Guns 'N' Roses *Paradise City* played. Josh's old cell. In Kyle's pocket.

Kyle pulled it out; Rodney grabbed it from his hand and flipped it open to check the caller I.D. "Snap!"

"Snap?" Cassie repeated. "Would you care to elaborate?"

"I'd love to. That was Henderson. He called from his own cell. Henderson gave *this* cell to Savine . . . and Kyle grabbed it when he was at the lab—"

"Aye, a nice story indeed," Brendan growled at Rodney. "Funny as I cannae see the point . . ."

"If you'd allow me to continue? Anyway, as I was explaining to the lady here . . . Henderson is with Zade. Henderson's phone has GPS capabilities."

Cassie's eyes rounded. "So if he has his phone . . ."

". . . then we can find him," Rodney finished. "Ergo *snap*."

"Have you ever used his phone to find him?"

Everyone looked at Rodney, their eyebrows raised.

He paused for dramatic effect. Finally he shared, "You don't have access to a GPS phone and not play with it! Of course I've tracked him."

42

"Internet, a GPS receiver and a mobile phone with an internal GPS receiver." Rodney pulled out the chair and sat at the armoire housing the computer. "Like I said already, that's all you need." He typed in the web address. "I've already downloaded the application to Henderson's phone so this shouldn't take long at all."

It didn't. An area visual filled on the computer screen.

"Anyone recognize any of this geography?" he asked.

"Amazing. Yes, it's about a twenty-minute walk from here," Richard said.

"Rodney, you finally came through with something." Cassie grinned wide.

"Wait until you see the bill for my services."

Richard said, "I'll go tell Father what we're planning. I'll let him know where he can meet up with us."

Henderson tried once more. Lucien Savine would be pleased to hear that they'd have their werewolf in short order. Again the phone rang, but Savine didn't answer.

Rodney picked up the cell, checked the caller I.D., then looked up to nod at the expectant faces around him. Moving to stick the phone in his pocket, Rodney stopped and set it to mute. "Wouldn't want to spoil Henderson's surprise. Hearing Guns 'N' Roses out in the forest just might give us away."

Brendan nodded. "Smart thinking, lad."

Rodney jerked his head around and lifted a brow. Everyone tensed.

"Thanks, dude," he said.

Cassie breathed out relief. "Do you think he's getting suspicious? Henderson, I mean. This is the second time he's called and no answer. If he gets suspicious . . ." Playing devil's advocate came naturally to Cassie. But their plan was so shaky anyhow, she could spend the rest of the evening pointing out where it fell short. No one needed to hear it. "Or maybe I'm just worrying about nothing."

The atmosphere was ripe for Kyle's pessimism. "Well, I'm worrying about plenty. I'm sure I didn't sign on for hiking twenty minutes to my death."

"What *did* you sign on for?" Cassie asked. "As of yet, neither you nor Rodney has said why you're here."

Rodney shot Kyle a warning look.

"Rodney doesn't trust the mail," Kyle said.

"Should've known I wouldn't get a straight answer."

Penelope returned from her room, dressed in jeans, sweatshirt and boots. "It's getting dark. We should leave."

Richard and Brendan led the way. For the first part of the trip they could follow a path; after that they had to rely on Brendan's ability to see in the dark.

"Great, I think I just stepped in bear dung or something," Kyle whined.

"Probably deer droppings since there haven't been bears around for five hundred years," Penelope explained.

"Well, that sets my mind at rest. Who cares, bear . . . deer, it's still dung and I stepped in it. Wouldn't a seeing eye dog be better?" Kyle had been complaining about the lack of a flashlight for the past ten minutes.

Cassie reeled around. "Only if the seeing-eye dog was trained to attack so I could sic it on you. Why did he have to come along anyway?" she asked, turning on Rodney. "Couldn't he have stayed at the castle?"

"But who would we offer to Zade in exchange for Ceese?"

Kyle spread his arms and said, "Hey, I don't remember that being part of the plan."

"It may become part of the plan," Rodney informed, "if you don't keep your mouth shut."

As they walked, the moon rose higher in the night sky. Full as it was, it lit the forest track—and deer droppings—nicely. Brendan had left them to go find Merideth because Richard could now see landmarks and such. He could lead on his own.

Brendan returned in short order.

"You found him?"

His brother nodded.

"Is he where I told him to wait?"

"Aye. He's with Josh. They're in position. I suggest we move on. We're getting close, so we'll need to remain silent past this point." Brendan fixed Kyle with a hard stare. "Those who cannae keep quiet can head back to the castle—on their own."

Kyle zipped his lips and flicked away the imaginary key.

The canopy of leaves overhead thickened the closer they got to the cave. They could see the effects of the moon: silver-tinted foliage, an iridescent glow to everything around them, but not the entire moon itself. They'd depend on Brendan to tell them when the time came to act.

They had walked for five more minutes when Brendan made a motion with his arm. They had reached the initial posting point. As the plan went, Brendan would now take Richard to their father. He did so without incident and returned to the group.

Moisture in the cool night air condensing against the warm earth created a low ground fog. Penelope pulled her arms around her. Brendan eased over and whispered in her ear, "Stay beneath it and close to the ground. The fog is like a blanket."

Penelope recalled that Ceese had once told her the same thing. "I'm fine," she mouthed. She'd rather be prepared to jump up and run should the need arise.

Brendan sat down himself and leaned his back against the

trunk of a large tree. He closed his eyes as if to rest. The others made themselves as comfortable as the situation allowed and awaited the next phase of their plan.

The signal came an hour later. Brendan opened his eyes, checked for Rodney, and lobbed a stone at him. Rodney scrambled to his knees at the sight of the big man holding pinky to mouth and thumb to ear. It was time.

Cell in hand, Rodney stepped exactly in Brendan's footsteps to avoid snapping a twig or otherwise alerting their prey. The element of surprise was crucial. Fortunately, they didn't have to walk very far.

Penelope, Cassie and Kyle watched the silhouettes' progress.

Rodney waited for Brendan's next signal. He thought about how Henderson used this very phone to trick him. The scientist knew Rodney wouldn't answer if his name showed on the caller I.D. so he'd used Josh's cell instead.

And Rodney had fallen for it. *But thanks for the idea, dude. Two can play at this game.*

The two men stood at the edge of a small clearing where Brendan could see the moon. He looked up at it briefly, then turned to Rodney and nodded.

Rodney flipped the phone open, selected Henderson's number and pressed send. *Payback time.*

Growing more impatient, Henderson finally worked up the courage to confront Zade. "What are you waiting for? Shouldn't you be out getting ready or something?"

With his back to Henderson, Zade stood. With his night vision, Henderson could see something was very different. Previously, Zade could stand upright inside the cave. Now he had to stoop.

"Not that it matters," Henderson backed down. "I've no doubt you know exactly what you're doing."

Zade turned to face him and Henderson's eyes grew wide at the sight. Saber toothed tiger-like fangs and clawed hands transformed into being before his watching eyes. "Just go on with what you're doing. Never mind me."

Ceese pulled her knees closer to her chest.

Henderson's cell vibrated in his pocket. He pulled it out and answered, "Lucien?" he said while moving to the front of the cave to ensure a better signal. "Good news. We'll have our werewolf tonight."

"So sorry to disappoint," Rodney stepped forward when Henderson exited the cave. "Okay, not really. I'm happy to disappoint."

Henderson froze and dropped his phone.

But where are Ceese and Zade?

Rodney looked behind Henderson and then back to Brendan and the others.

A scratching sound above drew their attention. Behind Henderson, on a ledge above the cave entrance, they saw it—neither wolf nor man. Eyes aglow and fangs bared, the black coarse fur bristled as a menacing growl rumbled from the depths of the monster: a completely and terrifyingly transformed Zade.

Henderson glanced back over his shoulder to see what had everyone's attention. He turned back around and grinned. "He's on *my* side," he said to Rodney. "Who do you have on yours?"

"Ceese," Rodney breathed out.

She stood in the cave's entrance and walked slowly out. She looked toward Rodney and Brendan and then through them—as if she didn't see them at all. She then turned and looked at Zade.

For their plan to work, Ceese needed to stay away from Zade until the eclipse was eminent—their plan to kill Zade with Brendan's silver slugs when he was at his weakest depended on this.

But Ceese just stood there.

"Run," Brendan breathed his encouragement.

"Run," Penelope pleaded from where she and the others still hid.

"Please, run," Cassie seconded.

They all urged Ceese quietly. Still, she stood fast.

Rodney opened his mouth into a full yell. "*Rrruuuun!*" he screamed as loudly as he could.

In the silence that followed, Ceese did just that—she ran fast.

Zade pushed off with powerful legs and landed with an earthshaking thud.

The chase was on.

43

Henderson fumed at the sight of the rescue team jumping out of the shadows. His anger swelled when Richard, Merideth and Josh blew by him. *It can't end like this. I won't let it.* But what could he do to stop it? Taking flight through treetops, he'd follow them until he could think of something.

Zade could've easily overtaken Ceese, Brendan knew. He felt reasonably sure Zade would wait for the golden opportunity—that brief moment before the eclipse when nothing could stop—or kill—a werewolf. By his calculations and experience it shouldn't be long now.

While the others ran on, Kyle slowed a little at a time until everyone had passed by. He had little incentive to run. He hadn't been keen on the killing aspect of the plan earlier and nothing had changed. The sight of a transformed werewolf clinched it—he had no desire to see the monster a second time and especially not up close.
To make matters worse, Josh was now a part of the team. Kyle shivered. It didn't matter that his vampire friend hadn't expressed an immediate interest in cursing him—the darkness, the creepy shadows, werewolves, vampires . . . Kyle dropped out of the chase and let the others run past.

Henderson trailed distant enough to escape notice but close enough to keep tabs. He spotted Kyle wandering alone. His face crafted a cruel smile. *What luck!*

Kyle jumped and nearly hit his head on a low branch when Henderson landed in front of him. His eyes darted this way and that as he backed up. "Oh, man. Not you again." But he wasn't in his dorm room now—there were no walls to stop him from escaping. He stepped backwards quickly . . . and stumbled. Kyle fell to the forest floor with a thud and a grunt.

Cassie followed Richard and managed to keep pace. Without warning, he dropped to his knees. She careened off to the side to avoid a collision. Short of breath, she croaked, "Richard is down." No one heard the barely audible cry for help. Cassie took a few deep breaths, cupped her hands and tried again, "Richard is down."

Brendan, Penny and Merideth circled back around. Richard's eyes rounded as he clutched his head between his hands.

"Brother," Brendan admonished lightly, "we need to keep moving. We need to catch up with Ceese."

"Henderson," he managed, "—Kyle."

They all looked around. Kyle wasn't with them . . . and neither was Josh.

"Wait," Cassie said. "I've seen Richard like this before, back home. He was shaving—there was a homeless man—" She stopped, her eyes wide with fear. "Oh no," she gasped. "Henderson must've found Kyle. He's trying to curse him."

Henderson's hot breath caressed Kyle's neck.

"Please be a dream. Please be a dream," Kyle whimpered.

"Oh, it's no dream. But don't worry, it won't hurt—much." Henderson opened his jaws wide, revealing those horrible fangs glistening with saliva. He leaned in close, fully aware of Richard's efforts to stop him—just as he did that time with the homeless man. Henderson didn't mind fighting Richard this time. If he kept Richard occupied, no one would be there to help Ceese.

Flying low, Josh picked up on Kyle's scent. He headed towards it and saw Henderson straddling his friend.

"No way, dude." Josh landed in a run. "If anybody's gonna curse him, it's gonna be me."

Henderson whipped his head around.

Josh lunged at him. With no time to avoid the bone-crushing collision, Henderson was knocked airborne. He flew through the air until he slammed back-first into a huge oak. This time it was Henderson who landed with a thud and a grunt.

He shook his head and looked up. Slowly, he pushed up with one hand to his knees, then, pulled up onto his feet, rumbling a throaty growl.

"Come on," Josh said. "You want some more of this?"

Henderson, favoring his left leg, simply limped off. He had sustained enough punishment and frustration from this lot.

"Yeah, you better run," called Josh.

Kyle should have registered relief, but a frown and wide-eyed stare told different. "You were just kidding about cursing me, right?" A nervous twitter fluttering his words.

What was this? Kyle actually sounded worried. Kyle, who always got the upper hand and always managed to make Josh look stupid—he sounded worried. Josh narrowed his eyes and raised his eyebrows. "Maybe. Maybe not." He hid his wide grin until he'd turned his back towards his obnoxious friend. *This is fun. Being a vampire definitely has its perks.*

Zade stood in front of Ceese. He hadn't actually caught up —Ceese had stopped running and turned back to face Zade.

"She's given up," Penelope said. "Ceese has given up."

"This is nae good," Brendan added. "Our plan depended on Ceese being safely with us."

Rodney sputtered, "What about the gun, your gun and the silver . . .?"

"It won't stop Zade. Not while he is at his most powerful," said Richard. "Oh, why didn't we consider Ceese's reaction?"

"Do something! One of you must be able to do something," Cassie cried.

Merideth stepped in, "If I may, there *is* something that can stop a werewolf—can stop Zade." Everyone whirled around to face Merideth.

"Your knife, Brendan," Merideth finished.

"Aye, it has the power."

A twig snapped in the clearing. Zade clutched Ceese's arm and pulled her toward him.

"Oh, come on, Father," Richard urged. "Is this really the time to humor—"

"Brendan's knife, with my blood," Merideth wasn't finished speaking. "If it is introduced at exactly the right moment, when Zade is at his weakest, it will send him straight to Hell."

"But he'll be at his strongest just before he's at his weakest. He'll have ample time to curse Ceese."

"But he'll draw it out. It's all about taunting for Zade. It always has been. Look at him. He could curse her now but he hasn't. Zade's pride gives us ample time."

Brendan had the knife in his hand. Richard grabbed it from him.

"Here," Merideth ripped his shirt open to reveal his chest. "Put it here."

Richard gasped. "No, I can't. I—I won't sacrifice one for the other. Don't ask me to do that."

Merideth took hold of the end of the knife and guided the point to the center of his chest. "I'll be fine, Richard. Remember, I'm a vampire. Take what you learned in darkness and bring light, Son. Finish it."

Brendan felt the surge of lycanthropic power Zade undoubtedly felt. "It's happening, Brother. It will nae be long."

Richard gripped the hilt of the knife tighter, his long hair forming a curtain of blond as he tilted his head forward. He started to work the knife in. At Meredith's initial gasp, he halted. "I can't do it."

"You can," his father reassured. "Besides, you promised. You said when the time came you'd do whatever it took."

"Do you love me, Father?"

"There's some irony, isn't it? If a vampire could love, this one would be one of the few who could love you forever, Richard. As it is, they can't love at all. Not truly. But as I've told you, things are different with me. I can't say it but you must know I feel it and always have."

The feeling of absolute power peaked. Brendan watched Zade lift his arm—he yelled at Richard, "Now. Do it now!"

With one smooth motion, Richard plunged the knife, drew it out and then expertly whipped it at Zade.

44

The knife pierced Zade's heart. His arm, raised to strike Ceese, fell to his side. Zade's face remained stoic—no sign of surprise nor pain. He didn't even attempt to hold onto Ceese when Rodney raced forward and pulled her to safety.

The eclipse had completed. The werewolf had no supernatural power on which to draw. And as powerful as Zade was, it had to be quite unnerving. After standing with both arms at his sides, he sank to his knees and sat back on his haunches. Before everyone's eyes, the werewolf transformed back to his human form.

Zade looked down at his chest and stared at the protruding knife. He went into action, grabbed it by the hilt and pulled at it. He glanced anxiously at the moon and tugged harder—his eyes gleamed with fear. To remove the blood-coated knife before evil touched him once again was the only thing that might save him. Zade's supernatural strength—the strength he had become accustomed to—had drained. Hands shaking, he twisted and pulled, with one eye on the copper red moon.

His audience stared. They too watched the knife and the moon in turn. Still, none could tell which occurred first, the knife yanked free or the end of the eclipse. They could only assume the latter because in an instant, Zade was engulfed by fire.

The surge of flames died down and left nothing but charred ground. Ceese wandered over to the spot and Rodney followed. "He's gone," Rodney said softly. "He can't hurt you anymore."

Her eyes moistened and she bolted off into the forest.

"Ceese," Rodney called after her. "Wait."

"Let her go," Penelope said from where she stood with the others. "She needs time to figure things out."

Rodney had company with his worry. Merideth struggled from where he leaned against Brendan's shoulder. "Cee Cee."

He took several unsteady steps before Brendan caught him by the arm. "Ye are nae in condition," he said. Richard grabbed his father's other arm and together they eased him to the ground. Merideth drew a ragged breath.

Richard said, "You're not well." He looked around at the others. "A knife piercing a vampire's heart has no lasting effect after it is used against another. I just don't know what's wrong."

Merideth tried to sit up. "Cee Cee—" A bout of coughing interrupted and weakened him further. He fell back to the ground and his sons rushed to his side.

"He needs to feed." Josh walked up with Kyle. He stared at the wound in his friend's chest. "What happened?"

"I don't think we have time to tell you," Richard said. "I think you're right about his needing blood though. Can you take him back to the castle? You can get him there quickest. There's still a supply of blood in the refrigerator."

With surprising gentleness, Josh gathered Merideth into his arms. "Come on, dude. Time to fly."

Kyle stared in wonder. "Now there's something you don't see everyday."

Ceese ran and tried to find the pack. *Why is this so difficult?* She'd never had this kind of trouble before. She had to stop several times to catch her breath. She had to rely on common sense. *Nothing feels right.*

Finally, she spotted them. Already skirmishes had broken out in an attempt to determine the new leader. She held back and watched—uncertain of her welcome. *Will they accept me?*

The answer sounded behind her—a low growl startled Ceese and she jumped but did not turn. First off, it *sounded* like a growl, even to her. Second, as hard as she tried, she could not growl in response.

Tears streamed down her face as she watched the wolf mark a tree before it looked up to the night sky and howled. She knew what it meant. If she left now, she'd be safe. They wouldn't kill her.

She didn't belong. She turned and stumbled away; her chest heaved with sorrow.

45

Josh had helped his friend feed on one bag of blood but that wasn't enough—he desperately needed more. Unfortunately, Merideth had consumed just enough to restore his energy and put up a good fight. Both argumentative and combatant, he flung a lamp from a side table into the far wall when Richard insisted he take in more blood. Brendan backed his brother and Meredith flung the matching lamp. "I don't want to feed! I don't want to live! Cee Cee is gone . . . my Cee Cee, she's gone."

Through all the commotion the men heard neither the voices at the front door nor the parade of footsteps down the hall. Ceese had entered the castle followed by the rest of the group. She bypassed the parlor to follow Merideth's voice. She stood in the doorway, her face strained.

"Father?"

Merideth quieted at once and slowly turned around. He gasped at the sight. "Cee Cee. You've come back."

"I'd . . . qu-quite like t-to," she said, "if I could ever know for certain this is where I truly belong."

"You do belong here," her father said. "You belong with me—with Richard and Brendan. Your family."

She shook her head slowly. "I don't know *who* my family is anymore."

Rodney took a slow step forward. "Um—I might be able to help you figure that out." He reached into the back pocket of his jeans and held out an envelope—the one Kyle had delivered. "Remember when you told me on the lawn that day that you'd very much like to know who your father was? Well, I very much wanted to help you find out. I had a friend of Kyle's do a paternity test."

Ceese stared at his offering. "Rodney, I don't understand. What are you talking about?

Rodney continued, "A paternity test—you know, a test that can show whether someone is related to someone else. The results are in this envelope."

Cassie shook her head. "Sure, Rodney. What do you know about paternity tests? How could you provide the necessary elements?"

"I know more than you think," Rodney said. "Now, if you don't mind . . ."

Cassie rolled her eyes and turned her back.

Rodney put the envelope down on a table and took Ceese's hands between his. "Ceese, I asked Kyle to get a vial of your blood from Henderson's lab. I took a rabbit your dad, or-or Merideth had fed on, so they could get some of his saliva. I paid—or rather Geoffrey paid until I can pay him back—a friend of Kyle's to do the test. This friend does the grunt work for a number of medical labs. Anyway," Rodney pointed, "the results are in that envelope."

Ceese picked up the envelope but let it wilt between her fingertips.

She turned to Richard. "Could you look for me—please? I want to know. I just—if you could just tell me."

"Certainly."

Richard took the letter opener Penelope fetched for him and slit the envelope open. He pulled out the piece of paper he found inside and unfolded it. Before he could read it, he glanced up . . . first at his father then back to his sister. Ceese looked away but the rest of the group's eyes riveted on Richard's face. He looked down at the lab results and studied them for a moment. The room remained mausoleum silent.

"It seems," he said, "that according to the test—" He paused this time to clear his throat, "—that Father is truly and undeniably your father as well as mine and Brendan's." He paused to smile before continuing, "As if one couldn't tell by how stubbornly alike the two of you are."

Ceese just stood there.

"But this means nothing if you can't accept it," Merideth said.

Silent tears streamed down her face. "I accept it—Father." In a rush she went to him. "I've missed you so. I'm sorry I didn't believe you."

He smoothed her hair. "You're here now. That's all that matters."

"Aye," Brendan added. "It's good to have ye back, Sister. Now can someone help us convince Father to feed?"

"I'll feed," Merideth said. "But Richard, I'd like to speak with you first. Alone."

Everyone but Richard and Meredith left the room. Excited chatter and relieved laughter trailed down the hall and into a parlor still in disarray after the long rescue-planning session.

<hr />

Brendan hugged his sister and her friends circled around. Rodney's grin spanned side to side. Josh and Kyle patted each other on the back and gave playful pushes—one of which knocked Josh into Cassie and she fell back against Rodney.

Cassie pushed back at Josh. "Why don't you two just link arms and skip around the room?"

That brought a round of guffaws from the two.

Rodney piped up, "Why don't you two just *get* a room?"

Tears ran down their faces as they buckled over and held their stomachs. "Get a room." Kyle snorted and started coughing. "Did you hear that? Rodney said—"

"Qui-et!" Rodney yelled. "You two are a complete and utter embarrassment." He paused as he noticed Ceese. "Are you okay?"

Ceese's eyes had once again filled with tears but as soon as she smiled, Rodney exhaled. She held Brendan at arm's length to look up at him. "Brendan," she said, "thank you, thank you so—Brendan?" The smile wanned and she raised her eyebrows. "There is something different about you . . . I can't quite—quite put my finger on it."

"This is incredible." Brendan rubbed at his smooth beardless chin. "Do you realize how long ago I shaved?" He walked over to the window to check his reflection. "And, nothing has grown back. The stubble is gone. It seems, now that Zade is nay more, things are as they should be. Is it the same with ye, Sister?"

"Things *are* different for me," she answered. She walked over to sit with Rodney. "When I went to find the wolf pack, I grew tired—I can't run great distances without getting tired anymore. I even had trouble tracking the wolves."

"Funny," Rodney said. "Brendan actually sounds excited about things being back to normal. You don't sound excited, Ceese."

"What is normal to me is now gone. I'll have to get used to everything. It won't be easy."

"Aye, it'll take some getting used to. But at least the souls Zade took will have another chance to choose."

"Choose what?" Rodney asked.

"Where they end up when they pass on—you know, Heaven or Hell." Ceese said. "Zade drew his power from them. That's how he grew so strong. Those he cursed who never cursed another now get to choose again."

"What about those who did curse someone?"

Brendan answered that, "Alas, they went with Zade."

Ceese looked suddenly sad. "If only Joachim hadn't cursed another."

"Joachim dinnae curse anyone," Brendan said. "He was searching for the same thing ye looked for—redemption. And did ye find yours? Father was worried sick about ye."

"Who is Joachim?" Rodney asked.

Ceese answered the easy question first. "He helped me along after Zade cursed me. Zade was very jealous of the time I spent with Joachim. Zade took him."

"And so now he's back—among the living?"

"If what Brendan says is true. I'd do anything to see him again."

"Keep in mind," Brendan told her. "He comes back as a werewolf. He'll face the same struggles ye faced to find his way—to be redeemed—the way ye were, assuming ye are. Have ye claimed by faith what is yours to take?"

Ceese stared down at her hands. "Maybe we can find Joachim," she said.

"I'm pretty sure I won't be looking for any werewolves any time soon," Rodney announced.

"Forget about werewolves," Kyle rubbed his neck. "Has everyone forgotten about Josh? Wasn't the entire plan to bring him over here to help him get 'un-cursed' or am I missing something? I know I'll sleep easier once he is."

Brendan tried again. "Sister, ye dinnae answer my question."

Ceese stood silently.

But an answer under pressure was no answer at all. "Perhaps she'll have a reply for you later," Penelope offered.

"Yes," Ceese replied, less tense now that she was off the hot seat. "Let's work on a plan to find Joachim."

Rodney put his hands in the air. "Don't look at me. I'm not helping."

Cassie commented, "When do you ever willingly help?"

"He'll help," Ceese said.

"How can you be so sure?" Cassie asked.

"Because I sensed it." It wasn't so much what she'd said but rather how she'd said it that held everyone's attention. "I heard your thoughts."

The entire room fell silent.

***

"Yes, Father?" Richard settled in a chair next to the bed. "What did you want?"

"You did a good thing tonight."

"It wasn't easy," he said. "Stabbing you was the hardest thing I've ever had to do. At one point, I was certain I'd killed you. And the wound doesn't look much better. You really do need to feed."

"I—I will," Merideth said, "but first, I must know, I *have* to know. You've committed yourself . . . your soul? You do understand what I'm trying to say?"

"Well, yes. I suppose, though I'm not sure why it's important for you to know now. And it's only been two days since you asked me the very same question in the hall—the day my memories of you returned."

"I just want to make sure. And you found the *item* in the cave?"

"That was you who left, um, *that* there?" Richard avoided the word to protect his father from suffering. "But how did you carry it? With it being what it is, I mean."

"The construction of the box, the animal skin around it—it was enough to keep its essence contained much like coffins keep the lure contained so those darned vampire bats—"

Richard stopped him with a raised hand. "No need to finish," he said, the memory of vampire bats covering his flesh was not something he wanted to envision at the moment. "But why carry the, uh, box around at all?"

"Because you're going to need it."

"For what?"

"I can't tell you."

Richard rolled his eyes. "Perhaps I should just leave you so you can feed."

He started to get up and Merideth pulled him back down by an arm. "In a minute, after you listen."

Richard settled.

"You asked me the other day how my curse was different and I need to tell you."

"Now? Perhaps we could discuss it when you're more willing to explain everything," said Richard.

"I made a deal . . ." he continued, "with Cyn."

Richard's face blanched.

"I had to," he explained. "It was the only way. Allowing her to make me a vampire gave me the time I needed to find you, to find Cee Cee. But now I have to hold up my end of the bargain. That's why I needed to make sure you'd committed your soul. Cyn wants you, Richard, but she'll never be able to claim you if your soul is accounted for."

"She claimed *you*?"

"Temporarily." Merideth looked toward the wall.

"Why do I not like the way that sounds?"

"I wish I could explain."

"I don't understand."

"I'm sorry, Son, but you will shortly."

Richard drew breath to speak then closed his mouth. His eyes grew wide. Before him Meredith transformed.

Penelope was the closest to the door and the first to see Richard stumble into the parlor. He grabbed the open door for support but his legs quivered.

"What on earth?" Penelope helped steady him. "Richard, it looks like you've seen a ghost. I've not seen you this pale since you left for New York."

She wiped at his shoulder. Her eyes slowly walked up to his neck. "It . . . it . . . it's blood." Her words caught in her throat as she saw the marks on his neck—and that oddly familiar harshness that now marked his features and had marked his features in the not-so-distant past.

She stared and Richard returned it, seeing but not seeing, as through a dense fog. In an instant of recognition, the fog lifted. Richard's left brow rose.

"Mamá."

Announcing the 3rd installment

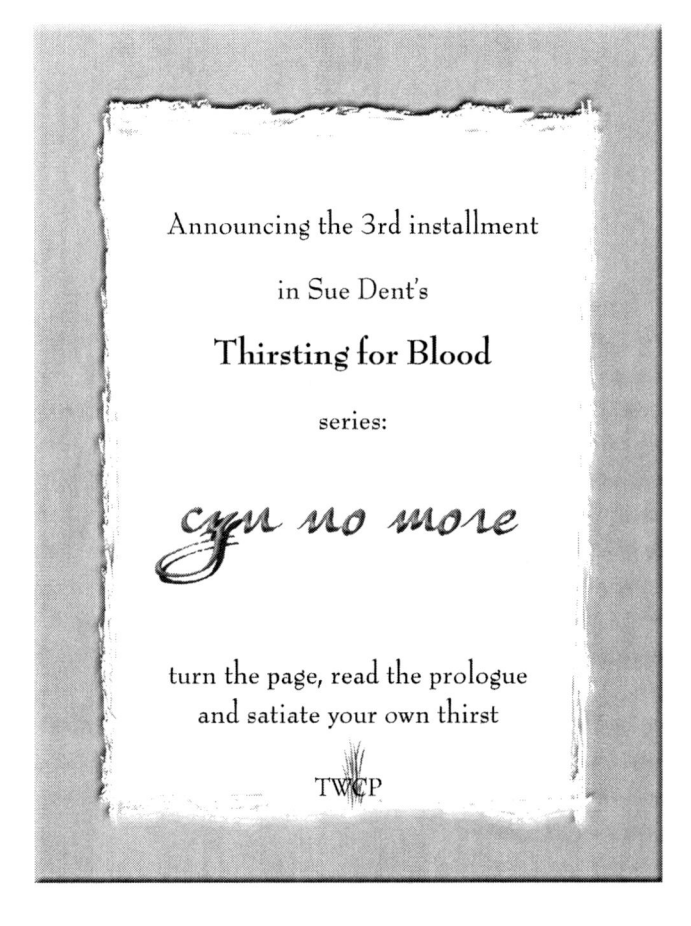

in Sue Dent's

Thirsting for Blood

series:

cyn no more

turn the page, read the prologue
and satiate your own thirst

TWCP

Prologue

He forced his eyes open, *so tired*. His mind screamed for rest. Gravity worked against him as he strained to lift his head. His first thought—to reach for the lantern he'd carried into the dark forest with him. Yet even with blurred vision, that cleared as he batted his eyes, he realized he didn't need the lantern to see. Not because darkness didn't envelope him, but because he could see just fine—despite the overwhelming pitch blackness.

But how?

Heavy clouds still covered the night sky but even without them, the thick leafy canopy would've made it difficult for light to reach the forest floor. He tried again to raise his head but stopped at the sound of a small voice just above him.

"Risiart," someone gasped his name in relief.

The voice brought him round quicker. Ceese. Yes, in recent months six year-old Ceese had taken to the Gaelic pronunciation of his name. *But what's she doing here?* Richard shook his head and clenched his eyes.

Why am I on the ground?

It mattered not how hard he tried, he could not recall much of anything . . . except . . . two blurred figures fleeing into the woods.

Then blackness.

But another memory arose, someone—could it be Ceese—someone praying loudly in Father's native Gaelic tongue right after stepping into the glade.

Richard's head now in her lap, Ceese smoothed his hair with her small hand as he struggled to remember more. *How long have I been out, I wonder. Why do I feel an urgency to seek refuge before the sun rises?*

"You're alive," Ceese said. "You're all right."

Her attitude towards him had changed so much over the last three months and Richard hadn't yet grown accustomed to it. She'd gone from the uncompromising, selfish demon-seed to a sibling who couldn't seem to care enough about her oldest brother.

Richard pushed himself up onto his hands. "We need to get you home."

* * *

Merideth, at his wits end, had all but run out of ideas on how to convince Richard, his oldest at twenty-four and Ceese, his youngest at six, that they truly needed to try harder to work out their differences.

Ceese, insanely jealous of the time he shared with Richard and his studies, would go out of her way to make her Richard's life miserable. Much to Merideth's dissatisfaction, Richard always dumped the matter back into his lap. He complained regularly that *Father* do something about her. Merideth, a man of great patience, took all he could before he finally stood firm.

"Don't," Richard begged Father as he walked after him toward the horse drawn cart, "leave me with that—that—*her*. It certainly makes more sense to take me along. What will you be teaching on tonight? Let Raewyn stay behind so I may go along as well. At least the urchin lis—"

Father turned on his heel, tight lipped and eyes a-glare.

Richard rephrased. "Did I say urchin? I'm sorry. I meant Ceese. At least the—umm—*child* listens to Raewyn." Ceese had just the day before, poured ink all over some of Richard's notes. Difficult though it was, Richard tried to sound caring.

Father's tight lips curved into an audacious grin. "Perhaps, then, you can draw some ideas from Raewyn."

Within the span of two seconds, Ceese rushed out of the house, across the small porch and down two steps. Immediately she attached herself to Father's right leg. "I want to go with you. Please don't leave me."

"You see," Richard said, "the feeling is mutual. And you know you don't want to disappoint her."

Father reached down and lifted Ceese up. "Richard is going to stay with you tonight," he said gently, "and I don't want to hear anymore about it. It would make me very sad if I knew you were upset about this arrangement. You don't want me to leave sad, do you?"

"I don't want you to leave at all," she pouted. "—not without me."

The others waited now. Julia stopped next to her husband and offered Ceese her own instructions. "You'll be good for Risiart, won't you? No trouble?" Though Merideth would mark it as a valiant effort, Julia's words held little emotion. She'd yet to overcome the trauma of the assualt that resulted in Ceese's conception.

Ceese's small head fell forward, her lower lip pushed out.

"Cee Cee," Father prodded, tilted her head up by the chin. "I need you to do this."

A deep forlorn sigh escaped. "All right. But only because you ask this of me."

Father kissed her forehead. "That's my Cee Cee. We shan't be gone long."

The wagon round the road's first bend, Ceese cut her eyes at Richard then sped off into the house. The front door slammed shut behind her, followed by the door to the room where the girls slept. *Perhaps the urchin will pass the time by ignoring me.* With an hour safely tucked away, it became clear Ceese might do just as Richard thought.

Then she cried out.

The fearful scream launched him from the table where he'd been scouring through scripture. He raced across the room and threw the bedroom door open. Ceese cowered in the furthest corner.

"Bad dream?" Richard guessed.

She pointed, whispered. "S—someone is at the window. It's him. He's come for me."

What the devil is she talking about?

"Who has come for you?"

As Richard moved to the window, someone or something scratched at the back door. At least the intruder no longer stood outside. He motioned for Ceese. "I'll ease you down," he said, unlocking and sliding the window open. "You go hide. Don't come out until I come after you. Do you understand?"

"What if he kills you, Richard?"

His eyes widened in mock alarm. "Your lack of faith in me is staggering."

She hugged his neck tightly, then dropped to the ground below, stared up at him. "I'll hide in the ash tree. He can't touch me there," she hissed.

Play along, he thought. There certainly didn't seem to be time for anything else. What an odd thing for her to say though. "Yes, fine—the ash tree then."

Ceese had no concept of how much time had passed before the steady plod of their mare and the creak of the wagon sounded. She did know Richard hadn't come after her. At the sight of Father's pale blonde hair glowing in the moonlight, she climbed to a low branch and dropped to the ground. She sprinted for the wagon.

"You children stay here," Merideth said sternly, handing the reins over to his second oldest, Brendan.

Brendan, at twenty-two protested, "I'm not a child."

Twelve-year old Christian and ten-year old Rolland, stiffened and drew breath to speak.

"Would you go against what Father has asked you to do?" said Sophie, silencing them, sounding so much like her influential older sister that Raewyn nodded her approval.

"Just wait here," Father ordered as he hopped to the ground and ran toward Ceese.

Julia followed, lifting her long dress from around her feet. Ceese lunged for Father the second he knelt to scoop her up. Julia covered her daughter's shivering form with her shawl.

"Why in the name of all that is good are you outside, child?" Father asked.

"Richard told me to hide outside until he came after me."

"Why would he tell you to do that?"

"To protect me," she answered through chattering teeth.

"From what?" he asked, barely able to make out her words. "Certainly not from the cold. We'll be lucky if you haven't caught your death already."

"There was a man at my window and then he came in the house—"

Before she could finish, Richard staggered out onto the porch. Julia gasped as he stumbled down the steps, one hand on the back of his head the other on the side rail. Ceese squirmed from Father's grasp, shed the shawl on the grass, and ran to where Richard had dropped to one knee.

With a ferocious hug, Ceese nearly sent her unsteady brother tumbling backwards. Clutching his neck tightly she said, "You're alive. He didn't kill you. And you saved me."

Richard stared ahead uncertain and nervous. *Will she put a rodent down my shirt again or perhaps another handful of crickets?* Yet her concern seemed genuine and no uncomfortable itching or scratching sensation followed. Richard stumbled to stand, lifting Ceese who still clung tight.

"What happened?" Father asked upon approach.

"There was an intruder but it seems he's gone now. I searched the house."

Father certainly had the right to look alarmed yet Richard saw something else in his expression.

"What did he look like?"

"Well," Richard said carefully, "he was waiting for me just outside the girl's room so I hardly had a chance to get a good look. I do remember his eyes though. They had a hard green-gold cast to them—like nothing I've ever seen before."

Julia gasped.

Richard quickly added "He's gone now and was probably just someone looking for food."

"Is that blood on your hand?" Father asked.

Richard stared numbly. "Yes, I suppose it is? Fancy that."

"Did he—did the intruder scratch you?"

Confused brows knitted. Had Father really just asked him that? "No. I'm pretty certain he hit me." He felt the back of his head and winced, "and with something very hard, too, though I'm not sure what."

Merideth nodded away the awkwardness of his comment. "Oh, yes, of course." He then reached out to take Ceese. "Come with me," he said to her, held his arms out. "Let Mother look after Richard's woun—"

Ceese latched on tighter. "No. I want to stay with Richard."

It took a moment for her words to sink in. "Now there's some irony," Richard snipped. "If only we'd known it would take my nearly being killed to get her to warm up to me."

* * *

Richard still struggled with his memory. The sentiment Ceese found for Richard that night remained. She'd followed him out earlier this evening when the stranger had come and here she was now. But why?

How had she known to follow and what made her think she could help? Richard wanted to understand.

"Why would you come after me? Why didn't you stay at the house with Brendan and the others as you were told to do?"

Ceese's eyes pierced his. "I saw evil."

"Evil? The man came after me so that I might read last rites to his friend. How did you see that as evil?"

"He was lying."

"What made you think he was lying?"

"I know when everyone is lying. I have second-sight."

Richard squinted and rubbed the bridge of his nose hard. "I told Father he shouldn't fill your head with such nonsense."

"It isn't nonsense. I'm the seventh born."

"Second-sight applies to the seventh *son* of a seventh son—"

"Father says it doesn't matter. It passes to a daughter as well."

And why am I having this debate? "All right then . . ." Richard looked around. "But let's get you back *before* the sun comes up, shall we?"

Ceese looked around as well. "But it's black as pitch and your lantern has gone out. How will we see?"

"Not to worry. I can see just fine."

Her eyes narrowed suspiciously. "How?"

"I'm not sure but let's not worry about that. Let's just take advantage."

He reached down, took her up, but instead of pulling her close, he held her at arms' length. *So innocent. So vulnerable. It would be so easy to take her—blood?*

"No!" he gasped, nearly dropping Ceese in a rush to put her down. As dark as it was, Ceese caught a glimpse of his fangs.

"You're like them," she breathed out and took a step back. "You—you're a vampire."

Flashpoint
Frank Creed

In *Book One of the UNDERGROUND* persecution in Chicago has reached the Flashpoint.

In the year 2036, all nations are run by a one-world government. The One State has only one threat: Fundamentalist terrorists—and has declared Bible-believing Christians 'terrorists'!

But the One State has not yet encountered Calamity Kid and e-girl...

2006 ELFIE —Best Sci-Fi Novel
2007 CFRB IMPRESS Award —Best Book Toured
2008 PLUTO Award Finalist

When peacekeepers bust a home-church in Ward-Six of the Chicago Metroplex, Dave and Jen Williams, alone evade capture. The only place to turn? A 'terrorist' cell known as the Body of Christ.

In their shattered world, they adopt codenames and slip between the Underground cracks. They must save their home-church before family, friends, and neighbors are brainwashed (or worse) by the One State neros.

Calamity Kid and e-girl fearlessly walk the valley of death, because He is with them. But they'll need every molecule of their re-formed faith to face down peacekeepers, gangers, One-State neros, and fallen-angels, in America's dark Post-Modern Humanist age.

Paperback: 978-1-934284-01-8

THE WRITERS' CAFÉ PRESS
.com

2037 Chicago Metroplex: Paramilitary Forces Fight a
WAR OF ATTRITION

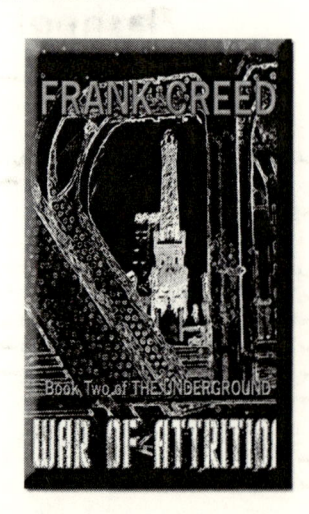

A suicidal sandman—

A traitor running for her life—

High-tech crosshairs aimed into the underground—

Ten months after Dave & Jen Williams join the Body of Christ, the Federal Bureau of Terrorism targets their muscle-cell.

Calamity Kid, e-girl, and the Body of Christ fight to evade their hunters, and confront the Unholy Trinity.

Will enemy-of-the-state, Legacy, surface to save the day?

COMING LATE SUMMER 2009
Paperback: 978-1-934284-04-9

THE WRITERS' CAFÉ PRESS
.com

Light at the Edge of Darkness
Cynthia MacKinnon, ed.

For more of Mr. Rice's fiction, check out these stories:

- At the Mountains of Lunacy
- Credo
- One Taken the Other Left

This anthology of 3 novelettes and 25 short stories comes from the finest writers of Biblical speculative fiction—all members of the Lost Genre Guild.

When forced to the edge of darkness, there's only one way back: embrace the Light.

... venture to futures where religious "Terrorists" smuggle frozen embryos to save lives and resist technologies designed to break their souls;
... explore dying alien worlds scouring the galaxies for hope;
... get abducted and discover the universe's secrets or the trial of a lifetime.

Teetering on the edge, escape inbred captors through a haunted labyrinth, survive a house where nightmares walk, or settle in for a martyr's tribulation.

Join an epic quest through the ridiculous, cross swords with monsters, sneak a glimpse at heaven, traverse the planes where angels and demons tread.

Follow these tales and more to the edge of darkness, to the brink of despair, and back to bask in the Savior's redeeming Light.

Paperback: 978-1-934284-00-1
Available at a discount at the publisher's site

THE WRITERS' CAFÉ PRESS
.com

SWORD OPERA

The Duke's Handmaid
Caprice Hokstad

Book one of a fantasy trilogy, *The Duke's Handmaid* is full of mystery, adventure, and even a little romance.

Keedrina is a young peasant who lives near a thriving seaport town. After marauders kill her family and burn her farmhouse, she meets Duke Vahn, who champions her cause, apprehends the outlaws, and dispenses justice. The duke offers Keedrina food and shelter in return for service.

Can the simple farmgirl find a family among the refined servants in the duke's house? Not if the prejudiced and conniving duchess has her way!

Paperback: 978-1-591603-37-5

Nor Iron Bars A Cage
Caprice Hokstad

Two baby boys are lost in the hostile country of Ganluc—one the firstborn son of royalty and the other a bastard half-breed born to an Itzi slavegirl and fathered by a licentious owner later executed for treason. Duke Vahn is determined to rescue both of these boys.

Scores of knights and bounty hunters who have risked their lives but none have found any clue to their whereabouts.

A bold plan is proposed and reluctantly, Vahn sends a strange trio off to Ganluc—-his brave captain, a middle-aged healer, and an Itzi slave.

Little does he know what challenges await both the trio and his own house, now forced to survive without its key leaders.

Paperback: 978-0-615163-60-4

Both books are available at barnesandnoble.com, amazon.com, lulu.com and by visiting the author's website at www.latoph.com

Leaps of Faith
Karina & Robert Fabian, ed.

EPPIE 2004 Finalist

An anthology of science fiction stories which cover the entire spectrum of the genre.

You'll enjoy stories from encountering alien life to space exploration; time travel to hard SF—if you believe in a future where science and faith live side-by-side.

- Can an ancient religion bring hope to first-line explorers for whom each trip is potential suicide?
- What does it mean when a physicist finds God's face in the stars?
- Is there a "saint gene" and can it be reproduced to create miracles?
- What happens to your soul when your body is shattered into quantum elements and reassembled on another world?
- How will the Christian faith transform alien thoughts and traditions?

Read as time travelers seeking to change Biblical history and space travelers harvesting "angels" are brought to faith by their experiences.

Experience tender romance and heart-pounding adventure.

Laugh at the foibles of man.

A 2004 EPPIE finalist for Best Electronic Anthology, Leaps of Faith promises the best in Christian sci-fi.

"Seldom does a book come along like Leaps Of Faith...I give Leaps Of Faith two thumbs up, and I look forward to similar works in the future."
Midwestern Book Review

Paperback: 978-1-934284-10-0

THE WRITERS' CAFÉ PRESS
.com

The role playing game based on Frank Creed's FLASHPOINT: Book One of the Underground.

...an immersive, creative experience where you can step into the world of FLASHPOINT, and take on the role of a hero!

COMING SPRING 2009

Paperback: 978-1-934284-04-9

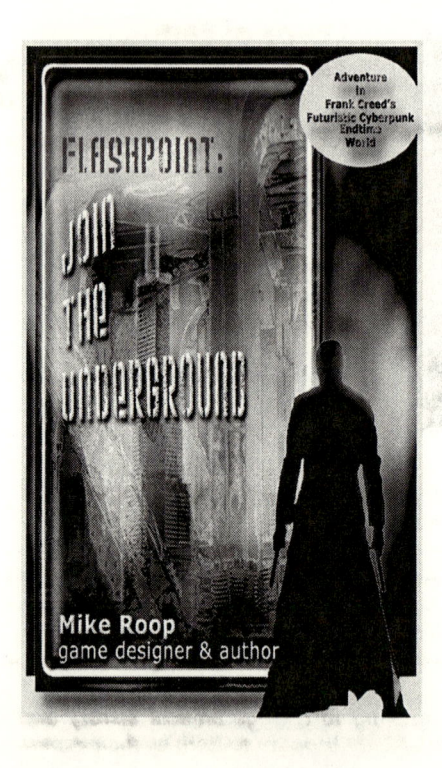

THE WRITERS' CAFÉ PRESS
.com

Printed in the United States
133887LV00002B/247-255/P